A swordsman of the brigade

Michael O'Hanrahan

Nabu Public Domain Reprints:

You are holding a reproduction of an original work published before 1923 that is in the public domain in the United States of America, and possibly other countries. You may freely copy and distribute this work as no entity (individual or corporate) has a copyright on the body of the work. This book may contain prior copyright references, and library stamps (as most of these works were scanned from library copies). These have been scanned and retained as part of the historical artifact.

This book may have occasional imperfections such as missing or blurred pages, poor pictures, errant marks, etc. that were either part of the original artifact, or were introduced by the scanning process. We believe this work is culturally important, and despite the imperfections, have elected to bring it back into print as part of our continuing commitment to the preservation of printed works worldwide. We appreciate your understanding of the imperfections in the preservation process, and hope you enjoy this valuable book.

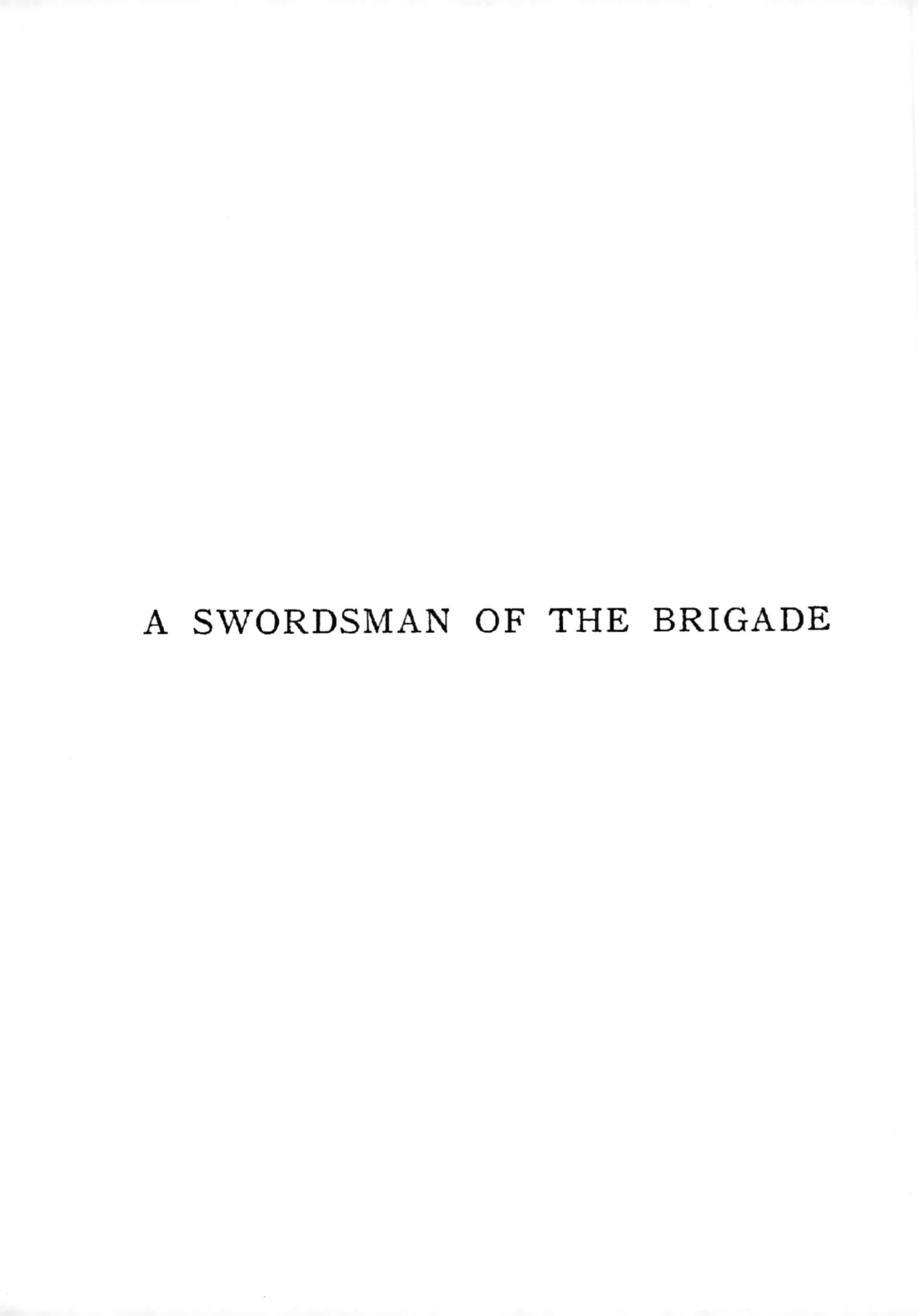

A SWORDSMAN OF THE BRIGADE

MICHEÁL O hANNRACHÁIN

A SWORDSMAN OF THE BRIGADE

BY
MICHEAL O hANNRACHAIN

SANDS & COMPANY
EDINBURGH: 37 GEORGE STREET
LONDON: 15 KING STREET, COVENT GARDEN

DEDICATION

To the memory of a father to whom I owe much, whose life's quest is over, and to one other, my mother, who whispered hope when days were black, I dedicate this book.—THE AUTHOR.

CONTENTS

CHAP.
- I. ONE NIGHT IN CATHAIR DOMHNAILL
- II. THE SPY AT "LE CHAT ROUGE"
- III. SPEIER—THE CAPTURE OF THE STANDARD
- IV. THE MOUNTAIN AUBERGE
- V. BETRAYED
- VI. FOOLED—I WIN THROUGH
- VII. IN HOSPITAL—A MEMORY OF THE HOMELAND
- VIII. O BRIAIN'S STORY
- IX. A GIRL'S APPEAL
- X. THE ESCAPE
- XI. THE WHIPPING OF THE CHEVALIER
- XII. THE CHALLENGE—THE DUEL—ARREST
- XIII. THE DUKE'S ALTERNATIVE
- XIV. AMONGST THE MOUNTAINS—LE COQ DORÉ
- XV. THE SIEUR STRIKES
- XVI. AN UNLOOKED-FOR FRIEND
- XVII. PRISONERS—DISILLUSION
- XVIII. AIMÉE COMES
- XIX. FREEDOM—THE FLIGHT ACROSS THE MOUNTAINS
- XX. PURSUIT—DEFEAT IN VICTORY
- XXI. REFUGE—A DEBT WELL PAID

CONTENTS

CHAP.
- XXII. AGAIN AT IVREA
- XXIII. DESPONDENCY—SHELDON'S AGAIN—THE CALL TO IRELAND
- XXIV. IN DUBLIN—A GENTLEMAN OF LEISURE
- XXV. A WHISPER FROM THE PAST
- XXVI. BY BULLOCK STRAND—A LOYALIST VOLUNTEER
- XXVII. LOVE IS NOT FOR ME—CHECKMATE TO AN ENEMY
- XXVIII. A WILD-GOOSE CHASE—A LITTLE SWORDPLAY
- XXIX. AN OLD FRIEND
- XXX. LOVE WHISPERS AGAIN—AN INVITATION
- XXXI. THE DAUGHTER OF MY ENEMY
- XXXII. FOR THE HEAD OF A TRAITOR—LOVE COMES TO ME
- XXXIII. THE PROTECTION OF THE LAW-ABIDING
- XXXIV. THE FROWN OF FORTUNE
- XXXV. CONSUMMATION—FAREWELL

A SWORDSMAN OF THE BRIGADE

CHAPTER I

ONE NIGHT IN CATHAIR DOMHNAILL

On a dark and tempestuous night in the beginning of the year of grace 1703, a stout little lugger crept out of a secluded creek on the coast of Kerry, having on board, myself, Piaras Grás, and many another lad who had given the word which enrolled us comrades of those other brave fellows who had trailed their swords across many a battlefield, and made their names synonymous with dashing bravery.

The night was suited to the enterprise. Across the sky scudded heavy masses of cloud through the rifts of which the moon peeped out fitfully. From the land the rain blew in heavy sheets, carried by a wind which moaned and whistled through the cordage of our little vessel.

But what cared stout Seamus Og, the master of the swift sailing smuggler, though winds blew high and skies looked black. Full many a time had he sailed his gallant craft in the teeth of wind and wave, carrying his cargo of brave recruits away to France. How many a time had not his lugger shown her heels to the cruisers of Dutch William, treading her way in and out of the creeks and inlets indenting the Kerry coast, where they dared not follow. How many a "wild goose" had taken his flight with him, to cleave his way to fame and fortune in the ranks of the Irish Brigade, or to find a grave 'neath the sod of some field of blood, where sword in hand he had struck home at the enemies of his race.

And here am I, Piaras Grás, son of old Seaghan Grás of Snaidhm, whose sword had flashed on Aughrim's day, sailing this stormy night away out towards the land of the generous Gaul.

. . . .

I had been all day at the fair of Cathair Domhnaill, having ridden over there on my black mare, Crom. A Dhia! how I loved that mare! My father had bred her dam in the days of his prosperity, when Seaghan Grás was known from end to end of Kerry's hills and valleys—aye, and far beyond—for his open-handed generosity, his princely chivalry; before those devilish laws, the product of hell, had come to blight his name and wreck his fortunes, leaving him a broken man in a little wayside cabin.

In the tall castle where his fathers had lived and ruled—where I had played in childhood—a surly Williamite undertaker now lorded it over the surrounding country-side. From the ruin of his fortune he had managed to save the mare, and bring her to that little cottage where his declining years had been spent. Here had I grown up into young manhood, witnessing from day to day all the bitter humiliations and insults to which a beaten people may be subjected by an arrogant conqueror. Here had I learned the bitter story of the hated laws which had reduced the old race and bowed them to the dust. Here had Crom been foaled. Here had we hidden her away from prying eyes.

How I had tended her; how often I had patted her arching neck; how I knew every mood and whim of my gentle Crom. And she—how she'd whinny with delight when I came near, and thrust her soft muzzle into my open hand. My bonny mare! And now my hand has given you death.

We had carefully hidden her away till that fatal morning. How gaily we pricked along the white road! How prettily she arched her neck, and tossed up her handsome head, as if disdaining the long miles which she sent flying behind! What little thought I had as we swept merrily along of what that evil day would bring forth! Could we see into that future which is hidden from us how differently we might act!

I was busy all day attending to the business which had brought me hither. The evening was closing in when I, mounted on my mare, rode out through the gateway of the inn kept by Micheal Mor, an old retainer of my father's. By some ill chance of fortune I dismounted at the inn door to transact a business I had forgotten till that moment. Throwing the reins to a buachaill standing by, I stepped inside. A few minutes sufficed, then I came out to mount for home. But as I placed my foot in the stirrup, a heavy hand was laid on my shoulder, and turning, I beheld the black face of Sir Michael Sickles.

"That's a fine mare you've got there, my fine fellow," he growled out. "A fine mare for a Papist beggar."

"Little the thanks to you for her fineness, you black hound," I shouted angrily, for my temper was always a bit fiery. "Take your hand off my shoulder, or——" and my hand went unconsciously to my pocket.

"Not so fast! not so fast! my gallant young spark," exclaimed Sir Michael, sneeringly. "I want a good mare just now, and that one of yours will suit me. Bring her up to me at the Castle of Snaidhm to-morrow. You ought to know the way, Master Grás. Or better still, I'll ride her home. The price the law allows will be paid you whenever you call, or will I give it to you now? I doubt not you have need of it," and he laughed hoarsely.

"You'll never own her, you dog," I shouted

furiously, drawing a pistol, and firing point-blank at the mare. The aim was true, and with a scream, almost human in its agony, my gallant Crom sank to the ground.

Sword in hand, the baronet threw himself on me, at the same time shouting loudly for help. Just in time I turned to meet his furious onset. With a cry of rage, I threw my empty pistol at his head, which, striking him in the face, caused him to stagger back a pace or two. But the distance was too short to do him much damage. However, it gave me time to draw my second pistol. Reckless of consequences, I fired almost without taking aim, and Sir Michael fell prone with the bullet in his breast.

Stupefied, I stood gazing down at the unfortunate man lying there, his blood dyeing the surrounding roadway. But a hand was laid on my arm, and a voice whispered in my ear: "Teith, a mhic mo chroidhe. Beidh na saighdiuiri annso ar ball."

The voice aroused me from my stupor. Hardly knowing whither I went, I allowed myself to be led back into the inn I had just quitted. It was barely time, for the sound of the hastening footsteps of soldiers was borne to my ears. The landlord, for it was he who had drawn me in, hurried me through a dark passage, and into a little room at the back of the inn. Raising a portion of the coarse drugget which covered the floor, he lifted a small door, from which a ladder led downwards. In a whisper he told me to descend, and when I had reached the bottom to remove the ladder.

As I descended into the darkness of the cellar, the door was closed down, the drugget dropped back into its place, and then I heard the retreating steps of the landlord. Groping forward in the Stygian darkness, I could hear the heavy tramp of the soldiers; hear their voices as they questioned Micheal regarding the occurrence whereby the King's peace had been broken, and the blood of a local magnate and loyal subject spilled. I could hear them tramping through the house; hear their oaths as they realised that their search was fruitless—that the bird had flown.

Looking back now through all the years which have flown by since that night when I lay there in the thick blackness listening to the pursuers who might come on me at any moment, I realise that never again did I experience such mental torture. I have charged up against the bristling bayonets of Dutchman and Hun. I have ridden through the thick smoke of many a German battlefield, where bullets whistled like hail. I have carried my life in my hands what time I rode through the allied lines with Duke Vendôme's dispatches in my keeping, but never did I feel the torment of mind which was mine on that night standing there, a youth of twenty, with only an empty pistol clutched in my hand.

That night, with the voices of these Sasanach bandogs sounding in my ears, not knowing when they might stumble on my hiding-place, my utter helplessness affrighted me. Should they have come on me then, I would have been caught like a rat in a trap, and having neither sword nor pistol wherewith to defend myself, like a rat I would have been slaughtered, for I had resolved not to surrender. A Dhia! even now the terrors of that awful night come back to me.

But when I rode amidst the hissing bullets, with my good sabre in my grasp, I was a man amongst men, ready and willing to give blow for blow. The blood bounded fiercely through my veins, and the battle-lust was on me.

Gradually the sounds died away. I heard the retreating footsteps of the soldiers, as they departed to continue their search elsewhere, and then all was silence. After the lapse of about half an hour, so nearly as I could judge, I heard a stealthy step overhead, and the trapdoor was raised. In the profound darkness I could see nothing, but a whisper reached my ear.

"Are you there, Master Piaras?"

"Yes," I whispered back. "Who calls?"

"It is I, Micheal," the voice of the landlord whispered. "Buidheachas mor le Dia, the soldiers are gone. But hurry, they may come back again at any moment."

Placing the ladder against which I leaned to the opening, I rapidly ascended, and in a few seconds stood beside my old friend.

"Now, a mhic mo chroidhe," he whispered, "be quick. Off with that coat of yours, and put this on," handing me a long cloak which completely enveloped me. "This caibin will serve you a turn."

When I had rapidly made the changes, he regarded me in the feeble light of the rushlight which he held in his hand, remarking:

"It won't be so easy for a spy to know you now."

Then thrusting a pistol into my hand, he went on:

"It would be dangerous for you to go home. There will be a watch on the house. The soldiers found your pistol with your name on the butt, so they'll be on your track. Take my advice and quit the country. There's an officer recruiting for the Brigade beyond at An Currán. Go there and find out Seamus Gabha. Tell him I sent you. Have no fear of telling him everything that happened. Away with you now, and God watch over you."

Extinguishing the rushlight, he cautiously opened a side-door, and peered out. He whispered to me that the coast was clear. Then a hand-clasp and I was away.

Walking swiftly forward beneath the twinkling stars, I soon left the sleeping village behind. Extreme caution was necessary, therefore I kept to the fields. It was well I did so, for I had not gone far when I heard the jingle of the harness of a mounted patrol on the road. I crouched down in the furze. But the men trotted past, and soon the beat of the horses' hooves was swallowed up in the distance.

Day was breaking as I came within sight of An Currán. From a peasant lad who crossed my path I inquired for Seamus Gabha. He pointed me out a tumble-down forge at the entrance to the village. Going to the door, I knocked. In a few minutes it was opened cautiously, and a black-bearded man, who appeared as if he had only risen from bed, peered into my face, inquiring in a gruff voice what I wanted. In a few words I told him I had come from Cathair Domhnaill, and had been sent by Micheal Mor, the innkeeper. The mention of Micheal's name seemed to produce a favourable impression on my black-visaged questioner, and in a more kindly voice he bade me enter, remarking as if in excuse of his brusqueness:

"These are dangerous times, and we know not whom to trust. Spies surround us on all sides. We must, therefore, be cautious, and careful as to how we bestow our friendships."

When I had entered, I told him of the happenings of the night. He listened in silence. When I had done:

"You must get away," he said. "Your life isn't worth a traithnin if the soldiers lay hands on you. The Brigade is the only place for you. During the day a wool-buyer will be here; he's an officer of the Brigade. Till he comes you must hide. Prying eyes may be about. But I'll put you in a place where it will take a clever Sasanach to find you."

So saying, he led me into the forge, and there in a recess under the fire-place which seemed to have been hollowed out for just such an emergency, he stowed me away. And then he brought me some cold meat and bread, which I devoured, for I was as hungry as a hawk. A jug of ale completed my repast, and with my hunger satisfied, worn out by fatigue and weariness, I stretched myself on the heap of straw with which my hiding-place was furnished, and was soon sleeping soundly.

I awoke suddenly with a start, to hear the sound of

loud, rough voices and the clink of spurs. Evidently these sounds had awakened me, or perhaps it was the sense of danger which sometimes grips at our sleeping faculties, causing us to start up affrightedly. I raised myself on my elbow and listened. They were evidently searching the forge. The few disjointed words which reached my ears were hardly necessary to tell me for whom they were searching. At last the sounds of their searching ceased, and I judged they had gone.

Starting at every sound, I sat up in my den. It was so small I could not stand erect. It was barely high enough to permit of my resting in a sitting posture. Oh, how I fumed and fretted! How I longed to be out under the sky once more! How I felt my manhood smirched and disgraced through having to lie there like the veriest criminal! What would I not have given for a dash across the heather of my native gleann on my gallant Crom! But never again would I bestride the back of that loved companion of my youth. No! The die was cast. I had done with the old life. There could be no turning back now. At last, merciful sleep came again to my aid.

I was awakened by a touch on my arm, and a voice whispered in my ear:

"Teanam ort. 'Se an t-am."

I permitted myself to be led into the little room which I had entered in the morning. There I found myself in the presence of a tall, broad-shouldered man of florid complexion. He was evidently acquainted with my story, and at once inquired if I were wishful to join the Brigade. I replied that such was my intention.

"Very well," he replied, "we want such men as you. You are only just in time. To-night Seamus Og's lugger sails for France."

In a few minutes I had pocketed the silver coin which enrolled me a bold brigadier. Then I gripped the hand of my good friend and protector, Seamus

Gabha, and out I stole into the night beside my soldier companion.

A walk of an hour or so through the storm which had sprung up brought us to the little creek where the smuggler lay. A long whistle from my comrade brought a boat stealing across the foam-flecked waters. We took our seats in her, and in a few minutes I was standing on the deck of the little lugger which was to bear me to the land of the fleur-de-lis.

And this is how I came to don the uniform of Sheldon's Horse, and sailed away to cleave my way to fortune.

Henceforth I shall know the fierce delight of the headlong charge. I shall see the red twinkle of the camp-fires shining through the night. In the land of the gallant Gaul there is fame and fortune to be won at the sword's point.

Hurrah! Hurrah! for the life of a soldier!

CHAPTER II

THE SPY AT "LE CHAT ROUGE"

THREE months have flown by since that stormy night when I gazed through the mist at the receding shores of my native land. Three months! Such months of ceaseless drill and preparation for the red work of war. At night the last mournful cadences of the bugle lulled me to sleep. In the grey morning light the shrill notes of the reveille startled me from sleep to the work and bustling activity of another day.

How gaily we swaggered it through the streets of the grey old Flemish town in our gay uniforms, our spurs jingling merrily at our heels. How we longed for the serried lines and the thunder of battle, and envied our more fortunate companions who had been drafted away to the army of the Rhine, where hard knocks were plenty but promotion certain. However, Piaras Grás can wait, his chance will come. Meanwhile, I can plume it with the gayest in the inns and taverns of this old fishing town, which has known the Spanish and English, but now owns the French as masters.

And it was in this old town of Dunkerque that an incident happened which had like to finish my career as a dashing guardsman.

We had gone down one night to "Le Chat Rouge" in the Rue Saint Julien to enjoy a flagon of Père Jacques' wine. There were about a dozen of us in our company, most of them of Sheldon's Horse, with one or two Frenchmen. We were enjoying our wine, and chatting about the campaign on the Rhine, whither we of Sheldon's Horse hoped soon to be sent.

Suddenly a tall, dark-complexioned, bearded man entered. He was dressed in the costume peculiar to the Catalonian seamen. Round his waist was twisted a red silken sash, and in his ears he wore large gold earrings. His long, black hair fell in wavy confusion down on his shoulders, and was partially covered by the red woollen cap, worn by the seafarers of that country. He was a stranger at "Le Chat Rouge," for though we were constant visitors, we had never seen him there before.

Swaggering to a vacant side table he called for wine. Little Annette, the host's pretty daughter, brought it to him. He threw a gold piece on the table in payment, and in silence set himself to the enjoyment of the liquor. In a few seconds the girl returned with the change out of his gold piece. But it was evident the fellow had had too much to drink. With a loud laugh he jumped to his feet, and throwing his arms round her, attempted to kiss her. Annette resisted violently, calling to us loudly for help. In an instant all was confusion. With shouts of rage we dashed to her assistance, but in our excitement only encumbered each other. Disengaging myself from the crowd I rushed at the bold stranger, who still held the struggling girl in his arms. With a fierce blow I caught him full in the face. Releasing Annette he turned to meet me. We rushed at each other, but he stumbled over a chair, and then—the big beard he was wearing fell away, revealing to my astonished gaze a clean-shaven face —an English face.

A shout of "Spy, spy" rose on all sides. With a quick movement the Englishman drew a pistol, and fired at the candelabrum which hung on the wall, bringing it clattering to the floor, and leaving us in complete darkness. After some delay a light was procured, and then we discovered that the stranger had disappeared. I remembered that I had felt someone brush past me. I told my companions of this, and with one accord we dashed into the street.

Fortunately we were just in time. Away down the street, slinking along in the shadows, we caught a glimpse of his red cap, revealed for an instant in the light of a smoky lamp. With shouts of "The spy's away," we plunged ahead on his track. In the eagerness of pursuit I far outdistanced my comrades. Ahead I caught a glimpse of the Englishman now and again. Through the Rue Saint Jean we rushed, our footsteps echoing loudly on the paved streets, and causing many a window in the tall houses to fly open, and then the tall masts of the ships lying in the Bason, rising up in the night like giants' arms, came into view. I was now close behind; scarcely fifty yards separated me from him.

Suddenly I lost sight of my quarry. We had come to the corner of a dark and almost uninhabited street, round the corner of which he had wheeled. When I reached it he had disappeared. I halted in confusion. I looked up and down the street, but it would have needed a cat's eyes to see in the thick gloom. Realising the uselessness of trying to pick up his track in that dark, and, to me, entirely unknown neighbourhood, I decided to give up the pursuit, and turned to retrace my footsteps. A light footfall sounded beside me. Instinctively I stepped back, but a stinging blow deprived me of my senses, and I knew no more.

. . . .

When I came to myself I was in complete darkness. A raging pain was in my head, round which a cloth was roughly bound, which felt wet and clammy to the touch. Slowly the knowledge of what had happened came back to me. I remembered the pursuit of the spy, and the sudden blow which had deprived me of my senses. Ah! this, then, was the explanation of the bandage round my head.

But where was I? This swinging thing which swayed and shook at every movement, surely it could not be my hard bed at the barracks? Was it a room at " Le Chat Rouge "? If it was, its beds were most confoundedly uncomfortable.

But hist! What was that? A stealthy step sounded in my ears, and a lantern gleam cut through the darkness. Instantly I lay back feigning insensibility. Slowly the footsteps advanced, and the lantern was flashed in my face. But not even by the twinkle of an eyelid did I betray myself. They should not know of my return to consciousness till I had found out where I was.

After a cursory glance the lantern-carrier turned and tiptoed noiselessly from my side. Through half-open eyes I watched him hang his lantern on a hook suspended from the ceiling—watched his retreating figure disappearing. When his footsteps had died away I raised myself on my elbow and looked round. By the lantern's light I perceived that I lay in a hammock. Overhead I could hear the sound of many feet, mingled with the lap-lap of waters. With a start I realised that I was on shipboard. But what ship, and how had I come there? Anxiously I gazed round, and suddenly the horrible thought flashed across my dulled brain that this was an English ship. Aye, and there painted on the lantern was its name, "Ambuscade." Vainly I racked my brains for an explanation of my presence in this place. But none presented itself. Whatever was the meaning, I felt that now I was on board, and knew of the presence of a hostile ship in the harbour, care would be taken that I did not escape. And quite apart from that was the fact of my being an Irishman in the French service. My danger was imminent; it behoved me to look to myself.

Again I heard the voices and footsteps of several persons coming down the companion-way. Again I lay back in my hammock with closed eyes. Again they approached me. But this time some involuntary movement on my part betrayed me. With an oath I was seized and lifted, none too gently, to the floor.

Before me stood my friend of the inn. He was now dressed in a kind of naval uniform.

"Who are you?" he demanded roughly.

"Piaras Grás of Sheldon's Horse," I replied proudly, looking him full in the face. I knew it was useless to attempt to deceive him. My uniform betrayed me.

"Do you know anything of an O'Carroll of the same regiment?" he asked.

"Possibly I might," I replied, resolved to gain as much time as possible, "but then there are so many O'Carrolls."

The question explained much. The remembrance of an affair, leading to the recovery by the dashing lieutenant of ours of some plans connected with the defence of the town from an English spy, who had escaped, came to me. Probably this was the spy from whom they had been taken, who hoped to make good his loss by the capture of the lieutenant.

"This O'Carroll to whom I refer," resumed the Englishman, "is tall and dark-complexioned, and wears a heavy black moustachio."

"Ah!" I drawled reflectively, "the lieutenant of ours. And what might you want of him?"

"It is not for you to question, sirrah," he growled, "but to answer."

"Well, you see, sir spy," I drawled, "I imagined you wanted information."

I was succeeding admirably in my design. In a few seconds he would be beside himself with rage, and an angry man is less watchful than a cool one.

"Do you know where the lieutenant lives?" queried my captor.

"Yes," I replied coolly, "but I won't tell you. Piaras Grás is no informer."

"Perhaps a little gentle persuasion will make you less squeamish," sneered my captor. "Besides I owe you something for that blow at the inn. Boatswain, your cat-o'-nine-tails. We'll make this rat squeal."

To this remark I did not see fit to make any reply. Piaras Grás never bandies words with a foe. The boatswain, a big, lusty fellow, dropped my right arm which he had been holding, while another sailor held my left.

No sooner had the boatswain disappeared than I twisted myself free. It wasn't a very hard job either, for I had been so passive that my remaining guard had relaxed his grip. With a trip I sent him headlong into a corner, and in a bound I was on the officer. My move had been so sudden he was taken by surprise. He attempted to draw a pistol, but I was too quick for him. Fair in the stomach I caught him with a tremendous kick, which sent him reeling across the cabin. Up the companion-ladder I sprang almost on the heels of the boatswain, cutting my shins badly against the steps. But what mattered these scratches. I was free.

No, dar mo laimh, not yet a while. A yell sounded behind me: "The prisoner's escaping."

A rush of feet across the deck made me pause with my feet on the last step. But this was not the moment for delay. With a bound I was on to the deck. The red glare of a lantern revealed me to the enemy. I tripped over a coil of rope lying on the deck, and fell heavily. Lucky for me I did, for a heavy missile went whizzing past. Had I been standing it would have laid my head open.

I jumped to my feet and raced forward blindly. But the sailors were closing in around me. A bullet would have stopped my career. None came. Doubtless they feared to use their firearms for fear of arousing the suspicions of the port authorities. Should I allow myself to be taken I was lost. Farewell then to Sheldon's Horse and all my dreams of glory. At the thought the lurking devil in me woke up. With a yell I sprang at the nearest form which I could make out in the darkness. Down he went before my furious onslaught, and I staggered across his prone body against the bulwarks. Without a moment's hesitation I placed my hands on the top and vaulted clear.

Down—down into the dark waters I plunged. The shock of their icy coldness almost took away my senses, but the feeling passed, and in a few seconds I rose to the surface. Treading water I looked round. Far ahead I could see the bright glare of the beacon standing at the end of the Pier. Its yellow gleam was like a ray of hope to me. Kicking off the heavy cavalry boots, which hung like lead on my feet, I struck out. My head still throbbed painfully, and I was weak from the loss of blood. In my weak condition my progress was slow, but the indomitable spirit of my race did not desert me. I knew it was not likely my assailants would pursue. After my escape they would be more intent on looking to their own safety. My feeble strokes carried me onwards, and at last, worn out, and almost at the last gasp, I felt the ground shelving under my feet. Staggering from the water I fell senseless to the ground.

In this condition one of the sentinels found me. When after ten days in the military hospital I was able to give some account of the happenings of that night, pursuit of the English ship was out of the question. Doubtless, fearing that I might bring the authorities down about his ears, my captor had taken flight, and was heard of no more. As for myself, I slowly recovered from the effects of my adventure, and was once again in the saddle. I had hardly got back to the ranks when our troop received orders to join the army of the Rhine.

Now, at last, my opportunity has come. What Fortune's hand shall stretch to me in the German land, I know not. Shall her smiles light up my path, or will my fate be that of so many of my compatriots? But to what purpose these questionings? Let come what may Piaras Grás will do his duty.

CHAPTER III

SPEIER—THE CAPTURE OF THE STANDARD

NIGHT in the Bavarian Palatinate. Cold and bright glance down the moon-rays on the placid waters of the Middle Rhine, flowing swiftly on its northern course towards the land of dyke and ditch, the Dutch Nederlanden. Away beyond rises up the tall spire of the old cathedral of Speier, looking down from its lofty height on the ancient town nestling beneath, whose streets have full many a time echoed to the shouts of the victorious invaders, who came with fire and sword, the shibboleths of their various parties on their lips, to level its walls and deliver its burghers to the fury of a soldiery maddened with the wine of victory. Dark and silent it stands out in the clear moonlight like some giant sentinel keeping watch and ward through the lonely watches of the night.

To my eyes, at least, it appeared so as I stood at my lone post this cold November night, leaning on my carbine, and musing on the battle which would take place on the morrow. But the moon shone down on other sights than that old cathedral town. Its rays glanced back from row on row of white tents. It tipped bayonet point and musket barrel as they stood piled ready to be seized at the morning's dawning.

From my post I could mark the extent of our lines by the camp-fires, which twinkled redly through the darkness. To my ears was borne the sharp "Qui Vive" of our sentinels as they watched lest an enemy might steal on us unawares. No other sound broke the stillness. All around men slept, and, mayhap, dreamed of the dear ones left behind in some village of old Normandie, or on some storm-beaten coast of far-away Bretagne, whom they might never see again. Or, mayhap, they dreamed of the glory which might be theirs. All around repose and forgetfulness reigned.

Musingly I gazed on the peaceful scene spreading out before me. How soon would its peace be broken by the red tocsin of war! How long ere its fairness be marred by its dread engines! How long ere torn, mangled bodies of Frank and Teuton would lie along these quiet valleys!

The word had gone forth that we would fight on the morrow. During the day, and well into the night, our chief, the gallant old Marshal de Tallard, bravest amongst France's soldiers, had made an inspection of all our forces. In fighting trim we had stood before him. It was a stirring sight to see the stout old warrior, riding along with his staff-officers, accompanied by torch-bearers, examining arms and accoutrements, dropping a word of kindly commendation here, or a sharp word of reprimand there. The Marshal was no drawing-room soldier, owing his position to the intrigues of courtesans at Versailles, but a grizzled war-dog, who had won his way by valour and prowess on the tented field.

But that had passed. The camp had become quiet, and the soldiers had disposed themselves to the snatching of such repose as they might, till the drum would beat its shrill reveille, and they would seize their arms to meet the shock of the advancing enemy.

Before us lay the army of the Allies, commanded by the Prince of Hesse Cassel. To-morrow's red work would be no mere skirmish, but a fierce struggle for the mastery, which would be furiously maintained on both sides. Would I see the end of that bloody conflict, or was I destined to leave my bones crumbling to dust on the banks of the lordly Rhine in the land of a stranger people, thrown unknown and uncared for into a pit dug by unheeding hands, where Gaedheal and Gaul, Teuton and Hun would lie side by side, united in the final grand equality of death?

What visions and memories crowd through the brain of the lonely soldier pacing his solitary rounds in the solemn night! What recollections of home and friends come stealing o'er him! Before my mind's eye passed in review the memory of my childhood, spent amidst the gleanns and woods of wild Ui Rathach. The free, happy days when I wandered through the whispering woods, seeking the hidden nest of thrush and blackbird, or that other day when, urged by a spirit of daring, I had climbed to the topmost branch of one of its tallest trees, and remained there, chained at this eerie height by unnameable terror, till the moon had come out, and I was discovered by a party from the castle. Ah! those careless, gladful days so far away, and yet so near!

Sharply and distinctly loomed up before me the sight of a gallant array of armed men, with my father, proud and stately, at their head. I almost imagined I could again hear the skirl and cronan of the pipes as they intoned right merrily the stirring notes of the "Cnota ban." Again filling my ears came the shrilling skirl and deep dordan, as the little band of brave glensmen and swift mountaineers marched away across the purple heather to join the forces of that worthless king from o'er the water. How I had urged and prayed to be allowed to march with them, but embracing me tenderly, my father had bidden me stay to watch over my mother till his return. And then the black days which had followed. To our home was borne faint rumours of victories and defeats. How our forces, struggling bravely, were gradually forced backward, till the black, bitter day, when the news of Aughrim's red debacle came to blast our home, as the lightning's flash blasts the ancient oak. My poor mother, whom I loved with all the hot, unthinking love of a fiery nature, already enfeebled in health, had sunk beneath the blow, and within three days was borne to her resting-place in the old churchyard. And I, after the first burst of violent grief had passed, remained on at the old castle, surrounded by a few faithful old retainers, watching for the return of my father. At last he came, back from Limerick's broken walls, a man bowed down and saddened by disaster, back again to his ancestral hall, where only sorrow and loneliness awaited him. Mo bhron! how different had been his home-coming from his outgoing!

But, Piaras Grás, you are growing sentimental. Rouse yourself, man! Rouse up! Shake off these morbid thoughts. On the eve of your career to allow such broodings to enter into your head. Think not of defeat or disaster. Think only of the promotion which awaits you! Think of the epaulettes which will, perhaps, grace your shoulders ere to-morrow's sun has gone down. The past is dead; the future lies before you.

The clank of arms breaks in on my reverie. I start bolt upright, raise my carbine to the ready, and my challenge rings sharp and clear through the frost-laden air. But a friendly "cara" greets my loud demand. It is the relief making its rounds. I present arms, fall in with the little squad, and in a few minutes am seated amongst my comrade-exiles, who, seated round their camp-fire, with merry jest and story pass the night, which for many of them will be their last.

. . . . . .

The sun of a short November day is shining brilliantly down on the plain where the forces of France and of the Allies are once more engaged in deadly strife. Away in front the red flashes of the artillery spit through the pall of smoke which hangs thick and heavy. The rattle of small arms is almost incessant. The shrill blast of the trumpet cuts through the air above the shrieking of shells and the roll of musketry.

The fight is going badly with us. The German cavalry have snatched many a dearly won trophy from our hands, which will deck the walls of some stately cathedral of the Vaterland. Some of our guns have passed into their hands, and even now thunder against us. Broken and disordered, our columns have been rolled back from the bristling positions of the enemy.

We of Sheldon's Horse had been inactive all the day. Impatiently we had listened to the rolling volleys, watched the shells hurtling through the smoke, seen our French comrades reeling backwards before the Imperialists. But now our opportunity has come. At last the blood-chilling wait is over.

Across the debris-strewn field come thundering a couple of regiments of Imperial cuirassiers, the earth trembling beneath the iron-shod hooves of their chargers, their standards fluttering gaily in the breeze, their trumpets braying the charge. On they come full tilt against the French line. And then an officer dashes up on foam-flecked charger to where our colonel, Christopher Nugent of Dardistown, waits seated on his horse. A salute. A few hurried words and then our trumpets give shrill voice. With sabres gripped tightly, away we go, like an arrow shot from its bow, our horses bounding beneath us as if they welcomed the mad mêlée. Shouting like madmen, we launched ourselves forward, the battle fever coursing wildly through our veins. And I, who had never before taken part in war's red revelry, shouted loudest of any.

And then the shock of our dread meeting. All round me sabres flashed and men shrieked. In that headlong charge many a brave boy who had lilted it right bravely in all our revels went down beneath the crushing hooves of war-maddened horses. The din of that dreadful strife was hellish. Steel clashed against steel. Curses, groans, shrieks, blended with the screams of infuriated steeds in that dread Inferno.

For a few seconds I saw only red. Instinctively I struck at the faces around me. Blinded, intoxicated by the fierce frenzy of battle, recking not of danger, or, rather, unconscious of it, I cleaved furiously, wildly with my sabre. Then dimly, as through a cloud, I saw the tall form of a standard-bearer, bearing aloft the colours of his regiment. He had got slightly separated from his companions. His reddened sabre was grasped in his right hand while his left gripped the staff of his ensign.

With a wild yell I spurred towards him. He swerved aside, trying to avoid my furious onset. In vain. Dropping my rein, I gripped the flag-staff. For a few seconds we struggled desperately for the possession of the trophy. Then a shearing blow from my sabre and my gallant foeman relaxes his grip, and falls backward from his horse with a shriek. My horse bounds forward and carries me onward, waving aloft the captured flag, which flutters as bravely as if it were still borne by the hands of the unfortunate German cuirassier into whose care it had been given, to join in the pursuit of the flying remnant of the cuirassiers.

Of the subsequent incidents of that eventful battle I remember little more. Our tremendous charge had paved the way for another French victory, and led to the surrender of Landau, which opened its gates to our troops three days after the victory by Speier.

But imagine my pride when as, drawn up after the battle, our gallant Marshal rode down our line, one of his staff-officers beckoned me to him. When I rode forward, with the captured ensign waving proudly over my head, and saluted, the stiff old veteran looked me up and down, and fixing me with his eye, asked me my name.

"Piaras Grás of Sheldon's Horse," I replied.

"Oh, un brave Irlandais," he remarked to the officer beside him, and then spoke a few words of praise to me, and rode on, while I, blushing like a schoolgirl, resumed my place in the ranks, amidst the plaudits of my comrades.

Some days afterwards I was summoned to the tent of the Colonel. I found him seated in a camp-chair, looking very pale and wan from the effects of the wounds he had received at the battle. He highly complimented me on my conduct, and informed me that I had been named ensign of my regiment, and he added, while he grasped my hand:

"Ensign, you have done well. Try to do as well in the future and speedy promotion awaits you."

And I, hardly knowing if it were night or day, found voice to reply:

"A Grás always does his best, mon colonel."

CHAPTER IV

THE MOUNTAIN AUBERGE

"Landlord, landlord, rouse up, rouse up!"

My voice echoed mournfully along the silent road, as I reined up my jaded horse before the door of the tumble-down inn, where I hoped to find food and shelter for the night. But no answering voice replied to my loud summons. Impatiently I threw myself from the saddle and hammered loudly on the door with the butt end of my riding-whip. After long and repeated thunderings a night-capped head was thrust through the narrow window up above it, and a hoarse voice growled out:

"What is it you require at such an unseemly hour of the night?"

"Lodging and refreshment for myself, and a stable for my horse. You retire early in this country, good landlord."

Without deigning any reply to my remark the landlord growled out in his most surly voice that he would let me in.

"Yes, and be quick about it, good landlord. This is no night to be abroad," I replied.

And without a doubt it was a bad night. The wind blew through the tall pines in fitful gusts, sending the dead leaves whirling above my head. Away in the distance, where the forest was thinner, I could see the rapid flashes of lightning as they lit up the dark mountain sides for an instant, and then went out, leaving the blackness blacker than it was before. The rumble of the thunder grew momentarily louder, echoing and re-echoing amongst the clefts and defiles till the crash and rattle grew almost continuous. Already the rain had begun to fall in large drops, which came whirling a-down the shrieking wind into my face. In a few minutes it would be a regular downpour, which would render my progress through this wretched country dangerous, if not altogether impossible.

However, here I was within sight of shelter, however indifferent. Fate had been kind to me so far, and it would be ungracious not to accept her good offices. But this landlord was a fearfully long time about opening the door, and I was just striding over to hammer on it again, when with a great clatter and rattle of bolts and bars it swung open, revealing him standing in the opening, shading with his open hand a candle, which threw a flickering and unsteady ray across the mountain road which I had been travelling.

"Now, monsieur," he shouted loudly, so as to make himself heard above the storm, "enter."

"But my horse, landlord," I said, inquiringly.

"I will see to him," he replied.

"No," I answered him quickly, "my horse is my own care. I stable him myself."

I knew these scoundrelly innkeepers only too well. Besides, my life had often depended on the fleetness of my horse, which had never failed me.

"Peste, monsieur, we cannot stand here all night," he growled, angrily. "I will put up the horse presently."

"No, good landlord," I replied steadily. "I see to him myself. A good horse requires all one's care."

"Diable!" he muttered. And then in sudden anger he burst out:

"The foul fiend take yourself and your horse. What a time of night to be abroad."

"Oh! fie, fie, landlord," I remarked in a pained voice. "What a reception to give your guest."

With muttered curses and oaths, he led me round by the corner of the inn, and opening a door in a shed, motioned me in. Beside this ramshackle place the inn itself seemed a palace. But better this than facing the raging storm through the passes, and so, with a philosophic sigh, I accepted this gift of the gods. I made my horse as comfortable as the limited resources of the place would allow; all the while the landlord stood aside looking on scowlingly. Then I turned and accompanied him back to the inn.

In silence he set before me some cold meat and a stoup of wine. Then seating himself in front of the fire, which he had stirred into a blaze, he sat staring moodily into it, while I discussed the dainty viands set before me. Dainty, did I say! The meat seemed to have been torn asunder by the dirty fingers of the landlord; the bread, black almost as the soot left behind by the blazing logs, went near choking me. I have never held by the doctrines of Epicurus. My campaigning has been fatal to epicurean tastes, which are bad companions by the camp-fire or on the march. But were I so inclined, my epicureanism would have received a frightful shock, and I would have turned from the table in disgust. Not being a follower of the jovial old Greek philosopher, I attacked the food with stoical indifference, and thanks to my ravenous hunger and the wine, which fortunately was good, I managed to make a fair meal enough. Experience had taught me the wisdom of enjoying whatever chance threw in my way without taking too much thought as to the manner of its serving.

As I sat sipping my wine, I could see that the host was regarding me with suspicious, if covert, glances. When I had finished, I pulled my chair over to the fire, and endeavoured to engage him in conversation. Possibly this boorish fellow had some information to give away. But I should be cautious not to add to his suspicions.

"A very lonely place this you live in, landlord," I said, tentatively, drawing my chair close into the shadow thrown by the projecting chimney. I wished to have his face in full view.

"Yes," came the gruff reply.

"Do you find it good for business?" I went on, unabashed by his gruffness and apparent want of desire for talk.

"Sometimes yes, sometimes no," and the landlord was gruffer still.

"I' faith, a very chatty aubergiste," I thought to myself, but there are ways of reaching the surliest landlord's heart.

Carelessly, I drew out a cigarro, and lit it in a leisurely fashion. As the aroma of my cigarro spread itself through the room I could see his eyes glisten, as he furtively glanced at me. Ah! I had found the way. I drew out another cigarro.

"Would mine host accept it?" I ventured politely. "I always like a smoke before bed."

Eagerly he stretched his hand for it. Evidently the poor devil had few opportunities of procuring such Spanish cigarros in this out-of-the-way spot. And then he sat enjoying it with all the abandon of a voluptuary.

I had now a good opportunity of studying his countenance. It was evil enough in all conscience. A low, retreating forehead overhung a pair of small, red, ferrety eyes. His cheeks and chin were covered by a short stubbly beard, which but ill concealed a deep cut which ran down along one side of his face almost to his chin. His nose was bent and battered out of all shape, and flattened so much that one looking sideways would imagine that his countenance was not graced by that useful appendage. Seldom had I seen a more villainous face, or one less likely to inspire its beholder with confidence. But what would you? War makes us acquainted with strange landlords. We cannot be too fastidious.

"That is good wine of yours, landlord," I commenced again. "Fit for the king, or the king's collectors."

"Oui, monsieur," he returned. "I try to supply my customers with the best; but it grows more difficult every day."

"Ma foi," I went on. "What matters it whether the king or his collectors have note of it or not, an' it be good."

"Oui, oui, monsieur," he said at last, "the king has good eyes, but his subjects like good wine." And he looked at me cunningly.

"Our tastes before everything," I laughed, falling in with his humour. Whereat the landlord guffawed, doubtless deeming me a good fellow not troubled with too many scruples.

"I was very fortunate to come across your good inn," I went on when the laughter had subsided. "This is not a very pleasant night to be out. But you seem to retire early in this country."

"What would you have, monsieur?" replied the host, now thoroughly in humour; "so few pass this way after dark."

He paused, and then resumed: "Monsieur, you will pardon the rough food I placed before you, but this evening a troop of soldiers were here, who ate up everything I had in the house. Germans they were, who swilled beer like swine. The captain asked me if a Frenchman had called at my inn. He was carrying dispatches, he said, and if I——" He stopped, and then went on: "They left about an hour before you came, monsieur. Ah! they are banditti, those Germans."

Sitting there in the shadow I listened. It was as I feared. The road was watched. And here I was, weather-bound, in this wretched inn, not knowing when those Germans, who were watching for me, might make their appearance. But not by a sign or look did I betray the thoughts passing through my mind. Once I thought of facing the fury of the storm. But as I listened to the roar and rattle, I knew how useless it would be. Without any knowledge of the mountain passes, the morning's light might dawn only to find me stretched lifeless at the bottom of some tall cliff. No! it was better to take my chance. I would set my wits against those of my pursuers, and if the worst came to the worst, why, I had my pistols and a good sword. And so I sat watching the wreaths of smoke curling to the ceiling.

After his confidential outburst mine host became silent again. Mayhap, he thought he had been too communicative. I had no desire to arouse his suspicions by an appearance of over-anxiety for information, and said nothing more, save to utter a few commonplaces as to my willingness to put up with rough fare in the circumstances. And then his wife, as ill-favoured as her husband, came to inform me my room was ready. With a good night to the worthy pair, I mounted the narrow stairs.

Removing my boots, I threw them in a corner, making as much noise as possible, so that I might delude them into the belief I had retired. Then, blowing out the evil-smelling candle, I sat down to think. Here was I, Lieutenant Piaras Grás of Sheldon's Horse, riding with important dispatches for the Marshal Duc de Vendôme, engaged in the siege of Ivrea, over the Italian border, stranded in this lonely inn amongst these wild Alpine passes. Unluckily the news of my journey was out; the emissaries of the Imperialists were on my track. The landlord might be honest or he might not. Living so close to the Italian border, he would be, probably enough, a man of the two sides; to-day a Frenchman, to-morrow a spy of the Imperialists.

Suddenly the sound of stealthy footsteps on the stairs made me start up, and throwing myself into the bed, dressed as I was, begin to snore loudly. Outside the door I heard the footsteps pause; then, as if reassured by my loud snores, the listener moved away again. After a few seconds, above the roaring of the storm, I heard the opening and shutting of a door. Creeping to the window, which was protected by bars, I looked out. In the thick blackness I managed to make out a figure slouching away from the inn.

Who would be abroad on such a night? My instinct told me it could be none other than the landlord, who, tempted by the prospect of a rich reward, had gone to find the Germans. Noiselessly I crept over to the door. I was hardly surprised to find it securely fastened. Escape was cut off in that direction. Nor did the window offer any better chance, since the bars were set too closely to permit of my squeezing through. I realised that I was trapped completely.

But Piaras Grás was not at the end of his tether yet. With some little difficulty I lit my candle again, and searching through the apartment placed my dispatches in a hiding-place where it would have taken my good host a keen search to find them.

Looking to the priming of my pistols, I slowly undressed. A sound sleep would sharpen my wits and refresh my body. I was bound to the inn for to-night, at least. Little the use of distressing myself because of it. With which sage reflection I blew out my light, and was soon snoring in earnest.

CHAPTER V

BETRAYED

The sun's rays were streaming into the room when I awoke. The storm had passed away, leaving few indications of its fierceness. Dressing quickly, I went over to the door. I half expected to find it still fastened, but it yielded to my touch. I smiled to myself at the cunning of mine host, who took such care that I should have no suspicion of his delicate attentions. Ah! he was a clever fellow, that mountain aubergiste.

Lilting a merry tune, I descended to the room where I had had my supper the previous night. I caught the sound of clinking glasses and the singing of a deep-throated German drinking song. The landlord's search had been a success then, and my enemies were here. Dar m'fhocal, they had not caught me napping.

As I entered the song ceased, and the eyes of half a dozen German dragoons were turned on me. With a merry greeting I swaggered over to the fire, and threw myself into a seat in the shadow, where I could see everything which went on. The pause at my entry had been only momentary, then the beer began to circulate freely again. For a while I sat watching them furtively. But all the time I could see that one of them was eyeing me curiously. Should I happen to cast my eyes in his direction he would look away. Seated apart from the others, he did not seem to take much interest in their merriment. He was a typical Teuton, tall and fair-haired, with large, curling moustachios, but had little of the stolid, heavy look which marked the others. Noticing his glances out of the corner of my eye, I resolved to play a bold game. I knew I was standing over a mine which might burst at any moment beneath my feet. Already I was half-suspect.

Throwing myself backward in my seat, I sang out lustily to the landlord, whose villainous face appeared in the doorway just then:

"Landlord, what have you for breakfast? I feel as hungry as the devil himself. Hurry, good landlord, I would fain get to the road again."

Watching him keenly, I saw a look of surprise pass over his sullen countenance. Evidently he had not expected to see me there. But he replied that he would set food before me in a few moments.

"And, landlord," I added, as if in afterthought, "serve me up a couple of bottles of your best wine. Perhaps some of you gentlemen would join me in a bumper." And I addressed my question particularly to the tall, fair-moustachioed trooper.

My proposal was greeted with loud shouts of approval by the soldiers, who turned eagerly towards me. When the landlord had set the wine before me, I shouted out loudly as I filled the glasses:

"Now, comrades, a toast. Here's to Prince Eugene, and confusion seize the French arms. May we always serve under so brave a soldier."

I could see the sudden start of the fair-haired corporal, and the long look which the landlord, who had not yet quitted the room, gave in my direction. But neither made any remark. The room fairly rocked with the shout which rose from the others. With much clinking of glasses and many guttural "Hochs," the toast was drunk. Bumpers were raised to my health. And when the landlord, looking much puzzled, had set before me a substantial meal, they crowded round and plied me with questions as to whither I was bound, what service I had seen, and many others, which I found very embarrassing. But I replied to them all with apparent frankness and becoming condescension. By veiled hints and half-uttered innuendoes I managed to convey the idea that I was a secret agent of the Imperialists.

When at last I rose from the table and ordered the landlord to bring round my horse, I was congratulating myself on the cleverness with which I had hoodwinked them, and had half turned to mount the stairs again, and secure my dispatches.

But the sergeant of the troop, a grizzled old soldier, stepped up to me, and saluting stiffly, remarked:

"Herr Captain, you cannot go for the present. We must search you. We have information that a Frenchman carrying dispatches will pass this way, and our orders are to let no one pass without being searched. Orders are orders, Herr Captain, and you, a soldier, will see they must be obeyed."

"But surely, sergeant," I replied easily, "the servants of His Highness of Savoy may pass unmolested?"

"Herr Captain, our orders are not to let anyone pass," the sergeant replied.

Here was a pretty pass. I, an officer and a gentleman, to be searched by these rascals. What matter, when the wine is drawn one must drink it. I saw that it was useless to protest. Resistance would only injure me. Shrugging my shoulders, I signified my submission to the inevitable, but remarked that the Prince's servants were privileged, and that he would demand an account, should they be delayed or insulted.

"My work," I declared, "demands secrecy and dispatch. The Prince does not brook delay."

The sergeant was nonplussed and stood pulling at his grey moustachio for a few seconds, then turned away. But the fair-complexioned corporal came over to him, and they whispered together for a long while. As for myself, I sat down again, and taking a cigarro from my pouch, lit it and puffed away nonchalantly, awaiting the outcome of the conference.

At last the pair seemed to have decided on their course and turned towards me, the sergeant remarking apologetically:

"Orders, Herr Captain."

Without any further remark I pulled off my long riding boots and threw them to the pair, who examined them minutely. Then my garments followed one by one. But nothing rewarded their search. I had taken good care of that. When the search had concluded and I looked at their blank faces, I could not help remarking banteringly:

"Sergeant, what would His Highness the Prince Eugene say should he learn one of his officers had been searched. Ma foi! how he would rage."

The grey-haired old veteran saluted and murmured: "Our orders are strict, Herr Captain."

"Eh bien!" I went on airily, "the incident has been unpleasant, but it is over. I am a soldier and understand."

The sergeant drew himself up and saluted, and in a few minutes I was in the saddle pricking forward. The beauty of the scenery impressed itself vividly upon me as I rode ahead. At either side of the gorge through which my way led me rose up lofty crags, rising one above the other in savage grandeur, their sides covered with dense foliage, which served to tame much of their wildness and savageness. Through the breaks in their serrated line the sun peeped in now and again, its shafts turning the heavy morning mist into a curtain of shimmering gold. All around me was the gurgle and roar of foaming torrents rushing through their rocky beds, leaping and bounding from rock to rock in mad delight, and finally disappearing far below in the depths. A wild, fierce splendour was everywhere. It was not in my nature to be entirely oblivious of it, but grand and imposing though the scene was, and much as I would have gloried in it at another time, the safety of my dispatches was my chief care at present. I had pledged my word to carry them with all speed to Ivrea. My honour was at stake. Their loss would blast my whole career and cover me with shame. As I thought of them lying there at that accursed inn a shiver ran through me. But then, I thought, they were safe enough. The soldiers, after their ill success, would return whence they came. They would stick to the letter of their instructions, and search only the persons of such travellers as they might meet. The aubergiste himself, if he was still suspicious, would hardly think of looking in my room. So I assured myself they were still lying safely in their hiding-place. But I would not feel content till they were again in my hands. Thinking thus, I turned my horse's head in the direction I had come.

CHAPTER VI

FOOLED—I WIN THROUGH

SEVERAL hours had elapsed since my departure when I again rode up to the auberge. Throwing my bridle across the post which stood outside, I stepped in. There was no appearance of the dragoons about. I greeted the landlord, who answered me with his most ungracious growl, and appeared much surprised at my return. I told him I had lost a most valuable ring, and had returned to see if I might have left it in the room I had occupied. He seemed as if about to refuse me permission, but then thinking better of it he consented, though with a very bad grace. Without further ado I proceeded to the apartment, and in a few seconds the precious papers were again crinkling in my hands. With a sigh of relief, I turned to quit the room, but there on the threshold stood mine host with a mocking grin spreading itself over his ugly countenance.

"Ah! ah! monsieur," he grinned. "We see the little game and a pretty one it is. You thought to deceive Pierre le Bourru."

How I hated that grinning rascal! With a shout of rage, I sprang towards him. But he was wary. Quickly he slammed the door shut and I heard the shooting of a heavy bolt.

"Ah! ah! my clever soldier," he flung back. "Monsieur can cool himself till the Germans come."

Then his retreating steps sounded out, while his burst of mocking laughter almost drove me mad.

Furiously I paced my prison. Soundly I rated myself for an addle-pated fool. I, to be outwitted by this wretch, this scum of an innkeeper.

Just then I heard the trampling of a horse, and going over to the little barred window saw Pierre le Bourru riding away mounted on my horse. Truly this was a turning of the tables with a vengeance. My own horse pressed into service to bring the enemy swarming down about me. This dour-faced landlord had a pretty sense of humour after all. At the thought a fit of uncontrollable laughter seized me. I laughed till my sides ached—laughed till the tears ran down my cheeks. Then, seating myself on the side of the bed, considered the situation.

My previous knowledge told me that there was little chance of escape. Both the door and window had been taken good care of. My wits, sharp though they might be, could not secure me a passage through either. No! there was nothing for it but to await the advent of the enemy, for I was convinced they would soon be here. Meanwhile I would see what I could do to fortify my position. Dragging over the heavy table which stood in the centre of the room, I placed it against the door, which opened inwards, thus barricading it very effectively. Then I piled against it furniture of all kinds, so as to make it more secure. Having made these dispositions, I sat down again and waited.

I had not long to wait. In about half an hour after the departure of the landlord I heard the jingle and rattle of a troop riding hard towards the inn. From my point of vantage at the window I marked them; about twenty heavy dragoons, with a tall officer at their head. With the grizzled old sergeant whom I had hoodwinked rode Le Bourru, a satisfied smile on his face.

They dismounted. Their footsteps sounded on the stairs, and I heard the bolt shot back, but thanks to my barricade the door refused to move. With furious oaths my assailants battered on it, but it was made of stout oak, and their efforts were vain. In a pause of the din a stentorian voice called out:

"Within there. Open and submit to the soldiers of the Emperor."

"Come and take me," I called back.

"We are many. You are only one," the same voice replied. "Deliver your dispatches and you can go free. If not, we will take them and hang you to the nearest tree."

"So be it, monsieur," I called back again. "Come in and take them."

Silence ensued and then the blows commenced again with redoubled vigour. Still the door held and showed little sign of yielding. But another sound fell on my ear, and turning swiftly I was just in time to catch a glimpse of a helmeted head through the window. Ah! that devil of a landlord had shown them a way to outflank me. Another instant and I would have been too late. With a furious thrust of my good sword I spitted the dragoon, who was raising his musqueteon to fire, right through the shoulder. With a yell of pain he threw up his arms and dropped from the ladder, which had been raised to the window, down on to the heads of his comrades who were crowding up after him, who in turn toppled over on to the ground beneath. With a blow from a long piece of timber which I tore off the bed, I thrust the ladder away from the window, and heard it crash down. Peeping out cautiously, I had the satisfaction of seeing it break across in the middle. Nothing would touch me from that side, for the present at least, I thought grimly.

Meanwhile the attack on the door was going on unabatedly. It must soon yield. Already it was trembling and showed one or two great cracks. The greatest danger I feared was the possibility of bullets reaching me. However, I would be sheltered by the jutting of the wall, which formed a deep nook, and offered very fair shelter, while at the same time giving me command of the doorway. Failing a bullet I might hold that opening against a hundred. Suddenly the upper half of the door gave way with a loud snap, and the faces of the troopers showed through the opening. Before a lightning-like thrust one of them fell back.

Then the work commenced in deadly earnest. Several musquetoons flashed out, but their bullets did little damage other than to bring showers of plaster tumbling about my head. When a face showed over the barricade I lunged forward. Already several troopers had felt the bite of my steel. My pistols were of little use to me, because I would have had to expose myself too much to aim, and I feared to risk it.

There came a sudden lull, followed by a shivering blow upon the barricade. Instinctively I knew what had happened. They had secured a beam, and were using it as a ram. My barrier shook and groaned beneath the heavy impact. Recklessly I leaped from my shelter and my pistols spoke out. My shots were answered by cries of pain. Rapidly reloading, I fired again at random into the mass of men who were dimly visible. But the places of the fallen men were quickly filled, and beneath the tremendous blows the barricade yielded. A couple more blows and the doorway was clear. A rush up the narrow stairs, and throwing aside my now useless pistols, I was again hotly engaged.

The advantage of position was mine. In their eagerness the soldiers hampered one another. Lightning-like, my sword flashed hither and thither. Cut, thrust and parry, till my arm ached.

But the unequal combat could not go on for long. The weight of numbers was slowly forcing me back. What mattered all my science and swordplay against this swarm of yelling fiends! And then I caught the gleam along the shining barrel of a long pistol levelled at me out of the gloom. I stepped back into the friendly angle. Had I been standing in my former position Piaras Grás's adventure had ended here. Mayhap, the kindly angel who watched over my birth was hovering near at this instant. As it was, the ball grazed my neck, leaving a slight wound, which began to bleed profusely. At the sight the dragoons set up a fierce yell of delight. The yell was answered by my biting sword.

My backward step had left the opening uncovered for an instant. Only an instant; still long enough to lose me my advantage. Backward I was forced, disputing every inch. And then they were in, pellmell. With back to the wall I fought doggedly. My blade levied a bloody tribute. I was not the most noted swordsman in Sheldon's for nothing. But still the Imperialists swarmed like flies.

Suddenly a loud, authoritative voice rang out. There was a cessation of hostilities, and I leaned back against the wall. The tall German officer who commanded the troop stepped forward, saluting with his sword, a salute which I returned in kind.

"Herr Captain," he said, "may I make you a proposition?"

"Monsieur," I returned, bowing politely, "I will hear it."

"Ach, Herr Captain," he commenced, "it seems to me this business will take a long time. Now if we might settle it man to man. I am noted amongst my comrades for my fencing. You have given us proofs of your prowess. Can we not settle it between ourselves. If I defeat you, you will deliver us your dispatches, for, Herr Captain, we know you are carrying most important ones to Marshal le Duc de Vendôme at Ivrea."

"And, Monsieur l'Officier, what do I gain by your proposal?" I queried.

"Ach, Herr Captain, you see what you gain by a continuance of the combat," and he looked round smilingly. "We have the greater force, besides we have firearms."

"And, Monsieur l'Officier," and I bowed, "suppose I refuse?"

He smiled grimly. "In that case, Herr Captain, the musquetoons."

For several minutes I considered. The dragoons were resting on their arms, interested spectators of the scene. On the one hand I was fatigued and surrounded by the enemy, who, counting the captain, numbered at least a dozen still. What chance had I against them? At least a hand-to-hand fight with their officer would prevent the use of their musquetoons against me, and might by some unforeseen happening render my escape possible. On the other hand, what right had I to place the Duke's dispatches at the hazard of a personal fight. Even were I to purchase my life at their expense, how was I to appear before him with my pledged word broken. But a glance round showed me that no other way lay open. And then I looked at the German, who stood regarding me silently, and said with a shrug of my shoulders:

"Monsieur l'Officier, you leave me no choice. But with your permission," and I bowed, "I will smoke a cigarro. May I offer you one?"

He accepted the one I offered him, and we seated ourselves, he on the only chair which the room afforded, I on the sadly wrecked bed. My sang-froid evidently puzzled him, for he looked at me strangely. But I had gained my object. The respite would be of immense service to me when I stood before him, for, truth to tell, I sorely needed rest after my struggle.

As we smoked we chatted of the engagements we had been in, of the chiefs we had served under, of the many things which interest soldiers. Then he told me of his country, far-away Silesia, and I talked of the gleanns and valleys of Green Eire. Surely men are incomprehensible beings, and to think that in a few moments our swords would seek each other's breasts.

At last we throw away the ends of our cigars, and range out opposite each other. The swords hiss along one another; then with nerves tense, eyes watching every motion, the duel begins.

From the first I saw that I had the advantage. Taller than I, he had the longer reach, but my lightness of foot and swiftness of thrust outmatched his slower, heavier movements. Still he was no mean antagonist, and had he engaged me while I was fatigued, I would have been hard put to maintain myself. As we fought his coolness deserted him, and his thrusts became wilder. No doubt he had counted on an easy victory. Purposely I prolonged the fight, gradually forcing him towards the door, to which he had his back. A dozen times I could have run him through, but the time was not yet ripe. I had no desire to kill him. He had been generous, if unwittingly so.

Now the door was within easy reach, and unguarded, for the dragoons were all clustered round, eagerly intent on the outcome of the fight. Even my friend the landlord had slouched into the room and was gazing on, trembling, possibly, for the fate of his reward. And then I saw my opportunity. With a swift lunge I stabbed fiercely over the German's guard, and ran him through the chest.

In a bound I was through the doorway, and stumbled down the dark stairs, over some wounded men, who lay groaning on it. Through the parlour I rushed, past the hostess, who was powerless to stop me, even if she had the will, and was in the open. My horse was still standing where the landlord had left him. With a spring I was on his back. A couple of shots rang out, and I felt the searing pain of a bullet shoot through my left arm. My shout of defiance pealed out as I went flying down the road, my horse answering in gallant style to my urging. Glancing back I saw five or six of the dragoons mounting hurriedly, and on they came in hot pursuit. For several miles they hung on my heels, but finally I outdistanced them.

Late that evening I rode into the camp before Ivrea,

weary and spent, with my left arm hanging useless, but my dispatches safe. And when I stood before the Duke, and handed them to him, all soiled and bloody as they were,

"Monsieur de Grás," he remarked, "you have done wonders."

"Milord Maréchal," I replied, "I had pledged my word," and then the night came down.

CHAPTER VII

IN HOSPITAL—A MEMORY OF THE HOMELAND

The wound which I had received in my arm and the consequent loss of blood brought on an attack of fever which confined me to a bed in the military hospital for several weeks. But war had toughened my frame, and in about a month after my dangerous adventure I was on my feet again, albeit feeling a trifle weak, and looking worn and haggard. I still carried my arm in a sling, but was allowed to move about unrestrictedly. Eager as I was to return to duty again, the surgeons refused to allow me to go, and though I grumbled at the enforced idleness, I had to obey.

In the hospital I met several soldiers of Dillon's Regiment, invalids like myself whom the chances of war had forced to rest a while. It was only natural that we should feel drawn towards each other. We were of the same race, we served in the same Brigade, we spoke the same tongue. Matters surely which gave sufficient passport to each other's good graces. Daily we gambled and smoked together, assisting each other to while away the idle hours which hung heavy on our hands.

With one of these officers, Muiris O Briain, a lieutenant à la suite in Dillon's, I became particularly intimate. He was a grey-haired, grizzled veteran, one whose undoubted talents and length of service ought to have entitled him to a much higher rank than that of simple lieutenant. At home in a national army a colonel's epaulettes would have graced his shoulders. Here in the service of a foreign king he had to be content with the rather insecure position of lieutenant à la suite. From my first meeting with him I felt irresistibly attracted to a closer intimacy with him than with any of the others. Some subtle sense seemed to urge me on. I could not define to myself that craving, that longing, but there it was, ever present. His name conveyed little to me. True, I had often heard my father speak, particularly in his later days, of a Muiris O Briain who had been his friend. But with what happenings in his life he had been connected I could not recall. Perhaps I had never heard, for there are some memories of which our elders will not speak. But I soon came to know of the reason of his attraction for me.

One day we were seated alone, for most of the others had resumed duty. We were smoking and chatting of the homeland to which our thoughts so often wandered, when O Briain suddenly inquired:

"Grás, what name did your father bear?"

"He was named Seaghan," I replied. "Seaghan Grás of Snaidhm. He served from the Boyne to Aughrim with the King's Army. He was with the force which defended Limerick after that day, and when it had fallen, and our enemies had triumphed, he came back to Snaidhm to enjoy the repose which our masters had agreed to allow to us, but he did not long enjoy his rest in his old home. Ah, it was a sad day which saw the fall of Limerick!"

"Aye, you are right," said O Briain. "Sad indeed! It reduced many brave and gallant gentlemen to the dust, and drove them out, wanderers from their own land. Ah, a sad and bitter day! And your father is dead?"

"Yes," I replied. "His heart broke after the downfall of our cause. He could not bear to look on the ruin which had overtaken the land—to see himself reduced to the position of a serf in the country where he had ruled as lord, a foreign undertaker lording it in the halls where he had spent his youth and manhood. One day we laid him in the old churchyard at Snaidhm. And I am here in France, the last of the Gráses."

"Boy," he cried, laying his hand on my shoulder, "I knew your father well. He was the man who saved my life on the disastrous day of Aughrim. Grieve not for him. At least he is at rest at home in the land he fought for, while I, his companion on many a field of blood, am here, a soldier of fortune, condemned never again to see my home. Is not he much happier than I?"

"Yes," I cried, seizing his hand impulsively, "much happier. But why do you say you will never see our country? Perhaps some happy turn of fortune may raise up the fallen cause. Perhaps we shall enjoy our own again. Then could you not return?"

I spoke with all the grand enthusiasm of youth. But Ó Briain shook his head sadly.

"No," he said, "my heart tells me that I will never again see the sun sinking down into the sea out over Mothar Ruadhain; never again gaze on the white horses as they came trooping in from the wild Atlantic. A Dhia na nGrás! how it all comes back to me. The blazing sun sinking lower and lower, down into the trough of the sea. The quiet, gentle breeze blowing in across the waste of waters. The cry of the sea birds borne to my ears. Often I have stood on the tall cliffs and watched the waves lashed to fury by the wild gale dashing themselves against them, seeking to tear them away from their world-old foundations. But no more I shall gaze on those scenes of my youth. They are gone out of my life, and I am alone, a homeless wanderer. Wife, country, friends, all, all are gone, and I am here, a swordsman in the service of a foreigner, battling in causes with which I have no concern, quarrels which fire me not. Ah, boy, how much I have seen!"

His eyes held a far-away, unseeing look. He seemed to have forgotten my presence.

"Come," I cried, wishing to rouse him from his melancholy, "tell me of your former life."

He started and looked at me. Then recollecting himself, he cried:

"Forgive me, my young friend. For the moment I had forgotten. But these thoughts of dead days surging in on me carried me away into the past. However, you will not find Muiris O Briain offending again with wailings. I am a soldier, but even a soldier forgets himself sometimes." He smiled half sadly. "But you would like to hear my story."

"Yes," I replied. "My poor father often spoke of you."

"Ah, he remembered!" said O Briain. "My story is brief, but you shall hear it. It is like many another which might be related by our comrades-in-arms."

CHAPTER VIII

O BRIAIN'S STORY

"I WILL begin by saying that in the whole of Clare there was not a happier man than Muiris O Briain of Ruadhan when in March of '89 King James landed at Kinsale. Young, light-hearted, care-free, I had just been married. How beautiful my Maire was! How I loved mo chailin fionn! How I treasured every word, every act of hers! Ah me! how soon our dream of bliss was over! When the news of the outbreak of war came to our home she bade me go to take my place with the others in defence of our land. For the foreign king who used us as pawns, I cared nothing. The country called. For it I risked all. I can see her yet standing by our gate in the morning sun waving her scarf to me in farewell as I marched away with my gallant company, her kisses still fresh on my lips. By the Boyne we fought when the King had fled away. Through the campaign which followed I was the companion of the brave men who, buffeted about as the shuttlecocks of foreign policies, still struggled on. Belied, traduced, betrayed we were by men who thought only of the good of their parties, not of our country's. My God! My God! Will it be ever thus? Will we never fight for a policy of our own; must we always spend ourselves in entanglements with policies of men alien to us, building up their strength that they may pull ours down? But I have forgotten. . . . My gallant lads were by my side through all. With them

I hungered and thirsted, went barefooted and ragged. They never grumbled. They died when their time came for the cause they thought right.

"During this time I had ridden several times to my home at Ruadhan. My dear one welcomed me with words of joy and love. Then after a few hours spent in her company I rode away again to take my place in the ranks, cheered and comforted by my visit. What need to speak of our struggle! The world has seen how it was maintained against odds the most overwhelming. And then came the awful day of Aughrim, when what had been almost a victory was turned in a moment into black, bitter defeat. Some time previously I had met your father. From the first we were close friends. On that day we fought side by side. Our swords flashed together as we drove the foreigners down the Hill of Kilcommedan and into the morass. And then the disaster came which lost us the day, and began the downward descent of our cause. The death of our general, slain as he led the final charge, snatched success from our hands. I, sorely wounded, was brought away from that fatal field, and it was your father who saved me. It was he, who, accompanied by some of his faithful men, brought me after a long and toilsome journey to my far-off home, and then, having placed me in safety, tended by my beautiful Maire, turned his face to Limerick. Boy, I never saw him again, and now he is dead."

I uttered no word. My companion's story had stirred up bitter memories. He went on:

"To him I owe my life. Monuar! how much better it would have been had he left me there; had I died on that field knowing that I had done my duty. I would have been spared the lonely years with their painful memories. . . . But," as he noticed the look of pain pass across my face, "forgive me, boy, if I have pained you. Your gallant father did not know. He was not a seer who could scan the future, nor was I. Would to God I had been! . . . For weeks, aye, months, I lay on my bed. But love drew me back to life. Maire tended me night and day. In the frenzies of my fever it was her white hand laid on my brow which calmed my struggles. When I rose from my bed, spent and wan, it was her dear arm which guided my tottering steps. . . . The struggle had gone against us. The treaty had been signed. Our army had sailed away. Our position as vassals of the foreigners was secure, so 'twas said. But how secure it was we soon knew.

"It was known that I had been active in opposing the conquerors. My name was included in the list of those outlawed, for whom there was no grace. But for some time I lived in peace. Possibly our home away by the wild Atlantic waves was too remote from the seats of power; possibly the victors were too busy in attending to richer game. But the fatal day came all too soon. I possessed a small estate, not very valuable, yet sufficient for my needs. Poor though it was, it aroused the cupidity of an undertaker named Trasker, who lived near us. It was declared forfeit to the informer, and we were forced to fly. We took refuge in the mountain shieling of a poor retainer, and I might have been happy, for my dear one was by my side.

"But the black undertaker who had acquired my few acres soon learned of the hiding-place of one who was an outlaw, who had not taken the oath of allegiance, who had drawn his sword against the Government in power. I was abroad one day when to our cottage came this hell-born wretch. He was on my track, and was accompanied by half a dozen soldiers. My poor Maire told him I was not at home, but the foul wretch endeavoured to force her to his embrace. Enraged at the resistance she made, and alarmed by her screams, the scoundrel emptied his pistol into her fair bosom, and mounting his horse rode away. A Dhia na bhfeart! the sight which greeted my eyes when scarcely half an hour afterwards I returned——"

He paused and turned away. I saw the war-scarred frame quiver under the sobs which burst from him. M'anam, how terrible it is to hear a strong man weep! Gritting my teeth to keep back the lump which rose in my throat, I turned away my head. But dashing the tears from his eyes, O Briain resumed:

"On the floor just inside the threshold lay mo chailín aluinn. The blood still flowed from the wound in her breast. With a cry of anguish I raised her up.

"'What fiend has done this?' I cried.

"'Trasker!' she gasped. 'He came to arrest you.'

"'The hound!' I cried. 'His own blood shall flow for it. But I must bind up your wound, and then seek assistance.'

"''Tis useless,' she replied, her poor voice scarcely above a whisper. 'I am going from you, Muiris. Promise me that you will leave the country at the first opportunity.'

"'I promise,' I replied, my voice choked with grief.

"'I am content,' she said, 'Dia go deo leat i mbaile agus i gcéin. Kiss me, Muiris, before I go.'

"Passionately I pressed my lips to her paling ones. A smile passed over her beautiful face, and with scarcely a sigh she passed away in my arms."

He bowed his head on his hands, and was silent a long time. Again he went on:

"There beside my murdered love I swore to be revenged on her murderer. At night I went to the village which lay a few miles away. Accompanied by some of the poor people who had known her, I laid her to rest on her mother's breast, beneath the walls of the ruined old abbey where our tyrants had forbidden us to bury our dead unless it were consecrated to the usages of the new faith. She had no shroud but her cloak, no requiem save the sad night wind blowing in from the sea, no light save the rays of the pale moon rising up over Mothar Ruadhain. In silence we worked, in silence we prayed. But before I turned away from that grave which held all that had made life dear to me, I again, on bended knees, renewed my vow of vengeance."

He paused, and I could see the tears coursing down his rugged cheeks. And I, my eyes wet, bent my head.

"I think I became mad after that," the low voice resumed again. "I cared not what became of me. The people—ah yes, they protected and sheltered me, but they had troubles and griefs of their own. I wandered up and down through the country, searching, searching, always searching for the devil, Trasker. I could have gone to his house, but that was guarded. No, he would come to me, and then—— For weeks and weeks I watched and waited. Food, rest—they mattered not to me. A pair of loaded pistols were my only possessions. They were enough. And then one night I met him. . . ." His voice rose exultantly. Even at this distance of time he felt the fierce joy of that meeting. "Aye, I met him. It was on the road which runs by the cliff. Crouched down in the shadows I watched him approach, riding slowly. He was whistling to himself, unconscious of danger. Ah, he did not know I was there! I sprang out on the road, and shouted to him to halt. In the moonlight I looked a veritable fiend, with my unkempt beard and hair. And so I was; so I was," he whispered.

"Pulling up his horse, he demanded my business.

"'You will soon know,' I cried, seizing his rein. 'Dismount.'

"He tried to draw a pistol, but I sprang on him, and seizing him in my arms dragged him to the ground. In my madness I had the strength of a dozen men.

"'Now,' I cried. 'Look to yourself, George Trasker. Either you or I die to-night.'

"'Who are you, madman?' he cried.

"'You pretend you do not know me, dog,' I shouted. 'But too well you know Muiris O Briain, whose wife you murdered.' In the moonlight I could see the terror leap into his eyes. 'Here, take this pistol. Hell-born devil, I will give you a chance for your life,' and I pushed a pistol into his hand. But the cur wished to save his vile life.

"'O Briain,' he cried, his voice shaking with fear. 'You are a poor man. I will make you rich again. I will restore your lands.'

"'Can you restore my murdered wife to life?' I shouted. 'What care I for lands or gold? I seek only vengeance,' and I struck him on the mouth.

"Again he tried to parley with me. Aye, he even kneeled to me, but I laughed and spat in his face. Suddenly he raised his pistol and fired at me, but the bullet only grazed my cheek. Springing to his feet, and casting the empty weapon into my face he turned and fled. But as he reached the cliff I fired. With a wild yell he leaped out, and went crashing down on the beach far below. And I, looking down on his ghastly, upturned face, whispered in my heart:

"'Maire! Wife! You are avenged.'

"Amongst the cabins of the peasantry I hid myself till the hue and cry raised by the authorities had blown over. Then I crossed to France, and again took up my place in the Regiment of Clancarty. With it I served for several years, and had risen to the rank of captain, but the Peace of Ryswick in '98 caused the reduction of many of the regiments of our Brigade, and destroyed the chances of advancement of many a brave fellow; and you see me now—grey-haired, war-battered, a simple lieutenant à la suite. But I care little. My vow of vengeance has been kept. On many a field of blood I have struck at the forces of the Government, of which Trasker and his like were minions. I have no other care; no other wish. I live on having no possessions but my sword, no memories but those of a murdered dear one—a murdered country.

Hopes?—ah, they are dead! Some day soon my life will go out in the hurly-burly of the charge, and cast into the pit where so many nameless ones shall lie; Muiris O'Briain will be at rest, and his spirit—happy in its release—shall seek that country where it will meet again that dear one whose body lies beside the old abbey walls near to Mothar Ruadhain."

His voice died away. For a long time we were silent. At last he raised his head, and laying his hand upon my shoulder, said:

"That is all. You know now how I came to know and love your father; why I pained you by saying it would have been much better had he let me die at Aughrim. But, Grás, for your father's sake let me be a friend to you. Should you ever need one do not fear to call on me. You are young. A friend, even though he be a beggar, may be useful at times."

I gripped his hand and pressed it warmly, and as I did so I little thought how soon I would sorely need a friend. I left him then. He was still oppressed with the gloom of his sad story, nor could I banish his sadness. Mo bhron, how many stories were like to his! How many men of the Brigade had wrecked homes, blasted hopes, to mourn!

CHAPTER IX

A GIRL'S APPEAL

My arm rapidly improved. I hoped soon to receive the order which would release me from hospital, and send me spurring away on my fleet-footed charger to join my squadron. My spirits rose at the prospect, and I went about whistling and singing in my light-heartedness. But I reckoned not with Fate. It had other things in store for me. One evening the ring of spurs sounded outside my door. Springing to open it, I perceived an officer standing on the threshold. He handed me a letter from Monsieur le Duc which ordered me to report myself at his quarters next day to take up duty as aide-de-camp. For the present I was to attach myself to Dillon's Regiment till I would receive further orders. The letter would be sufficient introduction to the regimental commandant—M. le Comte Arthur de Dillon.

When the aide had withdrawn, I hastened off to see O Briain, who had again resumed duty.

"Ha!" he cried, when he had read the letter. "You are a fortunate fellow, Piaras. There are many in camp who would give their eyes to be appointed to the Marshal's staff. The Duke has taken a liking to you."

"I wish he hadn't," I grumbled. "I would much rather return to my own regiment than remain here in the Duke's service."

"Hush!" cried my friend. "Let no one hear you say so. The Duke is a stern disciplinarian, and would not approve of your questioning his command. Come, we will go to see our colonel."

M. de Dillon received me very kindly, and having read the Duke's letter, assigned me quarters in the regimental cantonments. Next day I reported myself at the Duke's quarters. It was yet early, and I had to wait some time before he came to me. Apparently he had only risen from bed. His hair was frowsy, and his dress untidy. Altogether he appeared not to have quite recovered from the effects of a night's carouse. Withal he had a handsome face, though it was sadly marred by dissipation. As I stood saluting he inquired kindly if I had fully recovered from my illness, to which I replied that I felt fully fit to undertake any duties he might assign me to. He appeared pleased, and remarked:

"Monsieur de Grás, you will wonder why I have not sent you back to your regiment, but I like the men of your nation, and would like to see more of you. Your service of the other day has shown me that you are a brave soldier."

I saluted in recognition of the compliment. With such flattery M. le Duc had gained the goodwill of his soldiers, who loved him in spite of his faults, and they were not few.

"You will report yourself here daily," he went on. "I have little doubt you will fulfil my expectations of you. Till to-morrow you are free, then my chief of staff will assign you duties."

He turned away, and feeling myself dismissed I returned to my own quarters. Thus I found myself in the service of the Duke—a unit of his personal staff. I wondered to myself whether it would turn out well or ill for me. It was not a position which fell every day to the lot of a poor lieutenant, and I ought to have been satisfied with such a mark of favour; but even so I would have preferred to have gone back to Sheldon's. However, the first duty of the soldier is obedience. He must learn to subordinate his will to that of others.

For some days I followed the routine of duty laid down for me, and then an incident occurred which came near blasting my whole career, and placing me before a firing platoon; or, at the very least, consigning me to a lonely cell in the Bastille. But looking back at it now I cannot say that I regret my action in the matter, however much I may regret its consequences; nor do I think that, placed again in like circumstances, I would act differently.

One day I received from the Duke's own hand a letter to be conveyed to a part of the cantonments which lay some distance away from the little village where Milord Duc had his quarters. He had instructed me to deliver the letter only to the person to whom it was addressed: "M. le Chevalier de Frobin, Colonel of the Regiment of Béarn." Mounting my horse I galloped off to the residence of the noble Colonel. Striding up the steps of the house —one of considerable pretensions—where the commandant lived, I knocked, and being at once admitted, was conducted into a pleasant morning-room, while the soldier-servant went to seek his master.

Left to myself I gazed round the lofty room, which was furnished in very luxurious style, much more luxuriously than one would expect the quarters of an officer engaged on active service to be. But the commandant, I reflected, was extremely fastidious in his tastes, and wished to surround himself with all the elegancies of his Parisian hôtel. Seated there in the high-backed chair I mentally drew a portrait of him. Tall, well-built, he was dandyish in his style of dress—the true court-gallant. Young (he was scarcely more than my own age), dark-complexioned, with black hair and moustachio, he was a very handsome man. But his black eyes, set closely together, gave to his face a rather cruel, sinister look, which detracted somewhat from his handsomeness. For the rest he had the reputation of being a brave soldier, a great gambler, and a most accomplished roué. From the first I had taken a dislike to the dashing Chevalier. On the few occasions we had met at the Duke's quarters he had been courteous enough. Nevertheless he always grated on me; nor could I tell why. Intuition, doubtless.

Suddenly the stealthy opening of a door interrupted my train of thought. I looked expectantly towards the door by which I had entered, expecting to see the Chevalier enter. But then, he would hardly come so secretly. I almost cried out in astonishment as I saw advancing from behind a heavy silken portière which draped the further portion of the room, a girl, her fingers on her lips as if to enjoin silence. As she came towards me I had time to note that she was tall and beautiful, of a dark, Italian type of beauty, with great black eyes, which held a look blended of hope and fear. She could not have been much more than twenty years of age. So astonished was I that, after my first start of surprise, I sat gazing mutely at the fair stranger coming towards me. When she reached my side she bent her head, and whispered in my ear:

"Monsieur, one who is wretched craves your help. Torn from my home and held here a prisoner by this wretch, de Frobin, I have no one to appeal to. Will you assist me?"

I regarded her in astonishment. She, a prisoner at the mercy of the Chevalier! In truth it was horrible to think of. I felt myself going cold at the thought. Knowing, fearing, could I refuse to listen to her appeal? But cold reason whispered to me, dare I consent? If I were to consent to listen what would be the outcome of it? Would I not arouse his enmity? And what then would be my chances against the powerful Chevalier, the friend of the Duke, and one highly thought of at Court? The Duke! Might he not understand and protect me? But I knew sufficient of him to force me to the belief that he would side with his favourite, who could command his ear in a way I could not. However, I was an Irishman. I could not be deaf to the voice of distress.

Interpreting my silence unfavourably, the girl said, as she half turned away: "Ah, you also! You are in league with this roué," and I could see the bitter tears gather in her eyes.

"Heaven forbid!" I cried, in a low voice. "If I can be of any service to you, mademoiselle, command me."

"Kind Heaven be thanked!" she breathed fervently. Then hurried on as a quick footstep made itself heard in the hall. "I cannot speak now. The Chevalier must not know that I spoke to you. If you would learn more come to-night at nine. If Heaven is kind I will be at the little green door beside the grove. Now, not a word to anyone."

Before I had time to reply she was gone. Hardly had she glided behind the portière when the Chevalier came in. He greeted me pleasantly enough, and having read the letter I had brought, requested me to inform the Duke that he would be at his quarters at eight.

Back at my duty again I pondered over the girl's strange appeal. The affair puzzled me very much. Several times the thought came to me that it was a trap designed by someone who might feel aggrieved at my staff-appointment, to entangle me with the Chevalier, and through him with the Duke. But I rejected this possibility. I could not believe my appointment could lead to such a plot. Was the girl mad, I wondered? But no. No light of madness gleamed from her dark eyes. Nor could I believe that she was fooling me; that only the desire for a little secret intrigue had prompted her. No, her distress was too evident for that. I would have spoken with Muiris O Briain but for the silence she had enjoined on me. So I shrugged my shoulders. My honour was pledged. I would at least hear the girl's story.

The hours fled away, and nine o'clock found me

at the tryst. I had scarcely taken my stand by the little green door, having left my horse tied some distance away, when I felt a touch on my arm, and a voice whispered:

"You have come, then."

Turning, I perceived in the darkness the form of a girl, my suppliant of the morning, for I recognised the low, sweet voice. Bowing, I replied:

"Mademoiselle, I never break a promise."

"Oh, thanks, thanks for your trust," she cried. "God has at last sent me a friend. Oh, how I have prayed for this!"

"Mademoiselle," I inquired in a low voice, "what of the Chevalier?"

"Fear not," she hastened to reply. "He rode away in the direction of the camp about an hour ago. Susanne, the woman who watches me with never-sleeping eyes, has gone to the camp also, doubtless to see some soldier lover, leaving me in charge of another maid who is less careful in her watch than she. I managed to prevail on her to allow me to walk in the garden. Thus I have found my opportunity."

"Let us hurry then, fair mademoiselle," I said, for I had no desire to be discovered in such a place. "Your story is not yet known to me. I do not know why you wish for my help."

"My story is short, and easily told," she began eagerly. "When you hear it I know you will not refuse me help. I am held here captive by this roué, daily exposed to all the dangers which an unprotected girl in the hands of an unprincipled man can be exposed to. I am the daughter of the Vaudois chief, Henri Neffer, who has long held out against the French, and fought for his legitimate prince, Victor Amadeus. As such he has been pursued relentlessly by your forces, but my father knows our Alpine fastnesses. . . . Ah, monsieur, I know you are a French soldier, but you are also an honourable gentleman."

She paused. There was an accent of fear in her voice. I could feel, rather than see, her eyes fixed anxiously on me.

"I hope so, mademoiselle," I replied. "My loyalty to my flag does not prevent me from being that."

"I thank you," she said, and then went on. "One day to our mountain home came a force of Frenchmen, guided by one who had sold us for gold. They were led by this Chevalier de Frobin. My father was absent with the greater part of his band. Even so the few brave men who were on guard made a fierce resistance, but they fell one after another, and I became the prize of the leader. Ah, monsieur, did you know all I have gone through since that unfortunate day! The insults to which I have been daily subjected. How sorely I have been tempted to end it all!"

Her voice faltered and broke. She bowed her head in her hands and wept bitterly. For a few minutes I was silent. Her distress pained me. All my doubts of her had gone. The horror of her position, a captive here in this house, appalled me. But what could I do? To appeal to the Duke against the Chevalier, I felt would be worse than useless. He would only feel amused at the gallantries of his friend. Besides, this girl was the daughter of Henri Neffer, the guerilla chief, who had so often and so successfully struck deadly blows against his convoys of supplies. If no worse fate befell her, he would hold her as hostage for her father's good behaviour. What then was to be done? For something should be done to rescue the girl from her unhappy position. Ha! If she could escape. Gently I laid my hand on her shoulder.

"Weep no more, mademoiselle," I said. "If I can aid you, I will do so."

She seized my hand and covered it with kisses. And I confess her action made me hot with embarrassment.

"May God bless you for your goodness," she cried.

"Pray God that He may assist us," I said, "for indeed this task is a difficult one. Mademoiselle, have you any friend who would receive you if you were outside our lines?"

"I know only one," she replied. "A poor shepherd who lives amongst the mountains about three hours' ride from this. If I could reach his cottage he would convey word to my father."

"Good!" I ejaculated. I had been thinking out a plan. If I could procure the assistance of Muiris O Briain I was convinced I could manage the affair. Muiris could wait close to the Chevalier's with horses till I came to him after being dismissed from duty. Then if the girl could slip away from the house we could ride as rapidly as possible to the shepherd's house she had mentioned. Of course there was the difficulty of getting through our lines. A girl riding with two officers at night-time would arouse dangerous comment. If we should be stopped and questioned I feared it might be fatal to our scheme. And then there was the danger of being met by patrols. It was clear we could not venture to take the girl undisguised. Ah, why not disguise her as one of ourselves! That would make everything easy. I rapidly outlined my plan to my companion.

"But," I said, "for your greater safety you must become a man, a soldier. We dare not risk attempting to pass the lines with a girl."

"I see that," she replied, "and I will assist in every way possible. I will become a soldier even for the time. Mon Dieu, I would do more than that to escape from this house."

"I will make myself responsible for the procuring of a uniform," I said. "But how can I convey it to you?"

She thought for a moment.

"I have a beautiful bracelet," she said, "which Susanne, my gaoler, covets very much. I have little doubt I could bribe her with it to convey a bundle or letter to me. You understand, she might not be averse to a little intrigue if it paid her."

"No, no," I cried, "that would never do. The woman would take your bribe, and then betray us. No, we must not trust our secret to her. Is there not any other way?"

"Unless you might come to me secretly," she said. "Ah, that is it! Do you see that window from which the light streams out?" and she directed my gaze towards a window which was brightly illuminated. "That is my sleeping apartment. If you could come unseen, you could climb by the ivy which covers the wall. It is thick and strong."

"That is the better plan," I said. "Much safer than to place ourselves in the power of a third person. But you must be careful not to rouse suspicion. Go on as if nothing had happened, as if you were resigned to fate."

"Have no fear," she replied. "Aimée Neffer can be careful. She will play her part."

"I will come again to-morrow night when darkness has fallen. Be you on the watch till you hear my tap at your window. Can you keep a light burning?"

"Yes," she replied, "I will do so. But hark! They are seeking me. I must away."

Even as she spoke a call in a woman's voice rang out on the night air.

"Farewell, my generous friend," she whispered. "Kind angels guard you for my sake, and your own."

And then she was gone. Going to where I had tethered my horse, I mounted and was soon back in camp.

CHAPTER X

THE ESCAPE

Muiris O Briain threw himself into the affair with a will after I had explained to him the danger in which the girl stood. True, he pointed out the danger which might come to me if the part we were about to play should reach the ears of the Chevalier. He even had a wild idea about calling out that gentleman, but I set myself against such an absurd proposal.

"What good would a duel with him do this poor girl?" I asked. "Even if we were to defeat him, she would still be a prisoner. True, by that means we might bring the affair to the ears of the Duke, but I fear that would do little good, merely exchange one prison for another. And probably I'd erect a prison for myself, for the Duke does not approve of duels between his officers when on campaign, even if the gallant Chevalier were to agree to meet either of us."

"Aye, I suppose you are right," growled Muiris. "We can only fall back on your plan in that case."

We arranged everything to our satisfaction. I had discovered that the Chevalier had been ordered for special duty the following night.

"That will be our chance," I said. "We must have everything arranged for then. While he is away the watch on the girl will be less strict."

"That is so," said O Briain. "We are agreed then?"

"Yes," I replied. "You will see to the horses. And not a word to anyone."

That night I went again to the Chevalier's. Stealing through the garden, I climbed the ivy which I found afforded a good foothold, and tapped at the window from which the light shone out. Cautiously it was opened, and Aimée Neffer looked out from the darkness, for she had extinguished the candles.

"Hush!" I whispered. "It is I, Piaras Grás."

In a few words I told her of our arrangements.

"I will come to-morrow evening," I said, "and will bring with me an officer's uniform. Dressed as one of Dillon's, we need have little fear of discovery. I will come as soon after nightfall as possible. You must then dress in the uniform as quickly as you can, and descend by this ivy without any undue sound. You will not be afraid of the downward descent?"

"I am a mountaineer," she replied simply.

"Good. And you must be alone as much as possible to-morrow evening. Feign sickness, sulk, or do something that you may retire to your room when the night comes. They will hardly suspect a sick girl has any other intention than that of retiring to rest. It will remove you out of the reach of watchful eyes. If we can allay suspicion till the morning all chance of pursuit will be gone."

"I will manage it," she replied. "I am locked into my room each evening. Susanne sleeps in the next room. But I am often sulky, and refuse to allow her to come into my room. At such times I drag a table across the door. I will do the same to-morrow night. . . . Oh, mon ami, I tremble to think that we may fail!"

"What! Afraid!" I cried. "The daughter of Henri Neffer ought not to fear. You will soon be amongst your native mountains again. You must not think of failure."

"And I had thought that I was brave, but I see now that I am only a weak girl, affrighted by a little danger. Ah, mon ami, what risks you are running for my sake!"

"Do not speak of them," I said. "There are a

hundred men in our regiment who would run similar ones. What matters all the risk if we succeed, and we will succeed. Adieu then till to-morrow evening."

"Adieu," she whispered. "I will be brave. When you come you will find me ready." Then I swung down the ivy and was away.

. . . . . .

The night which was to see our attempt fell black and threatening. Had we ourselves had the arranging of the weather we could not have arranged it more suitably. It was about an hour after dark when O Briain and I rode up to the clump of trees beside which he was to wait. Leaving him there I stole forward. Soon I was tapping at the window. It was opened and Aimée Neffer gazed into my face. I handed her the bulky bundle which I had tied to my belt, whispering:

"Everything goes well. We could not have selected a better night. And you, have they any suspicion?"

"I do not think so," she replied. "They imagine I am asleep."

"Hurry, then. Hurry!" I cried. "I will await you below."

At the foot of the ivied wall I waited. But the delay was not long. Soon I heard the rustle of the ivy, and then the girl laid her hand on my arm, and whispered:

"I am ready."

"Come then," I said. "Draw your cloak closely round you for the night is an unpleasant one, but it is all the better for our purpose. O Briain awaits with the horses."

I felt her start, and hastened to reassure her.

"He is a brother-officer, mademoiselle. One whom I can trust. Without his aid I fear I would have been unable to help you."

My assurance satisfied her, for she whispered:

"If he is a friend of yours, monsieur, I am content. Let us go on."

In a few minutes we reached the place where O Briain waited. He called out in a subdued voice as we glided towards him:

"Is that you, Piaras?"

"Yes," I replied with similar caution. "Has anything occurred?"

"No," he answered. "Everything is quiet. But I did not think you could have been here so quickly."

I laughed, and, mounting, we urged our horses onwards through the darkness. The rain beat into our faces as we pressed forward, but we regarded it as a blessing. Nothing more fortunate could have happened. The pouring rain would keep everyone under cover except those whose duties compelled them to be abroad. If by any mischance we should meet a patrol they would think we were on special duty. I had little fear of danger till we reached a point where the road branched off to the mountains. This place I knew was guarded by a strong outpost, fortunately of Dillon's Regiment. I would avoid it if possible, but if not I had taken means to find out the password. Still I feared if we were stopped the presence of our female companion might compromise us. I therefore whispered an injunction to her to be silent whatever happened. Hardly had I done so when the tramp, tramp of a body of men coming towards us struck on my ear. There was no chance of turning aside. Even had there been I would not have done so. Had they seen us it would seem strange that three French officers should avoid one of their own patrols. So we rode on.

When the challenge came I answered, and then, almost stunned with the knowledge, I heard the voice of the Chevalier saying, as he rode up to us:

"Ah, Lieutenant de Grás, you ride late. Morbleu! it is a devilish night."

"Aye," I laughed. "One which might be better spent in camp. But weather has little consideration for soldiers."

"No," he cried. "A bottle of wine and a pack of cards would be better work on such a night as this than outpost duty. But whither are you bound?"

"To the Col yonder."

"Ah, you are not far from it now. Messieurs, a good night to you," and he gave his men the order to march.

"M'anam," whispered O Briain to me as we spurred on, "what ill wind drove the Chevalier in this direction to-night?"

"It must have been an ill one indeed," I replied. "But it was fortunate for us that the night was so black, else he would have recognised the mademoiselle, and then the game was lost."

And then I turned to reassure the girl whom I felt must have been sadly alarmed by the unlooked-for meeting with her enemy. We did not approach the pass where the Dillons held guard. Instead, guided by our fair companion, we turned away from the road we were pursuing, and made our way through a rocky defile which would carry us away beyond the outpost, and far outside the French lines. We had to lead our horses over the rough, broken ground, and once nearly ran into a small outlying party. It was only the ring of a musket-butt against a stone which warned us of its proximity, and we turned aside just in time. We met with no more danger, and when we had toiled on for a couple of hours more, ever striking deeper and deeper into the mountains, I judged we ought to be close to the end of our journey. Hardly had the thought come to me, when Aimée Neffer exclaimed:

"Monsieur de Grás, we have almost reached the end of our flight. Five minutes more, and we will be at the cottage of Gaspard, of which I spoke to you."

Standing beside her we gazed on the scene of savage grandeur spread out before us. During our ascent the storm had died away, and now the moon sailed through a calm, peaceful sky. Its pale light showed us the mountains rising up all around us, grand and magnificent, their cleft and riven sides clothed with dark pine forests. Away in front of us a foaming torrent leaped down the mountain side, bounding, tumbling from rock to rock, glittering silver-like in the moonlight. The sound of glacier-born waters was everywhere, laughing, babbling, shrieking as they flung themselves down to the plains below. The moan of the mournful night-wind wandering through the dark forests came to us. I confess I felt a feeling of gloom and loneliness creeping over me standing there on that mountain side. Possibly my companions felt it too, for O Briain cried:

"M'anam istigh! This place oppresses me."

"Yes," remarked the girl. "'Tis a lonely spot. But the cottage of Gaspard lies yonder," and she pointed towards a small grove of pines on the right. "Come. Let us go."

I followed the direction of her pointing finger, but could perceive nothing. However, she led on unerringly and in a few minutes we stood before a little cottage in a small clearing. It was dark, and for all the appearance of life about it, might have been uninhabited. But Aimée Neffer knocked loudly, and raising her hands to her lips uttered a peculiar cry. Hardly had it died away when the door was thrown open, and a tall, black-bearded man stepped out. He was armed with a long-barrelled musket. As he caught sight of us he raised his piece to his shoulder.

"Peste!" he cried. "This is no place for French spies."

"Hold! Hold, Gaspard!" cried the girl with a ringing laugh. "Do you not know me?"

"Now God be praised!" cried the mountaineer, lowering his musket. "'Tis the chief's daughter."

"None other," she replied. "And these gentlemen," pointing to us, "are my very good friends. If it were not for them I would not be here."

"'Tis a pity," I heard him growl. "How easily I could put a bullet through their heads."

And watching the glitter of his eyes from beneath his heavy brows I knew how gladly he would do so. But the girl whispered in his ear, and he turned away.

"We part here, my brave friends," Aimée Neffer said, turning to us. "I had little thought that I would owe so much to Frenchmen."

"We are Irishmen," interjected O Briain.

"Ah, they are brave men, but our mountaineers owe them little love. Monsieur O Briain, I shall always remember the service which one brave Irishman has rendered me."

"'Twas but little, fair mademoiselle," replied gallant Muiris, and he raised her slender hand to his lips. "May you never again find yourself in the need of a friend, a chailin dubh dilis." And then he turned away to follow Gaspard who was to see us on our way.

"Monsieur de Grás," cried Aimée, addressing me, "what can I say to you? How can I thank you for all that you have done for me? I shall always remember. In the future I may be able to pay back some little of my debt."

"Mademoiselle," I hastened to reply, "you owe me nothing. Were it not for O Briain, what could I have done?"

"Mon ami, you cannot deceive me," she cried. "Only I know how much I have to repay you. Adieu, and may the future only hold bright fortune for you."

Before I could prevent her she caught my hand in both hers, and pressed it passionately to her heaving bosom. She bent her head, and I heard her sob.

"What, mademoiselle!" I cried. "Why do you weep?"

She made no reply, but turned and fled in through the open door of the cottage.

"A strange girl," I muttered to myself. "For a

few seconds I stood expecting her reappearance, but she did not come. Then, turning, I followed the others who had gone some little distance. I felt puzzled, and not a little disturbed by the girl's passionate outburst, and her strange leave-taking. Looking back when I had gone a little way, I thought I caught sight of a figure outlined in the moonlight, gazing after us. But mayhap it was only fancy.

Guided by the taciturn Gaspard we quickly made our way down the mountain. I knew that it was only his devotedness to his chief's daughter which prevented our surly companion from turning his musket against us. At last when our watch-fires began to twinkle out in the plains afar off, he left us, snapping out an uncivil " good night," which sounded more like a curse. Alone we continued our way back to our cantonments.

CHAPTER XI

THE WHIPPING OF THE CHEVALIER

A COUPLE of weeks ran swiftly by after that midnight ride. During those weeks, though I had met the Chevalier once or twice, he had given no sign that he suspected me of having assisted his fair prisoner to escape. In the rush of duty brought about by the increased activity with which the Duke was pushing forward the siege, I had little time to think of other matters, and the whole adventure was becoming blurred, fading from my memory, pushed away by more pressing cares. But it was brought back again with staggering suddenness.

One night as a number of us were seated in a ruined old house which stood well beyond the radius of fire, where we whiled away many an hour which lay heavy on our hands with a game of écarté, or a hazard at dice, the Chevalier swaggered in. His coming surprised us, for it was seldom he honoured our poor little salon with his presence. Evidently he had not come for play, for he seated himself, and stretching out his legs gazed superciliously round, all the while that he twirled his long moustachio.

"What brings the Chevalier here, I wonder?" asked my opponent, Captain de Lussan of the Regiment of Vaisseaux. "I hardly think it is for play."

"'Tis not likely," I replied, but instinctively I felt that his visit concerned myself. However, I continued to play coolly, though I did not lose sight of the visitor.

Suddenly I saw him start, and rise quickly to his feet. His gaze was directed towards me, as he rose and sauntered across the room. Halting at our table he remained looking silently on as our cards flicked from our hands. When the hand had been played, he bowed low to me.

"Ciel! but you do play prettily, Monsieur de Grás," he cried, sneeringly. "A word in your ear. Are you as successful with the cards as you are in playing the gallant?"

Captain de Lussan sprang to his feet, protesting loudly against such interference with play.

"Monsieur le Chevalier," he cried, "'tis not usual for outsiders to interfere with players. If you wish to play you can do so. But we must not have interruptions of this kind."

"Easy! Easy, M. le Capitaine!" said de Frobin. "I have a little affair with this gentleman."

"But you could have settled it outside," protested the other.

"Ah, M. le Capitaine, this is the place," replied the Chevalier. "Where all may hear. Privacy is seldom craved for by gentlemen of the type of M. de Grás, except on certain occasions. Is it not so, monsieur?" and he looked at me.

But I made no reply. The time for words, and perhaps deeds, would come later. The affair at our table had attracted the attention of everyone present. The click of the dice and the flick of cards had begun to die away, and many curious glances were cast in our direction.

"Monsieur," the Chevalier went on, addressing himself again to de Lussan, "I did not think that honourable gentlemen would play with a vaurien such as this, who thinks to bring himself into the prominence which he craves by meddling in the affairs of men so much higher in rank than himself."

Still I made no remark. My silence was enraging the Chevalier. Raising his voice so that it rang through the whole room, he cried:

"If this young friend of mine were of equal rank I would force him to fight with me. Since he is not, I will proceed to chastise him so that he will know the consequences of further meddling in affairs which only concern his superiors."

He sprang towards me, raising a whip which he had kept concealed up to the present. Apparently I had been as unconcerned as if his remarks had not been heard by me. Now I sprang up, and interposing my chair between myself and my enemy, inquired calmly:

"May I inquire, M. le Chevalier, of what you accuse me? If then you cannot condescend to fight with a poor lieutenant we will see about this chastisement of which you talk so glibly."

"'Tis well known to you what I accuse you of," cried de Frobin. "You, vaurien, who came like the galérien you are to steal in the night. You, who are not fit to wear the King's uniform. Ah, galérien, how unfortunate it is for you that I met you that night with your mountain wench! Had I only known! Do you understand now, gueux?"

"Ah, how easy you make it, monsieur," I remarked. "Eh bien, if you hold it a crime in me to assist a lady to escape from the house where she was held against her will for his own vile purposes by the noble gentleman who owns it, I will confess to it. I do not know, of course, by what standard that gentleman measures his conduct, but I, a poor lieutenant, hazard the opinion that he, rather than the rescuer, deserves the title of galérien. What is your opinion, monsieur?"

My enemy was beside himself with rage. Without replying, he kicked aside the chair and made a rush at me. We struggled for a few seconds, but I wrenched the whip from his hands. Holding him tightly, I gritted out:

"Now, monsieur, you will apologise for your vile conduct and words in regard to the lady of whom you have spoken. Your insults to myself I despise."

"Never," he shouted. "Dog of an Irishman, never!"

"Monsieur," I cried, "you craved for publicity for your chastisement of me, now you shall have it for your own."

But a hand was laid on my arm.

"De Grás," a voice, the voice of de Lussan, whispered, "the affair has gone far enough. You will ruin yourself."

But I shook off his hand. I believe at that moment I would not have listened to the voice of Milord Maréchal himself. I was in a white heat of passion. With a vicious swish the whip sang through the air and twined itself round the shoulders of my enemy. Swish—swish—swish it sang till my arm ached. The Chevalier cursed and struggled wildly, but it was little use. As in a vice I held him. At last, tired out, I flung him into a corner where he lay for several seconds. Snapping the whip into a couple of pieces, I cast it to him.

"M'anam, M. le Chevalier," I cried, "you will now know what it is to insult a lady. She, fortunately, is beyond your power. If, however, you find that your rank does not now preclude you from seeking revenge on me, you will find me willing enough to give you satisfaction."

With the look of a fiend de Frobin got on his feet.

"De Grás," he cried hoarsely, "you have won this time. But we will meet again. Take care who wins then."

He strode out amidst the hush which had fallen on the assemblage. When he was gone they found voice. From varying standpoints they discussed the occurrence, but most of them agreed that though the punishment I had meted out had been severe, it was well deserved. But they shook their heads. They feared I would suffer for it. Questioned by some of them as to the reason for the quarrel, I related it from the beginning, suppressing only the name of the girl. It was better that they should hear the

F

story from my lips than from those of the Chevalier's friends. Muiris O Briain, who had come in while the Chevalier's punishment was proceeding, came over to me.

"This is unfortunate, Piaras," he said. "This de Frobin will work you harm. But if he should challenge you I hope you will allow me to act for you."

"What!" I cried, "and defy the Duke's anger?"

"Aye, even that," he replied. "M'anam, Piaras, but you did lay on. I fear your meeting with that girl will turn to your disadvantage. If you had not met her you would not have to face all this trouble."

"Muiris," I asked, "what if she had been my wife or sister?"

"Aye, you are right," he said. "You acted as your father's son should act. . . . You will send his seconds to me?"

"Yes," I replied, gripping his hand. I was coming to know what his friendship meant.

CHAPTER XII

THE CHALLENGE—THE DUEL—ARREST

To my quarters the following morning came two officers. After the usual courtesies which pass between gentlemen on such occasions had been exchanged, the older of my visitors, a little, dried-up man, but a beau to his finger-tips, whom I recognised as the Comte de Bellerive, stated the object of their visit. He spoke pompously and condescendingly, in a manner hardly likely to soothe me.

"M. le Chevalier de Frobin," he began, bowing almost to the ground, "has entrusted us with the direction of an affair which concerns you, M. de Grás "—again he bowed—" and himself. He alleges he has been grossly injured and insulted, both in person and honour. But he does not wish to be harsh with one who may not understand the code which governs such matters. He might enforce his undoubted right of compelling you to fight."

"Ah, he might!" I remarked. "And does he not?"

"No," replied the Comte. "He does not wish to exercise that right. He thinks it would be unfair. You know how noted a duellist he is. He therefore offers you an alternative."

"And the alternative is?" I inquired suavely.

"That you make l'amende honorable in the presence of the same persons before whom you insulted him the other night."

"Ah! how kind, how generous!" I mused aloud.

Surely the Chevalier was revealing himself in a new light.

"Ah, but he is generous!" echoed the little man, but his companion gave a quick glance at me, as if he were not quite so satisfied with my attitude as the Comte seemed to be.

"You will understand his position, I am sure," went on the Comte. "He, a noble of France, cannot waive the rights of his rank. If you were of equal rank——"

"But I am not," I put in. "I am only a simple lieutenant, and not worthy of the honour of being run through by this nobleman's rapier."

The Count looked quickly at me. He seemed to feel that he had put the case crudely.

"What is your decision?" cried the other, who was becoming impatient.

"Suppose I were to refuse to make this amende of which you speak?" I asked.

"Then," said the Count, who could not keep silent, "our principal, M. le Chevalier de Frobin, will require you to fight. He will waive all the privileges of his rank that he may meet you."

"Messieurs," I said, "I will accept the duello. You, Monsieur le Comte, will convey to your most noble principal the expression of my regard for his kindly condescension and consideration for one so lowly. You will find my friend, M. Muiris O Briain, lieutenant of Dillon's Regiment d'Infanterie, at his quarters. He will be prepared to discuss details with you. Messieurs, I have the honour to bid you adieu."

Bowing profoundly, they passed out. I smiled grimly to myself as I thought of the elaborate fooling. Were they fools, or did they honestly believe that I was prepared to make abject apology to this man whom I had thrashed with his own whip? I laughed aloud at the nonsense of it. Surely they did not know Piaras Grás. Forsooth I was to save the honour of the Chevalier at the expense of my own;

to make myself the butt and jeer of the whole camp, because my opponent was placed by fortune in a higher position than my own. Surely these men did not understand; or was it that their understanding had been so clouded by the prejudices of rank and its privileges that they could not understand?

And then my thoughts wandered to Aimée Neffer. What would she say if she knew of this outcome of her escape? Would she regret that I had placed myself in such danger for her sake? But I shrugged my shoulders. No doubt she had forgotten me by now, or else looked on me as a quixotic fool whom she had used to her own advantage. The Duke! What would be his action, I wondered? If it should come to his ears I feared I would pay bitterly for it. But I would not draw back now, whatever the outcome. At least if I incurred his displeasure it would be as a brave man, not one who shirked the consequences of his action.

In the evening Muiris O Briain came to me.

"Piaras, a mhic," he cried, "I have been arranging your little affair. Our friend, the Chevalier, has taken little time about calling you to account. The meeting takes place to-morrow morning and I have chosen swords as the weapons. But his seconds told me they had offered you an alternative."

"Aye," I replied, "they were willing to accept my abject apology, to be made before all those who witnessed the scene last night."

"What, they made such a proposal!" cried Muiris. "They must have been fools to think you would accept such an alternative."

"More likely men obsessed with the idea of privilege," I said. "Need I say that I refused?"

"No; I would not expect you to do otherwise," said Muiris. "But, Piaras, I understand he is a fine swordsman."

"So I have heard," I replied.

"But keep up your courage. You know something about swordplay yourself. And you must win, Piaras. We cannot afford to give the victory to this boaster."

Then he rushed away to see after some other matters. I tried to banish all disturbing thoughts about the morning's fight from my mind. But, try as I would, I was not successful. The combat itself troubled me little. I would do my best to win. But the black shadow of the Duke seemed to stand out before me threateningly. If the others made such a fetish of privilege, how much the more he, a duke of France! It was in his power to ruin me if he so wished. Thus I tortured myself, but if I had seen the other consequences which were to spring from that unfortunate meeting, I almost think I would have made l'amende honorable.

. . . .

The cold, grey dawn of early morning had not long come as we stood in front of each other, ready to commence our deadly work. The face of the Chevalier bore a look of deadly hate, and as he looked at me I could almost feel the glittering, closely set eyes burning through me. For myself I felt no particular anger. I had no other thought than to get finished with the troublesome business as soon as possible. Standing there I felt cold, and wished that it was all over. We were far removed from prying eyes, I thought, and only the dull booming of the guns which had already begun to hurl their missiles against the devoted city came to our ears. That far-off booming was the only evidence we had of the proximity of the camp from which we had ridden away as the stars began to pale in the heavens. Perhaps, I thought dully as their voices softened by the distance came to me, it was the last time I might hear them.

But they were a long time arranging the details. At last the little, dried-up Comte came hastening towards me. He bowed elaborately, and said:

"Monsieur le Lieutenant, our principal again

offers you the chance of withdrawing from this duel. He begs you to think of the Duke's anger."

"I have done so, but I must face it," I replied coldly.

"He does not wish to ruin you," said the Comte.

I began to get a little angry.

"Monsieur le Comte," I cried, and my voice was rather loud, "I cannot understand why you come to me now at this time. Have I not already given my answer?"

Muiris turned at the sound of my angry voice, and cried out warningly to me. He had been engaged with the other second, and had not noticed the strange proceeding of the Count. He sprang forward.

"Not another word now," he cried. "Monsieur, I am surprised that you should lend yourself to such a thing. The time for that is past."

"Your pardon, monsieur!" cried the little man, backing away; and for once he forgot to bow. "I had not thought——"

And then the word was given, and our weapons crossed with a vicious hiss which seemed to speak of the deadly hate which guided at least one of them. As they hissed and rasped across one another I found myself thinking curiously of the motives which underlay the Chevalier's action. It was hardly alarm for me as to the consequences which might ensue. With such a superb swordsman it needed the full concentration of my mind on the work in hand. I could not afford a divided attention. As I found myself forced back before the swift riposte which almost reached my breast, a light broke in on me. He had played to unsettle my mind. And I, fool that I was, had fallen into his trap.

Suddenly O Briain uttered a sharp exclamation. The point of the Chevalier's sword had drawn blood from a slight wound in my right shoulder. It was only a scratch, and it steadied me.

"Monuar," I heard a tense whisper from

O Briain. "Seachain! Seachain, a mhic. Think only of this duel."

Aye, it was necessary! No more extraneous thoughts must disturb me. I gritted my teeth as I thought of the subtlety which might have cost me so dear. My whole energies now engrossed in the struggle, I pressed my opponent with grim determination. I was dead to outside matters. There existed only myself and my opponent. For several minutes we feinted and parried. Then with a sudden turn of my wrist which sent a tingle to my shoulder, I sent my opponent's weapon flying from his grasp.

"A Rí na nDúl!" shouted O Briain, as I dropped the point of my sword. "Sin éacht."

"Strike, galérien!" shouted de Frobin hoarsely. "Nom de Dieu, strike!" But I made no sign.

"Does the Chevalier desire to continue?" asked O Briain of the Count, who came hurrying forward. "My principal is satisfied. Is it not so, Piaras?"

I nodded my head, but the Chevalier broke out furiously:

"Bah, galérien! I accept no favours at your hands. The fight must go on," and he glared at me, a malignant blaze in his eyes.

The Count stepped to his side, but he waved him aside, calling loudly:

"My sword."

Testing it, the Count handed it to him and stepped back. Again the word was given. For a long time we fought with little advantage. Nothing was to be heard but the sibilant whisper and clash of our weapons as they twined and interlaced in our tierce and parry; the sound of our deep breathing; and now and again the booming of the guns. I knew now that the Chevalier was bent on my destruction, but I shrank from the thought of aiming at his death. However, I saw that it would be necessary to disable him in such a manner that he would be unable to continue the fight. I bent all my energies to this.

Warily we watched each other, nerves stretched to

their utmost tension, feeling, testing with our blades if the guard of the other was weakening. And then suddenly I saw the opening which I desired. I sought to take advantage of it, when across the air to our ears was borne the sound of galloping horses. Startled by the sound, the Chevalier swerved slightly, and my sword, seeking its intended opening, entered his body. He had swerved only a little, but that little meant all that tremendous space that lay between life and death. My sword deflected even by that hair's-breadth had reached a vital part, and now indeed my opponent would not be able to continue.

Dropping my bloody sword point I sprang to the side of the unfortunate man, who had staggered back into the arms of the Count. He regarded me with a look full of burning hate.

"De Grás," he struggled to say, "you have won again. But beware the Duke! Will you win from him?"

A horrible spasm crossed his face.

"He may avenge me yet," he gasped out, his voice scarcely above a whisper. But that whisper conveyed all the pent-up hatred of the man.

We had been so engrossed that we had not noticed the approach of several horsemen till a loud voice cried out:

"Morbleu! What is this? A duel, by all the gods!"

Looking up I saw that the speaker was Milord Maréchal himself, who sat on his powerful bay, his magnificent white plumes waving proudly, gazing on the scene. Dismounting, he came forward, crying:

"How is this, messieurs? Did you not know how I regarded this duelling?"

Catching sight of the face of the dead man, he started, and muttered to himself half aloud: "Mon Dieu! The Chevalier de Frobin dead."

Then he thundered out:

"Speak, some of you."

The Comte de Bellerive stammered out: "Milord Duc, the Chevalier challenged this gentleman"—pointing to me—"and this is the result."

"And a magnificent result it is," cried the Duke, "by which I have lost one of my best officers. And who is this gentleman who has dared to run counter to my wishes?" He glared at me.

"Ha! Lieutenant de Grás," he cried, "my dispatch carrier. Why have you done this thing?"

"Monseigneur," I replied, saluting, "I had been challenged, I should fight. Unfortunately the affair has turned out badly."

"Badly indeed for the Chevalier," replied the Duke grimly, "and it may turn out badly for you and all concerned. Messieurs, you will report at my quarters. M. le Lieutenant, your sword. You are under arrest."

I handed my sword to him, and he bade me mount my horse, which was standing near by, and accompany him back to camp. Turning, he gazed for a few minutes into the lifeless features of his friend, whose body now lay on the sward covered with a cloak.

"Poor de Frobin," I heard him mutter, "he was a brave soldier. We'll never clink glasses again."

That was all. Then he was the iron soldier once again. Springing into his saddle he spurred on towards the distant camp. I rode with the group of officers behind, his waving plumes seeming to nod at me in menace. My thoughts of the unfortunate man lying back in the woods slain by my sword were sad. To think that his death had come by my hand, even though it were by accident. Ah, why did not the Duke send me back to Sheldon's before this thing had happened?

Ah, Aimée Neffer! Aimée Neffer! what your safety is costing me! But as her pleading face rose before my mind's eye, I felt I could not have acted otherwise, even had I foreseen all this.

CHAPTER XIII

THE DUKE'S ALTERNATIVE

I HAD been confined to my prison for a week. It was a weary time. Only my thoughts to keep me company, and an occasional word with the soldier who brought my meals. I learned at this time how terrible are the lives of those condemned to be shut away for years and years from the companionship of friends, from the sight of God's beautiful earth, brooding, ever brooding over the sad thoughts which may not be kept away. As time went on I began to grow despondent. You will understand me when I say that no coward's craven fears oppressed me. I did not fear death, if such were the Duke's wish. I had faced it a dozen times without shrinking. Neither did my conscience prick me as regarded the Chevalier's death. That had been an accident. But I was not hardened enough, nor cold-blooded enough to regard my connection with it entirely unmoved. I would have given much had it never happened. Had it been in the fury of battle——! But the past is dead. We cannot recall it. No, it was not all this. It was the uncertainty of the whole thing weighing on me; the waiting from day to day with no other occupation than a monotonous pacing from wall to wall, till it seemed as if the hours grew into days, the days lengthened into weeks.

Then one morning my prison door swung open, and an officer stepped in. Outside in the passage a file of soldiers grounded arms. 'At last they had come for me. Well, anything was better than the misery of waiting. The officer addressed me:

"Monsieur le Lieutenant, M. le Maréchal Duc de Vendôme requires your presence at his quarters."

"I am ready," I replied, and placing myself in the centre of the file was conducted to the presence of the Duke.

At our entry he looked up and signed to the officer to go. When we were alone, he sat for some time regarding me in silence. I grew fidgety beneath his cold, steady stare. At last he spoke:

"M. le Lieutenant," he said. "I was just thinking whether I would have you shot."

I made no reply to his words. They did not call for it, I felt. What reply could I make? And it requires a curious kind of hardihood to comment on such a statement. I did not possess it.

After a pause, possibly to note the effect of his words, the Duke went on:

"This duelling has lately lost me a number of good officers. It is well known in camp that I do not approve of private quarrels amongst my officers when on active service. Should this go on I see a time when I will have no one to lead my regiments. We are becoming more dangerous to one another than are the swords or bullets of the enemy."

Again I was silent. To attempt a reply to such statements would have been foolish.

"Ah!" ejaculated milord. "You do not reply. Why did you fight with the Chevalier?"

"Because he challenged me," I replied.

"It pleases you to be facetious," cried the Duke, frowning. "But, monsieur, remember that you have been responsible for the death of one of my best officers, and best friends."

"And no one regrets it more than I," I cried, eagerly. "But, milord, the fight was forced on me."

"Ah, and how was it forced on you?" he asked, tapping the gold snuff-box which he held in his hand.

As briefly as possible I told him all that happened

since my first meeting with Aimée Neffer up to the morning of the fatal duel. Only one thing I kept back, the name of the girl. I felt that the knowledge that I had assisted in the escape of the daughter of such a doughty opponent of the French as Henri Neffer would not prepossess him in my favour. Curiously enough he did not ask for it. To tell only truth, he appeared to pay little attention to my story, seeming to be more interested in an examination of his beautifully chased snuff-box than in what I was saying. But though seemingly so inattentive, he had not missed any part of my narrative, for he remarked when I had done:

"It is again the old story, cherchez la femme. And you whipped the Chevalier, a noble of France. Monsieur, you are a bold man. But I well know how bold, how reckless you Irishmen are. And I like you for it. Monsieur, you have done well in not attempting to lie to me. For some time back I have known something of what you have told me. Had you lied I would have placed you before the firing platoon within the hour. Even so your life is forfeit. Your crime can only be purged by an extraordinary service. You owe it to the King whom you have deprived of a brave soldier. I could order you to instant death, or send you to the Bastille to live out your life there. But I will do neither. I will offer you an alternative. M. le Lieutenant, you are young. You love life."

Again his fingers tapped his snuff-box. His voice was as calm as if he were merely engaged in some light, frivolous gossip instead of juggling with a man's life. He looked at me with his cold, steady gaze.

"Milord Maréchal," I replied, "if I said 'no' you might call me boaster or madman; if I said 'yes' you might call me coward or fool. I will only say then that while I do not fear death, having faced it on many occasions, I have no wish to die, but even if such is not my wish, I would not crave for life."

"Ah, monsieur, you are a diplomatist," cried milord, and a slight smile passed across his face.

"A simple soldier, Milord Maréchal," I said, "diplomacy is beyond me."

He smiled again, and took a pinch of snuff.

"M. le Lieutenant," he said, "you are too brave and clever a man to shoot out of hand, or to send back to Paris. But I cannot allow you to go without punishment. I have spoken of an alternative. It will give you a chance for your life. I will set before you this proposition which you may accept or reject as you think fit. But remember if you reject it you will take your stand before the platoon within the hour. I will say to you that my proposition is one involving great danger, possibly the loss of your life. If you carry it through successfully you shall be restored to the military rank from which I have suspended you. If you do not succeed I think it will be hardly necessary for me to punish you. The Sieur de la Genèvre will have taken care of that," and Milord Duc leaned back in his chair, regarding me the while as if he were trying to read my thoughts.

Standing there before him, I think I bore his scrutiny well, gave little sign of the struggle going on within me. I may have paled a little, but I suppose it would have been only natural. Very few of us are so tired of life that we can regard entirely unmoved its loss. And I was young, as the astute Duke had taken care to remind me. Only in the commencement of my career. It was indeed a frightful position to be in, and that through no deliberate fault of my own. The Duke was avenging his friend only too well.

"I will set before you this proposal of mine which may save you from the platoon," resumed the Duke. "Up amongst the mountains beyond Susa," and he pointed to a map spread out before him, "commanding the pass which leads from Briançon to that place, stands the castle of the Sieur de la Genèvre. Formerly an ally of ours, he has lately gone over to the Duke of Savoy, Victor Amadeus. To our convoys coming through the pass he has done much damage. You understand?"

I murmured "Yes."

"This castle of the traitor is almost impregnable. It would take an army to conquer it. And I, monsieur, have not that army. Neither have I the time to spare. I set before you then the task of securing this man, and bringing him here where he will be held as hostage for the good behaviour of his followers. I do not disguise from you that the task is a difficult one. But it is one which one or two men can effect more easily than a regiment. A regiment would rouse opposition which would render their efforts useless. One or two brave men may effect the task. You follow me."

"Yes," I replied.

"It may be necessary that the one who undertakes this task may have to gain admission to this stronghold. He may not. I care not by what means he accomplishes it, so that it is accomplished. The only thing which matters to me is the securing of the person of this M. de la Genèvre, and the bringing of him here. It is simple. If you succeed you will have your life and military rank restored. If you fail you will not escape, I think, with your life from the Sieur. Either way lies death. There it is a possibility. Here it is a certainty. That is the difference. What is your choice?"

For a long time I made no reply. I knew not what to say. If I refused this alternative my career was ended. If I accepted and went on this quest my career might also end. Whichever way I looked only death beckoned. But in the camp it stood close to my side. Amongst the mountains it was shadowy, more remote from me. Shrugging my shoulders, I cried:

"Milord Maréchal, I accept the chance. I will try to cheat ill-fortune."

"Bravo!" cried the Duke. "I wish you success."

I bowed.

"Have you, Milord Maréchal, any further directions to give me as to my proceedings?"

"None," he replied, "except that you be circumspect. And I need hardly say that your life depends on your success." Again his snuff-box came into requisition. "When do you leave camp?"

"As soon as may be," I replied. "And I may bring a friend with me. A lieutenant of Dillon's."

"Yes, yes," he replied. "Such arrangements as you wish to make I will have carried out." He rose as if to signify that the interview was at an end. "I trust, Monsieur de Grás, you will not have to face the firing platoon."

"The dice may turn to me, Milord Maréchal," I replied, and saluting turned on my heel.

CHAPTER XIV

AMONGST THE MOUNTAINS—LE COQ DORÉ

The evening was well advanced as we picked our way through the wild pass up which we had been advancing for hours past. Up above us we could catch glimpses now and again of the pointed roofs of the little bourg where our journey would end, perhaps for ever. In the clear mountain air they stood out distinctly before us, looking, up there embosomed within the encircling peaks, strangely aloof and removed from the mundane things we had left behind. In the background, towering up over the clustering roofs, a huge battlemented pile reared itself aloft towards the clouds. From one of its flanking towers a flag fluttered bravely. I could not make out the device it bore. Turning to O Briain, who in his character of serving man rode with me, and who was muttering between his teeth at the roughness of the way, I remarked:

"The man we seek lives yonder."

"And it looks strong and powerful to hold him," replied O Briain. "Though the road to it is so long and rugged, the village above looks pretty and peaceful enough. One would hardly think it harboured such a nest of hornets."

"No," I replied, "and one to look at me would hardly imagine that I was a man under sentence of death. Things are seldom what they seem."

"Let us not talk of death, only success," cried Muiris. "But hark! Someone comes this way."

Out of the pine forest which bordered our way, a man emerged into view. Across his right shoulder was slung a well-filled game bag. He was tall and loosely built, with black hair and beard. As he advanced he gave us good even, and I fell to wondering how many times the long musket thrown across his left shoulder had been levelled at the breasts of our soldiers, how many brave fellows had fallen before its spitting lead. However, I replied civilly to his greeting, and inquired if it was likely that we would find lodgings in the village.

"'Tis seldom we have strangers in our village," he replied, looking at us curiously, "but you may find what you seek at Le Coq Doré. It lies at the far end of the village."

I thanked him, and asked, pointing to the frowning castle:

"Yonder is the château of the Sieur de la Genèvre, is it not?"

I had hardly asked the question when I regretted it. I thought I noticed a knitting of the black brows, but he replied readily enough:

"Yes, our seigneur lives up there. But he is seldom to be seen. You know him, monsieur?"

My indiscretion had made me wary. I said with an air of indifference:

"No, I do not know him. But I have heard men speak of him in Turin, and of the good sport which one may find here! 'Tis hardly likely his château would be a very popular visiting place. I think few would venture to climb up there."

"Peste, no!" cried the mountaineer. "His friends find the way too rugged, so they seldom come. His enemies find it too dangerous, for our seigneur's men are brave, and they seldom miss. Eh! how this Duke Vendôme must hate him! No convoy of his can go through these passes without feeling his power. Parbleu! Our seigneur is a bitter enemy to these French."

As I listened to the boasting of this mountaineer, I

felt how difficult was the task I had undertaken. What if this fellow should suspect us? But how could he? The reference to Turin would lull suspicion. And it was hardly likely that the Sieur had spies in our camp. And even if he had what likelihood was there of his finding out about our mission. Courage! Courage, Piaras Grás! Put away your foolishness. It will hardly mean success, and your life hanging in the balance.

Nodding to the mountaineer, and again thanking him for his information, we moved on. 'Twas clear now how delicately we would be placed in this out-of-the-world place, how circumspectly we would have to move. We would be objects of doubt and distrust in the little hamlet, especially if we lengthened our stay. And however long the work required, we must remain on.

The path had become easier, and putting spurs to our horses we cantered bravely up the street of the little bourg, and drew rein before a dilapidated-looking house marked out from the rest by a large gilt weathercock which rose up over its pointed gable. Dismounting I threw the rein to Muiris, and strode inside.

"Landlord," I cried to the rather hang-dog looking man who came to meet me, "I require lodgings for myself and my serving man for some time."

"My place is but small," he replied. "I seldom have visitors. Does monsieur remain long?"

"It may be a week, a month, a year," I said carelessly. "But what matters it whether my stay be long or short, an' I pay you well for your trouble."

I pushed a well-filled purse beneath his nose, and watched his small, reddish eyes glitter with cupidity as he heard the merry chink of the gold pieces. Oh, a well-lined purse is a fine companion on the road. 'Tis wonderful how smooth it makes it.

"As I remarked, milord," and the good fellow was now all smiles, "we seldom have visitors, and my poor little inn is not what I would wish it to be. But if monseigneur would be willing to put up with the poor accommodation——"

"Say no more, say no more, good landlord," I cried jovially. "One who travels so much as I do will not be hard to please."

"Have you ridden far to-day, monseigneur?" asked the landlord, looking down at my mud-splashed boots.

"I have been in the saddle since early morning," I replied. "I have ridden from Turin in the plains below."

I spoke loudly, as much for the benefit of several fellows who sipped their wine while they listened to our conversation, as for the landlord's.

"The roads are in a devilish condition. And now, good landlord, will you set the table with the best your inn affords. Your mountain air has made me as hungry as a hawk. . . . Jean," I cried, going to the door and addressing Muiris, "put up these horses, and be quick about it."

Muiris, his face solemn and expressionless, touched his hat, and turned away with the horses. I could hardly forbear laughing, he looked so staid, and so like a gentleman's gentleman. But that would never do. Sharp eyes were about, and I must play my part. I turned back into the inn. The loungers were regarding me curiously, and calling the landlord, I threw him a gold piece, and ordered him to fill up their tankards. Then, as befitted a gentleman who despised such ignoble company, I mounted the stairs after the little grisette called by the landlord, in order to remove the stains left by my journey in the privacy of my room.

After a while the landlord came to tell me that dinner was served. In the room where the table was spread I found Muiris waiting for me.

"Ah, Muiris," I exclaimed, "why are you not seated?"

"Hush!" he admonished, looking after the landlord's retreating form. "May the serving man eat with his lord?"

"Ah, you are right," I said. "Then the serving man must serve his lord."

We both laughed softly. I think the one was endeavouring to cheer the other, to keep his mind from dwelling too much on the dangers which surrounded.

So I sat dining in solitary state with Muiris dancing attendance, albeit he was a little clumsy. The landlord came in and hovered round as if he wished to say something. In order to get rid of the fellow, I demanded:

"How now, good landlord? You wish to speak to me."

"Milord," he stammered, "as I told you my place is small——" and he stopped.

"Proceed," I cried impatiently.

"Your room," he got out, "your servant must occupy it also."

"Parbleu!" I ejaculated, scowling most ferociously at Muiris. And then I said resignedly, "Ah, this is the difficulty of having a serving man. But I must be satisfied. Landlord, see that his bed is drawn away as far as possible from mine."

The landlord went away bowing most profoundly. I had not hoped for this fortunate turn of affairs. Now Muiris and I could be together without causing too much comment, for it might have looked strange if I, a gentleman of quality, were to occupy the same apartment with my plebeian servant. Fortune was beginning to smile, and I said to Muiris:

"This is a difficulty got over. I begin to think we are going to succeed. Here, Muiris, a goblet to our success."

And taking care that no watchful eyes were about, we quaffed the flowing bumpers of rich red wine to the bright future. When Muiris had duly dined after his master, as a good servant should, he lighted the candles, and preceded that master to bed. Having sounded the walls all round for places where a spy might listen, we discussed our plans and retired, he, the plebeian, to his bed well screened from the eyes of myself, his lordly master. And I cannot imagine that had the Sieur de la Genèvre seen us that night in the chamber of Le Coq Doré, sleeping so peacefully, he would have thought that the worthy Fabien de Berac and his serving man were two Irishmen plotting against his liberty, and for his removal from his mountain stronghold.

. . . . . .

We were up betimes, and having breakfasted heartily set off on foot with guns thrown across our shoulders. We had decided to keep away from the village as much as possible, as we reasoned that our constant presence therein might make the inhabitants inquisitive. And suspicion must be lulled at all costs. If it should rest on us it would be fatal to our enterprise, and probably our lives. Away in the mountain passes we might stumble across information which would be useful to us. As a gentleman engaged in the pastime of hunting I would be less open to suspicion than in any other way. It appeared natural in these mountains which swarmed with game. Perhaps we might even have the good fortune to meet with the Sieur himself. But might he not object to strangers hunting amongst these mountains where he ruled? It was possible, but I must run the risk. I could think of no better plan. I must face risks, else it were better to return to the Duke, own myself beaten, and let the crashing muskets of the platoon end my story. But that was never Piaras Grás's way. No, I would go on. And when I spoke to Muiris of my plan he approved of it, and said it was the only way we could work for the present.

"Of course it has its risks," I remarked.

"Every plan has risks," he retorted. "It is certain we cannot remain all day long in this inn doing nothing."

All day we hunted, and at evening, tired out by our toilsome work, returned to the village. Game we had enough of, but as regards the human game we pursued we had learned nothing. Some peasants, wild-looking fellows who went well armed, had passed us. They looked at us curiously, as if they had never seen our like before. But silently they had passed on, and I had refrained from holding conversation with them. They might have told me something, but better to wait. Everything comes to him who waits.

So we continued for a couple of weeks. I was growing tired and dissatisfied with this continual hunting, and yet no more feasible plan presented itself, unless indeed we went boldly to the Sieur's château and demanded admittance on some pretext or other. I knew that the villagers were getting curious about our prolonged stay. They could not understand what interest would detain a gentleman in that remote village for so long, where men from the outside world so seldom came. Their eyes held a menace which foreboded little good to us. But I went back and forwards regardless of the black, scowling looks cast at us covertly. And Muiris followed at my heels.

Then one day a strange thing happened. We had tracked a chamois along a rugged path which I could see would lead us close to the Sieur's castle. As we hurried forward hot on the chase a loud cry of warning rang in our ears, and looking up to a rock overhanging the path we found ourselves covered by the long barrel of a musket held in the hands of a fellow who warned us not to advance farther. But we paid no heed to his warning till a bullet sang over our heads.

"Halt!" shouted the fellow. "The seigneur does not like strangers to come too close to his château."

"And why, good fellow?" I demanded.

"'Tis not for me to say," replied the man. "But on this mountain our seigneur rules without question.

As our enemies beyond," and he pointed in the direction of Ivrea, "know right well, he does not welcome strangers here or in his village."

"He rules life and death," I sneered.

"Aye," retorted the other; "none dare dispute his right."

"Undisputed monarch of the mountain," I sneered again. "Foe of Vendôme, friend of Savoy."

But O Briain whispered in my ear:

"For Heaven's sake come away. You may ruin all."

The whisper recalled me to myself, and turning on my heel I followed Muiris soberly enough. Had I spoiled all by allowing the unfortunate reference to the Duke to escape me? As we went the mocking laughter of the moutaineer rang in our ears, and his cry:

"Aye, foe of Vendôme!"

I bit my lip with vexation. What should I have known of Vendôme or Savoy? I fear I will have to curb my temper and guard my tongue more carefully before I can hope to succeed at work such as this.

"'Tis as I feared, Muiris," I said, when we had gone some distance. "We are being watched."

"Aye," he replied, "'tis evident enough. I do not doubt we are on the eve of a turn in the affair, be it for good or ill. And however it may turn, anything would be better than this groping in the dark."

He was right. The affair did take a turn, and a rather unexpected one. When we returned to the inn that evening we found a note awaiting us. It was addressed to M. Fabien de Berac. It was short and ran as follows:

"To Monsieur de Berac the Sieur de la Genèvre sends greeting. He does not think that strangers find his mountain passes very good for hunting. They are particularly dangerous, especially in the vicinity of his château. May he express the hope that, having now satisfied his desire for sport, monsieur will have a pleasant journey back to Turin."

"So!" I ejaculated, when I had finished reading, "the Sieur very politely tells us to begone," and I handed the letter to Muiris.

"Very politely worded indeed!" cried he. "One would hardly expect such polish from this mountain lordling. Of course you will go."

"M'anam," I cried, starting round angrily. But I saw the smile on his face and had to laugh myself.

"Is it likely?" I asked him.

"No, I think not. But the turn of the game has come."

"Aye, our blindfold groping is over. I wonder what his next move will be?"

We were soon to know.

CHAPTER XV

THE SIEUR STRIKES

WE remained on at Le Coq Doré. Of the Sieur's letter I had taken no more notice than if I had never received it. Thus four days went by. During that time we heard nothing from the man we now knew was our enemy. We made no change in our conduct, further than to keep our firearms well primed, our swords ready in their scabbards. But in the conduct of the aubergiste, Barnabé, we noticed a significant change. Had we not been on the watch for every little sign we might have set it down to mere gaucherie. But now everything had a meaning, and when we saw that the good Barnabé was getting lax and careless in his attendance on us we concluded that the Sieur was at work. It was now a meal kept late, again meat burned to a cinder, wine served up which tasted like vinegar. But we held on grimly, laughing to ourselves as we watched the efforts of our host to compel us to go, through the worrying of our stomachs.

And then he began to grow very unsteady on his legs. One evening it was a flagon of his villainous wine splashed into my face. A dish of venison scattered over the dirty floor through a stumble of his. But when it happened that the worthy fellow shot into my arms with a tureen of soup, covering my lace cravat and velvet coat with a horrible coating of grease, I confess I lost my temper, and administered such a succession of heavy blows about his plump cheeks that he roared for mercy. Accidents! Ah yes, they may have been, but my loss of temper was also an accident. After that he became surly and independent, where before he had been talkative and obsequious. He hardly disguised his wish that we should go, and commenced to hint it broadly enough.

"Monsieur de Berac," he inquired, as I was breakfasting on the fourth morning after the letter of the Sieur had come, "it is probable that you will soon be going away. You have no doubt seen enough of our mountains."

"'Tis not my intention," I said. "There are many interesting things yet to be seen, and my hunting has not lost its charm. I will not go yet a while."

"Few strangers make such a long stay," he remarked, as if to himself.

"Ah, but they may not be interested," I replied. "Now the château beyond would well repay inspection."

As I spoke I was watching him closely. A look flashed from his eyes which told me that he knew more than he pretended.

"Milord," he cried, "the château is not for inspection. The times are too dangerous. The Sieur has hanged a man ere now for venturing too close. Ah, milord, you little know what dangers lurk amongst our mountains. Accidents have happened many times."

"Aye, 'tis likely," I remarked grimly. "But, good landlord, you appear right anxious to get rid of me. Come, if it is a question of money——"

"No, no," he interrupted. "But I would not like accidents to happen. The Sieur——" He pulled himself up suddenly.

"Ah, this mysterious Sieur," I remarked. "Surely he has no connection with accidents."

But I spoke to the landlord's back. He had said too much, evidently.

"Muiris," I whispered, "our good landlord is trying to frighten us. Look well to your arms. We may need them soon."

The day passed without any untoward incident, and as the shades of night were closing in, we turned in at the door of Le Coq. I had instructed the landlord that we would be back at dusk, and dinner must be in readiness for me. When we entered we found that the inn was filled with a noisy rabble of well-armed fellows. I judged them to be of the Sieur's following, and plainly enough they were men who would stop at nothing, rascals who would do their master's bidding without any troublesome scruples. I paid them little attention, but pushed my way into the little room where we dined, followed by Muiris. They troubled not at all about making way for us. As I shouldered my way through I heard many covert sneers and allusions to myself.

"Ah, here come the gueux who hunts amongst our mountains," sneered one fellow, bolder than the rest. "Parbleu, comrades, is he not a coxcomb?"

His companions guffawed loudly at their fellow's witticism, but I paid no heed. I kept myself well in check, though my hand played with my sword hilt. In the dining-room no preparations had been made for us. The table was innocent of cloth or decorations. This scum of a landlord had then decided to starve us out. Dar fiadh, we would soon see.

"Landlord! landlord!" I shouted, "come here!"

It was a long time before he came, and then it was with an insolent air which did not tend to cool my sadly ruffled temper.

"How comes this?" I demanded, pointing to the table.

He stared at it as if he had never seen it before.

"Answer me," I cried. "Did you not know the arrangement, or have you suddenly gone dumb?"

"Monsieur," he said sullenly at last, and his voice was thick as if he had indulged rather freely in his wine, "you cannot dine here to-night."

"And why not?" I demanded.

"I have received my orders," he replied, sulkily.

"I have way no longer for strangers who, for aught I know, may be spies in disguise."

"A pretty landlord," I cried. "The mysterious Sieur has spoken."

He made no reply, but backed towards the door. However, I had no intention of letting him go so softly. My temper was beginning to rise, and the jeers of the Sieur's riff-raff, who had crowded round the door which the landlord had left open hardly served to calm me.

"The coxcomb will get no dinner. Let him come to the château. The Sieur will give him one," they laughed.

"Landlord," I cried, "I will go from this inn when it is my wish to do so. Have dinner served at once."

He paid no more attention to me than if I had been some mere routier, but continued his backward progress.

"Ha! you require a lesson," I cried, leaping towards him.

But he caught up a heavy tankard from a table, and hurled it at my head. It shivered itself into fragments against the wall behind. As if it were a signal the other rascals crushed their way into the room with loud shouts.

"Out with the coxcomb! Away with the spy! Have at you, misérable!"

"Seachain! Seachain, a Phiarais!" shouted Muiris, who had been silently watching the turn of affairs, springing to my side, his sword flashing. We fell back behind the table which stood in the centre of the room, and formed a slight barrier between us and the press of foes.

They came at us with a rush, but our swift thrusts sent two brawny ruffians howling back. But brave in their superior numbers the others pressed on, hoping to wear us down with their overwhelming attack. And we were hard pressed. Furiously they cut and thrust at us from all sides. So swift the blows came they seemed to be delivered by one mighty weapon. My masters, it is no easy thing for two to receive the attacks of a dozen, no matter how poor in skill that dozen may be. But somehow or other we managed to keep them in play. The way in which they were crowded together helped us, in that they could not use their weapons with all the freedom necessary. The apartment grew full of the sounds of fierce conflict. Shouts, curses, groans mingled with the clashing of steel and the crashing of glass, punctuated here and there by an odd shot. Above our heads the wild shrieks of the landlord's wife and servants calling for help added to the tumult.

And then suddenly a plan which would further limit their freedom of swordplay flashed into my mind. Why not use the table as a movable barricade? They, afraid to pass the ends of it guarded by our flashing blades, crushed back to the wall, would find their numbers a hindrance.

Shouting a warning to Muiris, I pushed the heavy table forward. My movement was successful. Now indeed their numbers became as dangerous to one another as to us. Their attack became more confused, and dearly they paid for that confusion. Already three or four of them had retired sorely wounded, and one still form lay on the floor.

Suddenly the men in front of us drew back as if moved by some strange impulse. Surprised by the unaccountable movement we hung back a little, still on guard, ready. And then I heard a slight noise behind. That lull, which our enemies in their foolishness had brought about, saved us. That noise would have passed unnoticed amidst the din of the struggle. Casting a swift glance backward I was startled to see a portière in our rear swing outwards, as if someone stood behind it. Plainly enough a door—of which I had not suspected the existence—had been opened. We were taken in rear.

"Outflanked!" I yelled. "Guard the front, Muiris."

And I spun round on my heel to meet the new attack. It was only time. The portière was thrown back, and two men sprang into view. It flashed across my mind that I had seen one of them before. Ah, I had it! The fellow who had spoken to us on the path on the first evening of our coming. But one of them stumbled in his mad charge towards me, and my sword passing through his shoulder gave him a wound it would take many a day to mend. Whether it was that my other opponent scorned the use of his sword, or, what was more likely, that he was not very skilled in its use, I know not. Whatever the cause he had not drawn it, but gripped a clubbed musket in his two brawny hands. M'anam istigh! that black-browed mountaineer was a brave fellow. Whirling his musket round his head like a flail he aimed a blow at me. My sudden leap aside saved me, but the musket-butt crashing against my sword snapped it off close to the hilt. Flinging it away, I sprang at my foe as he staggered forward beneath the impetus of his blow. We grappled with each other, fiercely struggling, for a few seconds; then with a sudden twist—one which I had learned years before in our Kerry gleanns—I tossed him on his back, and his head coming into violent contact with the floor, he lay as one dead.

Plucking his sword from out its scabbard, I returned to the assistance of Muiris. From the other flanker, who lay moaning pitifully, we need fear nothing. But the fight was nearly over. Disheartened by the failure of the rear attack, our assailants turned and fled out through the open door, and away. We had won. Panting and weary after our deadly strife, we remained in possession of the inn.

Around us was only wreck and ruin. The spectacle presented by the room bore witness to the passions which had been let loose. Broken furniture was strewn here and there. Glass and earthenware reduced to atoms by pistol ball or sword cut littered the floor. Splashes of blood stained floor and walls. After gazing round for a few minutes I turned to Muiris.

"The Sieur has shown his hand at last," I said.

"Yes," he replied, "but this defeat will only make him show it further."

"Time will tell," I said. "But we can only wait. Where is that rascal of a landlord? A goblet of wine would not be amiss. Our host has paid dearly for this night's work."

"Aye, more dearly than he thought of. But that wine. My throat is as dry as a limekiln. Ah, here comes our friend."

The good Barnabé looked pale, and I noticed that he wore a blood-stained bandage tied round his head. He looked at us with a dogged, scowling face, and I did not blame him for it. Had not his plan miscarried we would by this time have been fleeing through the mountain passes with the Sieur's rabble at our heels, or else be past the power of using our limbs in flight. After the very different upturn of the affair I did not expect he would regard us with the most kindly feelings.

"Ah, good Barnabé!" I cried. "You have been fighting. I trust your wound is not deep?"

He growled out a curse.

"Eh bien, it is the fortune of war," I remarked. "To-night we are victors; to-morrow, who knows?"

"Aye, who knows?" he growled. "The Sieur is a dangerous man to cross."

"M'anam! That mysterious personage is becoming quite a nightmare," I said. "Let us forget him for a while. Good Barnabé, after our strenuous labour we must have some wine. Muiris, will you accompany our host? And mine host, let it not be that vinegar you have placed before us since M. le Sieur thought he would look after our welfare."

He looked at me, his reddish eyes glittering, but said nothing. Accompanied by Muiris he went away, and in a few minutes returned bearing several bottles. Setting them down he was turning away, but I called him back, and filling up a goblet with the rich red beverage, handed it to him.

"A toast!" I cried. "May we be always as good friends as we are at present."

I thought he would have thrown the wine into my face, but he tossed it off at one fierce gulp. Ah, that wine! It was nectar fit for the immortal gods. It went coursing through my veins like fire, and made me a new man.

"Now," I said to the landlord, "this room looks very unlike the guest-room of the respectable Coq Doré. If some traveller should happen in you would be disgraced. A little clearing up will do no harm, and will enhance considerably the value of that long-delayed dinner which you will set before us."

I wished to keep good Barnabé within view as much as possible. We did not want him to work any more mischief. Muiris and I assisted him, and at the end of an hour we had brought some order out of the chaos. Very little sign of the struggle remained. The landlord had dragged away the badly damaged furniture, and then we carried away the body of the unfortunate fellow who had fallen in the fray to an outhouse. The black-browed wrestler who had tried to smash my skull with his musket-butt we tended last of all. He still lay where he had fallen. The blow which had rendered him unconscious had been a heavy one, but his skull was thick, and after a little we roused him up from his stupor, forcing copious draughts of wine down his throat. We sent him away then. The volubility of his cursing showed that he was little the worse of his heavy fall.

"And now, good landlord," I cried, "dinner, dinner, dinner!"

We sat down at last. However, I was cautious, and required Barnabé to taste each dish he set before us. But he had not tampered with them. He was a good fellow enough, though he had tried such scurvy tricks.

CHAPTER XVI

AN UNLOOKED-FOR FRIEND

Now that we had a little time to think I saw the gravity of our situation. The Sieur would not be satisfied with the failure of his attempt to drive us away. Of that I was certain. We had won for the present, but when our foe struck again he would take care that he would not fail. I feared we would go down before him, but better die fighting than return empty-handed. When would the attack come? I hardly imagined he would strike for the present. But I felt we must change our quarters on the morrow. Till then we must remain on at the inn. There was nothing else to be done, for we had no other refuge to turn to. Of course we could have saddled our horses, and fled away. But that could not be. Black night had long fallen, and how could we find our way through the passes? Even though it had not been so, I would not have gone. What! Fly before this rabble; run at the first whiff of danger; go to the Duke to hear his sneering laughter! No; whatever came I would follow this thing to the end. Men might call Piaras Grás unfortunate; they would never name him coward.

A voice broke in on my reflections. Some traveller had entered the inn. As I heard the sweet, girlish voice give greeting to the landlord, who had hurried out, I started. Looking towards O Briain I saw that he also had turned his head sharply.

"Muiris," I said, "we are to have a companion, it seems. That voice sounds familiar."

"I'd wager a year's pay against a louis that it is the voice of Mademoiselle Aimée Neffer," said O Briain.

"We'll soon know," I said. "Our good Barnabé is ushering her in here."

The door was thrown open, and a girl came in. A glance into the beautiful face, shaded by a jaunty little beaver with trailing white plumes, showed me that we had been correct in our surmises. The girl had ridden to the inn. So much was certain, for she was dressed in a most becoming riding habit, and in her hand held a gold-headed riding whip. She was followed by the landlord, who profusely apologised for the smallness and poorness of his inn. He regretted that he had not some more fitting apartment to which he might conduct her ladyship, but this was his best room, where his guests had their meals spread. If she, however, objected to the presence of two noble gentlemen who honoured his inn——

She broke in on his garrulity.

"Enough, good landlord," she said. "Your guest-room will be fitting for me. My stay will be only short. To-morrow I ride to the château of the Sieur de la Genèvre. Set a table here with the best your inn can afford. I am tired, and would retire as soon as possible. You will also see that my serving men are cared for."

He bent almost double, and assured her that he would carry out her commands. I sprang up, and, bowing to her, inquired if she would honour our poor meal with her presence.

"We have but commenced," I said. "Do not refuse to honour us by your acceptance, mademoiselle."

She looked at me, drawing herself up haughtily the while. She seemed as if she were about to reject my offer indignantly. But I went on:

"Mademoiselle Neffer, do you not remember?"

She looked closer, and uttered a little cry of delight.

"Ciel! Monsieur de Grás! Who would have expected to meet you here?"

"Our paths have crossed again, fair mademoiselle," I said. "The gods have pitied us."

She curtsied prettily, and gave me her hand. Then turning to the landlord who had been regarding us silently, she said:

"I will dine with these gentlemen. They are my friends. See that my sleeping apartment is prepared."

Barnabé set a place for her, and then went away. Our unlooked-for guest made a fair, pleasant picture sitting there in that room, which had so lately been the scene of such a fierce fight. Looking at her presiding with such grace, exchanging light, inconsequent banter with Muiris, listening to her merry, ringing laugh, it almost seemed to me as if the events of the evening had only been some hideous nightmare; that we had been transported to some fairy palace where fiery human passions had no place. One could hardly connect that gracious presence with the scene of turmoil and bloodshed of a couple of hours before. Ah, what a curious medley of light and shade, a strange, sad mixture of joy and sorrow, strife and peace, life is! I had grown silent and abstracted as these thoughts came trooping in on me.

Mademoiselle Aimée noticed my abstraction, for she remarked playfully:

"Monsieur de Grás, one would think that you were posing as a public penitent, you look so solemn and sad! 'Tis hardly flattering to your guest. But how comes it that you are here? This place is hardly one where one would expect to meet French officers. The Sieur de la Genèvre is not a friend of your people."

"Fate, fair mademoiselle," I replied, "has sent us hither. Too well we know how the Sieur de la Genèvre loves us. But, mademoiselle, let us speak of something else. The unfortunate circumstance which has driven us here is our secret. But since that circumstance has thrown us together again, even if it be for only a few brief hours, I can hardly think it unfortunate. But the Sieur de la Genèvre is your friend. We will speak of something else, an' it be your pleasure."

"Nay, nay," she broke out energetically. "Monsieur de la Genèvre is not my friend; say rather my enemy. One whom I detest, but whom the exigencies of policy demand that my father should regard as an ally. But, Monsieur de Grás, what can have sent you to this place? Pardon me if I appear insistent, but the strangeness of meeting you here, so far from your camp—here where your life is not worth a moment's purchase did the people know you for what you are—surprises me, makes me apprehensive. Mon Dieu! if they only knew!" She threw an apprehensive glance round as if she thought the very walls would disgorge enemies.

I made no answer. I could not tell her the true position of affairs. 'Twould only make her unhappy, and would not serve us.

"Ah, monsieur! are we not friends?" she asked. "Have you not saved me in the day of my distress? Amongst these mountains you are in danger. Why do you remain?"

"'Tis necessary that we remain," I replied. "But, mademoiselle, I beg of you, do not inquire further. You are but a girl."

"I am the daughter of Henri Neffer," she replied proudly. "Mon ami, I know that something strange has happened. As I rode through the village I saw that it was in a ferment. Excited groups stood round several wounded men, and when one of my men inquired he was told some strange story about French spies, and a fight which had taken place at Le Coq Doré. . . . Mon Dieu! Now I know what the landlord's bandaged head means, what yonder splintered table tells of. Messieurs, your lives are in danger.

Will you not tell me? I, a mountaineer, may be able to help you."

"Mademoiselle," I cried, "you know not what you ask. You know not what our mission is. We are French officers. We may be even engaged on work which you would detest. What! Allow you to associate yourself with our work, surrounded as it is with danger. No, mademoiselle; we must face this danger alone."

"Did you count the cost the other night when you aided me?" she asked, "when you exposed yourselves to the enmity of a powerful man? How do I know what punishment you may have undergone for your generosity to me—a stranger? Ah, monsieur"—and she turned to me—"do not refuse my poor aid in your necessity! For that that necessity is pressing I am certain. Else why the excitement in the village?"

"Mademoiselle," I said, "there is danger for us here, I will admit it, but it is not greater than that which awaits me at the camp. To return there would be simply exchanging a remote danger for a pressing one. No, mademoiselle, you may not aid us."

"Monsieur," she cried, tears in her eyes, "you are cruel. You will not allow me to repay the debt I owe you. And something tells me that I am in some way the cause of your present danger. Your aiding me has made the Chevalier your bitter enemy?"

Her question took me by surprise. I answered quickly:

"Mademoiselle, the Chevalier is dead."

"Dead!" she cried. "He fell by your hand. Ah, bon Dieu! I see it all now."

A Dhia! I could have bitten my tongue out for that foolish slip. Here I had revealed the very thing I had wished to keep from her. I could not now keep silent longer. The rest must be told, if for no other reason than to show her that she was entirely blameless in the matter. So I told her all. She listened in silence, and when I had finished, said quietly:

"Mon ami, my debt to you is much greater than I had thought it. Through me you are exposed to all this. If you had not aided me you would never have fought with the Chevalier de Frobin; you would never have been sent on this dangerous quest. I see now why you would not tell me; why you cannot return to your camp at Ivrea to face certain death. Mon ami"—and she looked at me, her soft black eyes wistful and sad—"can you forgive me for having brought you to this, condemned to seek one danger that you may avoid another?"

For answer I raised her hand to my lips.

"Mademoiselle," I cried, "the thought that I saved you from that villain counts for more to me than all the danger in which I stand. But do not fear. Piaras Grás will cheat misfortune yet."

"What men you Irish are!" she cried, smiling at my rather boastful words.

"You see now," I went on, "why it is that I cannot accept your help. It would expose you to dangers I would have you avoid, and would set you against this friend——"

"No, no!" she cried, interrupting me. "Say rather, ally. For myself, I dislike and fear him. At one time he made overtures to my father for my hand, but he rejected them. Since then he has not again spoken of it, but I fear that he often thinks of it. I would not have ridden here to-day only that my father had no other messenger to send. This new alliance of the Sieur's with our prince—Victor Amadeus—brings my father into touch with him. But, monsieur"—and she laughed—"I begin to grow afraid. What if you were to make me your prisoner? For after all I am as much the enemy of the French as is the Sieur. Even now I may be in negotiation with this enemy to work you harm."

"Have no fear, mademoiselle," I replied. "Your secrets are safe with me. I am a soldier, not a spy.

And I am myself a prisoner in this village, at least for the present."

"And you will not accept my assistance?" she asked.

"Mademoiselle," I said, "it pains me to think that I cannot accept it. But I cannot compromise you in any way. Believe me, I understand how great your offer of aid is, for am I not a French soldier fighting against your father's, your prince's ally? No, you owe a duty much above the claims of friendship to your cause, as I owe it to the nation in whose service I am. All I can expect from you is silence. Even in that there may be treachery to your people."

"If so I will do that treachery," she replied. "No one shall learn through me of your mission. But you will be careful. Danger is all round you. If you cannot fly from it, guard yourselves against it. . . . And now, my friends, good night. If we do not meet again remember that Aimée Neffer may yet pay her debt."

As I bowed low over her hand I said:

"Fair mademoiselle, you may soon get an opportunity of paying it."

And the landlord, coming in with candles, conducted her to her apartment. Ah, what true words we often speak in jest! When I gave utterance to the lightly spoken thought I had little idea that the debt would be paid so soon, or in such fashion. O Briain, who had been keeping a wary eye on the landlord during the latter part of our conversation, so that he might not listen, said to me:

"Think you it was well, Piaras, to reveal our mission here to Mademoiselle Neffer? Remember she is one of these mountaineers herself."

"Muiris, a bhuachaill," I cried. "I would entrust that girl with my life. She has promised her silence."

"Aye, it may be so," he said, "but for all that she is a Vaudois. And you remember the words she used that night by the cottage of Gaspard: 'The Irish are brave men, but our mountaineers owe them little love.' I campaigned against them with de Catinat's army in '95, Piaras, and I know they have not forgotten it. If she should desire to betray us, who could blame her?"

"Muiris, you are a miserable doubter," I rallied him. "She may be a Vaudois, but she'll never betray us. Though if she did it could do us little more damage than has been done already. Circumstances have betrayed us. Monsieur le Sieur is now as much our enemy as if he had received word from the Duke that we were here to work him harm. But whatever be the result of our adventure, I have faith in that girl."

He looked quizzically at me for a long time.

"Be careful, Piaras, a mhic," he warned. "I believe you are already half in love with our winsome little mountain maid. . . . And Mademoiselle Neffer is very beautiful," he added, half to himself.

"Come, O hound of watching!" I laughed, "let us to bed. I think Monsieur de la Genèvre will not make any move against us to-night."

But even so we looked well to our arms, and arranged that one should keep watch while the other slept. We did not wish to be caught napping. And so the night wore away.

CHAPTER XVII

PRISONERS—DISILLUSION

How long a time had elapsed I know not, only that the grey dawn was beginning to creep into the room, when I was awakened from my sleep by the crash of a door being forced in. It had been my watch. For some time after I had been awakened by O Briain I had paced the floor in an endeavour to keep myself awake, but the two or three hours' sleep I had had seemed only to have heightened the fatigue and weariness I felt. Seating myself on a chair beside the bed I filled a pipe, and lighting it, puffed away steadily for some time. But it was no use. I have only a vague idea when I dropped off to sleep. I have blamed myself many a time for the laxity I displayed on that occasion. I was a soldier, and should have kept my watch. But there is little use now in wailing. We cannot recall the past, however much we may regret it. Nature on that occasion triumphed over will and training. Hence the disaster.

With a cry of warning to O Briain I started to my feet. In the grey light of the morning I saw several men rush in through the wrecked door. I snatched up a pistol, but it was too late. A blow sent it flying from my hand, and then I was down, fighting madly, with three or four enemies above me who crushed me to the floor. I struggled furiously, but they wore me down, and in a few minutes had bound me tightly. That lapse had cost me dear. From his bed I could hear the deep-throated growls of O Briain, who had been served in similar fashion to myself.

"Light! Light! Barnabé," shouted a loud, hoarse voice. "I wish to see this coxcomb who has defied me."

"The Sieur de la Genèvre," I muttered to myself. "And we are his prisoners, not he ours. We have lost this time."

The landlord came in carrying several candles. He could not refrain from giving me a kick as I lay stretched on the floor.

"That for this evening's work," he gritted.

"Hold! Hold! good Barnabé," cried the Sieur, pulling him backwards. "These are my prisoners. Time enough for that. Do you know anything of them save what you have told me?"

"No, seigneur," he replied. "But here is a paper I found in this spy's coat the other day."

The Sieur snatched it from his hand, and looked it over. I started as I recognised it. It was the letter from the Duc de Vendôme appointing me to his staff.

"Ha! A French officer," cried our captor, advancing closer to me. And then I saw a fierce, vindictive-looking face with reddish-rimmed eyes which glittered strangely in the candlelight. Round his face he wore a scraggy, tawny-coloured beard which gave his face a funny look which reminded me of an ape. He was short in stature and very stoutly built. Altogether one would hardly associate the squat, ridiculous figure with the redoubtable Sieur de le Genèvre. As I looked I gave an involuntary laugh.

"Ha! monsieur, you laugh," he cried. "But laugh, enjoy yourself while you have time. Methinks it will not be long. Gustave de la Genèvre has a short way with spies. What do you know of this?" and he flourished the letter in my face.

I made no reply. What would it avail to affirm or deny my ownership?

"What connection has Monsieur de Berac with M. le Lieutenant de Grás?" he inquired.

"'Tis amusing to bear two names. It is lucky," I replied blandly, and I must confess that it is not easy to be bland when one is lying on a floor with cords cutting deeply into one's flesh.

"Ah, monsieur, it may be," he said, falling in with my humour. "But you will not find it quite so lucky to carry letters from M. le Duc. For if M. le Lieutenant de Grás is known to the Duc, it follows that Monsieur de Berac is also known to him. How does my reasoning please you, Monsieur de Berac?"

"Parbleu, monsieur!" I cried. "How wonderful is your comprehension! What a pity it is that a man of such subtle intellect should lose himself amongst these hills! Your reasoning has not a flaw."

"Eh, monsieur," he cried, his face flushing with anger, "you sneer. But why do I bandy words with you. Here, men. The quickest way is the best with spies. Take them out. You will find trees in plenty."

Already I had been dragged to my feet by two stalwart fellows, when an unexpected interruption came. The Sieur had strode to the door, but he halted in amazement as a girl stood before him. I was as much amazed as he, for a glance showed me that it was Aimée Neffer. She carried a candle in her hand. It seemed to me that she had not been in bed. She still wore the silken riding habit which she had worn earlier in the evening. Only her luxuriant black tresses were unbound, and hung down far over her shoulders. On her face there was a flush of excitement which made her more beautiful than ever.

"Parbleu!" cried the Sieur, starting back. "Mademoiselle Neffer!"

"The Sieur de la Genèvre!" she cried. "Monsieur, what good fortune has brought you here?"

"Rather, fair lady," said he, sweeping off his hat,

"what kind gods have sent you hither. But," suddenly recollecting himself, "the prisoners. Mademoiselle, you have arrived at a most inopportune time."

But the girl had been looking at us, examining us closely by the light of her candle. Suddenly she uttered a cry of dismay, and gripped the Sieur by the arm. He started round with a muttered oath.

"Mademoiselle," he demanded, as he noticed her looks, "you know these prisoners."

"Alas, how well I know them!" she cried. Then with a fierce gesture: "Who would know them better? This wretch here," and she pointed to me, "is the one who led the soldiers of Duc Vendôme against my father's stronghold, and burned it down. And this other grey-haired villain," pointing at Muiris, "is one whom I noticed particularly on that day. Oh, how I hate you. . . . Mon Dieu, monsieur, how you are avenging us!" and she turned to our captor, who beamed beneath her words of approval.

I was astounded. The whole thing had taken me by surprise. I almost shouted out my denial of her vehement denunciation of me, but, I thought to myself, what did it matter? In a few minutes we would dangle at the end of two ropes, and then what difference would it make? So I held my peace. But I felt a curious thrill of bitter disappointment pass through me as I marked her savage glances. This girl for whom I had exposed myself to such dangers. She who had protested so much. Ah, woman! woman! who will fathom you? Sick at heart, I turned my head away.

The voice of the Sieur came to me.

"Fair mademoiselle," he said, "a few moments now will see you truly avenged. You will have the pleasure of gloating over their strangled corpses."

"Sieur," she cried, "an' you love me, find some better way. Think! Think! You will hang them, but what good will that be to you or me?"

"Do you not desire revenge then?" he cried, amazedly.

"Aye, revenge," she retorted, "but let us sweeten revenge with profit. But send your men hence. I would speak with you alone."

He did her bidding, and then she spoke rapidly.

"Victor Amadeus, our prince, has many rewards for his faithful followers. Your delivery of these spies to him will secure you his favour."

"But, mademoiselle," cried the puzzled knight, "how will this profit you?"

"Do you not see?" she asked. "I gain revenge, for Duke Victor will hang them, but I gain something more."

"And that is?" he asked.

"Fortune for the man who has offered me his hand," and she smiled coquettishly into his face.

Sitting in the chair into which I had been thrust by the departing men I listened in horror to the proposition. Such vileness I had not thought possible. O Briain must be right. The girl was worthless. Even so, one curious thing puzzled me. She had not mentioned anything of the matters of which I had spoken to her. The landlord was not present, or this fine scheme of mademoiselle's might have been blown to the winds. But he had shuffled out with the others.

"Is it then that you love me, ma belle?" cried the Sieur amorously, and he endeavoured to embrace her. But she avoided him, and coming close to me, hissed into my face:

"Monsieur de Berac, how do you like my scheme?"

I returned her gaze coldly, and said bitterly:

"Vile woman, your scheme is worthy of you," and I added for her ear alone, "I trusted you. I did not think you were so vile."

In the candlelight I thought I detected a look of pain pass across her face, but she turned away and stood whispering to the Sieur for some time. Then she gave him her hand to kiss, and went away. As she went, she called back:

"Adieu then till to-morrow."

For several minutes the knight continued pacing the room, apparently in deep thought. Every now and then I heard him muttering:

"She will be mine. She will be mine. Dieu, she is a clever woman. This plan of hers will make Duke Victor my friend."

At last he shouted:

"Ho, my men! 'Tis time we were getting back."

His ruffians came trooping in, and we were again dragged to our feet. When they heard that they were to be disappointed of their sport they vented their rage in vicious kicks and blows, and amused themselves by offering wagers to one another as to who would draw the first cry of pain from us. But no cry rewarded their brutish play. At length, tiring of their efforts, they hurried us away from Le Coq Doré, towards the château. After a toilsome journey up the rugged pathway we halted before the grim, lowering pile. The heavy gates swung open, and when we had passed through clanged too again. Now indeed it seemed as if the knell of doom had sounded. What hope could there be here, alone, in the stronghold of our enemy?

Our captors hurried us into a large, square chamber lit by numerous candles standing in tall iron candelabra placed on the floor. The Sieur came over to me as I stood in the grip of two of his powerful ruffians.

"So, monsieur," he sneered, "you thought to defy the Sieur de la Genèvre. His château would repay inspection, would it? You are here now. Examine it well, for your time will be short."

I made no reply, only looked the contempt I felt.

"Monsieur l'éspion," he went on, tauntingly, "your master, Duke Vendôme, should have sent one who knows how to keep awake."

I winced. That unfortunate laxity of mine was a

sore subject. I was tempted from my calm by the taunt.

"Monsieur," I cried, "no doubt he would have done so had he known you were but a night prowler."

He uttered a fierce imprecation, and glared at me, his eyes glittering. As I watched him I thought my last hour had come. He dropped his hand to his sword, and half drew it. But he clashed it back again into its scabbard, and raising his hand struck me full on the mouth.

"That for you, dog of a spy," he hissed. Turning away he ordered: "Take them to the dungeons. You know the one, Michel," to the black-browed wrestler whom I noticed for the first time among my captors. "Messieurs, I hope you will enjoy my hospitality. I will send word to Duke Vendôme how you have fared, and how profitable your coming has been to me. Duke Victor will reward me well. A fair good night to you, but I fear I cannot say, pleasant dreams. Our rats are not very pleasant companions."

He bowed mockingly, but I laughed in his face. As to poor Muiris, he said nothing. He was still dazed and suffering from the ill-usage he had received in the inn. Through a long passage, and down several flights of stone steps, we were hurried. We were thrust inside a small cell, and then the door clanged shut, and I heard the bolts being shot into place. For a few seconds the echo of the retreating footsteps of our captors came back to me, then all was silence. Beside me I could hear the breathing of Muiris, and I almost blessed them for having thrust us in together.

"Muiris," I said aloud, "I fear I have brought ill luck on you. What can you think of me for having gone to sleep at that cursed inn."

"As to ill luck," he answered, "I knew the risks before we set out, knew that this was to be no mere gambade. And as to your sleeping, why, you were tired and weary. I might have slept myself, but that

I'm more seasoned than a youngster like you. Why should we blame ourselves? It will do us little good. But, Piaras, I fear the mademoiselle was only playing with us the whole time."

I was silent. Her actions puzzled me. Somehow I found it hard to crush out all faith in her. Were it not for her interference our dead bodies would now be swinging in the wind from some tall pine. But O Briain's voice came to me again, muttering:

"Ah, my poor head. It is bursting. Acht, dar mo laimh, maybe I'd pay the rascal who struck me yet," and his voice trailed off.

"Muiris, Muiris!" I called, but only his heavy breathing answered. He was asleep. And my own eyes began to grow heavy. I remember thinking dully of Aimée Neffer, how she had cheered us up with her merry laugh and inconsequent chatter. How winning she was! Alas, that she had ever come into my life! I had such faith in her, and now——

CHAPTER XVIII

AIMÉE COMES

It must have been several hours later that I awoke suddenly. Something had run across my face. With a loud cry I made a frantic endeavour to spring to my feet, but fell back heavily.

Ah, what a thing is sleep! How it wafts you away from the cares of earth, makes you insensible to its trouble and turmoil, brings to you sweet oblivion! My dreams had been pleasant. The gracious mountain maid had had a place in them. No doubts of her truth saddened me. To my dreaming senses she was only constant and true, incapable of guile or deceit.

But what was that thing which had awakened me; that thing with claws which had passed across my face? For a while I lay still, every sense on the alert, endeavouring to pierce the thick blackness. But my effort was vain. Fabled Styx cannot have been blacker than was this dungeon. And then again I felt the thing sniffing at my face. With an effort I rolled over. My movement frightened the thing away. Neither was it alone, for I heard a faint rustle as of many feet. The horror of our position burst on me, and I shouted frantically:

"Muiris! Muiris! Awake! awake!"

"What is it?" he questioned drowsily.

"We must free ourselves," I cried. "The place swarms with rats."

"Rats! rats!" I heard him mutter.

"Aye, do you not remember," I cried, in terror lest

he might fall asleep again. "Come, Muiris. Rouse up. We must do something."

"Aye, but what?" he asked, and I knew he was now alive to our danger.

I hardly knew what was to be done, but anything was better than to lie there like logs at the mercy of this horrible vermin. By rolling over I got close to where Muiris lay. At last I found his hands, and bending down bit and gnawed at the hard cords. Oh, how I worked! My teeth ached and throbbed. My lips were broken and bleeding from the chafing against the ropes. Muiris could do nothing but sit still. At last when I had begun to despair, when my back seemed as if it would break, my head hanging a dead weight on my shoulders, I felt the cords loosen. A few minutes more, and his arms were free, but they fell away to his sides, stiff and useless. But gradually the blood began to force its way through the numbed limbs.

"Now, Muiris," I cried, "a few minutes more, and you are free."

When it was done he worked at my bonds, and at last they fell away. In ecstacy I stretched out my limbs, even though I groaned aloud with the agonising pain caused by the released blood.

"And now, a mhic," said Muiris, "what next?"

"Nothing," I said, "but wait. We need not fear the rats now that we are free."

It was weary work waiting there in that damp, cold cell, leaning against the walls, slimy with moisture, or groping about to keep the rats off. But we managed it somehow, keeping up our spirits by various poor little devices. In this way a couple of hours dragged away when we caught the sound of footsteps hurrying along the vaulted passage outside our prison, and a ray of light entered through the grated opening in the door. We had barely time to spring behind it, and cower back out of sight, when the bolts were withdrawn and the door swung inwards. For several seconds we blinked our dazzled eyes in the light of the lamp which our visitor carried. Then growing accustomed to its glare, we beheld—Aimée Neffer. I cried out in astonishment, for I am free to confess that she was the last person I expected to see. I had been hoping that it was the Sieur, or one of his followers, for I had resolved to make a bold dash for freedom after having choked him into submission. But now——

Our visitor was speaking in low tones.

"Let us hurry, my friends. I have only a little time to spare."

I regarded her coldly and scornfully.

"Mademoiselle," I said, "it is unfortunate for us that you have come. I had hoped it was your lover. It would have given us a chance to sell our lives dearly, for I have no wish to spend any more time in this hole. Go back to him. His company is more fitting for you than that of honest men."

She looked at me with uncomprehending eyes.

"What do you mean?" she cried. "What has happened? Surely it is not that you doubt me?"

"Aye, mademoiselle," I replied. "Oh, you played your game well with your pretended friendship. What a fool I was to have trusted you! But I ought to have known that it could not be otherwise," and I turned away contemptuously.

"You jest, monsieur," she cried. "I have done nothing that justifies the use of such words."

"Ah, mademoiselle, you are a clever actress. I bow to you," and turning I bowed mockingly. "And it suits you to cultivate a short memory. Have you then forgotten the inn? Have you forgotten your suggestions to the Sieur? Have you forgotten your pretended friendship for us, your vindictive gloatings? I might have known. You, the daughter of a Vaudois rebel."

"I understand all now," she cried. "You doubt me. Think I am a traitress, that I have come here to gloat over your misfortunes. Ah, mon ami, believe in me." Her voice trembled. "Believe that I have only worked to save you. Yes, I have pretended to be your enemy, but only that I might aid you. Ah, bon Dieu, what I have gone through that I might serve you! How I have allowed this man whom I loathe to make love to me; how I have coquetted with him! Ah, monsieur, if you knew you would not doubt."

But I was stubbornly silent. Her words had all the ring of truth, but I had hardened myself against belief. A Dhia na bhfireán! what a fool I was in my blind unbelief!

"You have taunted me that I am the daughter of a Vaudois rebel," she went on. "'Tis true, messieurs, but even the daughter of a Vaudois rebel can recognise the duties of friendship. Kind God, she can even forget that the men who have befriended her are the enemies of her people."

She bowed her head on her hands, and wept bitterly.

For a long time I gazed at her in silence, listening to her bitter sobs. I gloated over her agony, was glad that my doubts and harsh words had given her pain. But my better nature began to reassert itself, her tears to reproach me. And I reasoned, what could she hope to gain by coming here? We were prisoners without means of escape. I turned to her.

"Mademoiselle," I questioned, "why have you come?"

"To save you," she replied between her sobs.

"But how can we trust you," I asked, "after what has happened?"

"Oh, how can you doubt me," she cried, looking at me reproachfully. Before her accusing glance my eyes fell. . . . "I know," she went on, "that my actions were open to doubt. But if I say to you that I was acting a part that I should deceive the Sieur as well as you? Had he doubted my enmity to you, you would not be here now. . . . Yes," as she noticed my glance wander round the reeking walls, "'tis a dreary place. But you know what his intentions were. Oh, I tremble when I think of his horrible design."

I knew right well that she spoke truly. To her we owed our lives so far. Had she not played her part so well at Le Coq Doré we would now be past the power of aid. I felt myself reddening with shame for my treatment of her. But I was proud. I could not confess that I had been wrong, yet a while.

"See!" she said, placing on the floor wine and bread, "I have brought you food. It is not so choice as I could have wished, but I could not procure better. You must eat that you may be strong for the attempt which we will make in a few hours. My friends, can you still doubt me?"

I almost yielded, but my stubborn pride was still too strong. I would not speak. She stretched out her hands with an appealing gesture.

"Mon ami," she cried, "what do I gain by coming to you? Should the Sieur suspect me he would not spare me, even though he is my lover." Her look of reproach caused me to hang my head . . . "You will not send me away—I, who am your friend."

At last I was conquered by her pleading.

"Mademoiselle," I cried, "I am a miserable wretch. I have been mad, ungrateful in thinking you capable of such baseness. I have pained you, have called you traitress, mocked your goodness——"

But she stopped me.

"Hush! hush!" she cried, her voice softening, a glow in her soft, black eyes. "I can forgive you anything, mon ami . . ." and she added playfully: "We are friends once more."

I did not trust myself to reply. She turned to O Briain.

"And you, monsieur," she asked, "have you no word to say to me?"

And he answered simply: "Mademoiselle, I doubted you, but I doubt no longer. I will trust you in everything."

She laughed happily, and swept him a little curtsy.

Then spreading out the food she had brought she bade us eat while she spoke of her plan. The floor of that damp dungeon was hardly an ideal banqueting board, but two hungry prisoners are not likely to grumble at the serving of their food. And we were hungry. 'Twas only now that I noticed how hungry. We had eaten nothing since our capture. The Sieur's men had evidently forgotten us, or if they had brought anything while we slept the rats had regaled themselves on it.

"How long have we been here?" I asked, for I had lost count of time.

"Almost a day has passed since you were brought here," replied Aimée. "This morning the Sieur sent a messenger to Prince Victor Amadeus to announce your capture. He ought to return to-morrow. Therefore we must make our attempt at escape to-night."

"But, mademoiselle," I cried, "I do not understand. How comes it that you are here? Forgive me the question."

"Why should he not trust me?" she asked. "Does not a man trust the woman who is to be his wife? For I have promised to be his wife. I blush to think of the things which I have done. I have deceived this poor fool, but it was for your safety."

And I had doubted her. I felt bitterly ashamed of my miserable conduct. How mean and contemptible I felt myself beside this noble mountain maid! I could hear O Briain mutter: "A Dhia na nGrás, and we thought her traitress!"

"Yes," she went on, "he trusts me, and believes that I have come to gloat over my enemies. But we must hurry. He might come to seek me. In this dungeon he believes you are safe, that there is no necessity to guard you. But he told me you were bound."

I pointed to the bonds we had cast off.

"Not too tightly to free ourselves," I said. "And 'twas well. Rats are unpleasant companions for bound men."

She shuddered.

"You must allay all suspicion till the time comes. If anyone found you unloosed it might cause the Sieur to place guards in the passage outside. That would be unfortunate, and might be fatal to our chances. I will come to you again as soon as I can. Then we will steal from this horrible place, and try to make our way out of the château. It is a plan full of dangers, my friends, but there is no other way."

"And now," she cried, "I must go. Allow me to bind you up again. But you need have no fear. A couple of hours more, and you will be free."

"Unless we are dead," I muttered. I was resolved once free of that horrible dungeon not to be taken back to it again. She bound us loosely, and then bidding us be of good cheer went away, taking her lantern with her. I listened to the echo of her footsteps dying away along the passage, and then cried to O Briain:

"There goes a true girl."

"Aye," he replied, "as true as breathes." And he added: "To think how vile I thought her."

Poor Muiris, and he never blamed me for having dishonoured her by my distrust!

CHAPTER XIX

FREEDOM—THE FLIGHT ACROSS THE MOUNTAINS

ONLY a few hours our fair protectress had said, but how long they seemed, dragging away on leaden wings. I know I counted the minutes as they passed, counted them again and again, and yet again, till it almost seemed as if time were standing still. Before, that damp, noisome dungeon with its slimy walls and swarming vermin had appeared miserable enough. But now in the renewed light of hope how terrible, how frightful it was. And then a thought would obtrude itself: what if Aimée Neffer should fail; if the Sieur should have his suspicions aroused! Thus I tortured myself, and almost thanked the rats when encouraged by the silence and gloom they crept from their holes, and commenced to gnaw at our boots. It was a blessed interruption. With kicks we sent them scampering back to their dens.

So long a time had now elapsed that I feared the plot had failed, and was about to give utterance to my thought aloud, when the sound of a light step hurrying along the passage caused me to pause. With dilated eyes I watched the shaft of light which came through the grating grow bigger and bigger, then as the bolts were pulled back, I whispered to Muiris:

"She is here."

As she came in through the door we relieved our pent-up feelings by a low cry of welcome.

"Hush! Hush!" she whispered. "The danger is great. I fear the Sieur begins to suspect. I could hardly get away."

While she was speaking she was severing our bonds.

"These were the only weapons I could secure," she whispered, thrusting a couple of stout hunting knives into our hands. . . . "Hark!" she cried, as the noise of heavy footsteps struck on our ears, "someone comes."

We stood listening. Quickly they advanced along the passage.

"Whoever it is can only be coming here," she whispered. "You must overpower him, and stifle his cries. If not he will rouse up the castle, and then all is lost."

The steps came closer. It seemed an age till the new-comer stopped outside.

"Mon Dieu," gasped Aimée into my ear, "it is the Sieur. He has followed me."

As the door swung inwards we crouched behind it hidden from his view. Then with a sudden spring I was on him, my hands gripped round his throat, strangling back the cry which rose to his lips. He struggled like a madman, but I choked him into quiescence. Quickly I stripped off his coat and boots, and put them on, and then, a gag thrust into his mouth, we bound him with the cords we had worn.

"The coming of the Sieur has not been so unfortunate," I said. "It has supplied me with arms and a disguise which may serve us well. If we could procure one for you, Muiris. No one will suspect you, mademoiselle."

"No, I do not think so," she said. "Will I not be in the company of the Sieur? But let us go. Every minute we remain here increases the danger."

A muffled sound caused us to look round. The Sieur had recovered, and was glaring at us. I have looked into the faces of men maddened by the lust of battle, but seldom have I seen such a look of hate as now distorted the features of our prisoner.

"Ah, monsieur," I cried, "you have recovered.

We are sorry that we have been so rough. But necessity, M. de la Genèvre, necessity. May your stay here be as pleasant as ours has been."

"Come," whispered Aimée, shuddering before the knight's baleful glare, "I begin to grow afraid."

I caught her hand, and pressed it reassuringly. I felt it tremble within my grasp.

"A merry good night to you, monsieur," I cried. "We regret we must leave you in the dark."

Thus we left him, and bolting the door after us, walked boldly along the passage. The securing of a disguise for Muiris was troubling me. Our risk was doubled by his having to go forward dressed as he was when captured. If by any mischance he should be seen by the Sieur's rascals we would be at once betrayed. Dressed in the Sieur's dandyish coat of fine yellow silk, with his plumed hat pulled down over my eyes, I might escape too many inquisitive glances. But we could only hope that chance might throw something in our way.

We reached the end of the vaulted passage, and were at the foot of the stone steps which led upwards from the dungeons.

"Extinguish the light," whispered Aimée. "We must go forward in the darkness. Be careful. A sound would betray us."

We crept up the stairs after our fair guide, and found ourselves in a passage similar to the one we had left, but that this one was lit by embrasures high up in the walls through which the moonlight streamed in. Before venturing out into it we peeped out cautiously to see if it were clear. Away at its far end we perceived a ray of light which seemed to filter out under a doorway. To our ears was borne the sound of voices raised in rude song.

"The Sieur's men," whispered Aimée.

But another sound came to us. The sound of footsteps. A man was coming towards us carrying a lantern. As I caught its gleam I pulled the others back into the opening.

"If he passes," I whispered to Muiris, "let him go. If not we must silence him. Mademoiselle, we would gladly spare you such scenes."

"I know their necessity," said the brave girl. "We cannot pause now."

The man came on, lilting to himself right merrily. Waiting there in the shadows we scarcely dared to breathe. He came opposite our hiding-place. It seemed as if he were passing on. But no. He turned to descend. Like a tiger I leaped at him, and struck a swinging blow with the haft of my knife. He fell without a cry, but ere I had time to seize it his lantern went rolling and bounding down the stairs. Its clatter seemed to fill the whole place. It echoed and re-echoed along the passages as if it were a thunder-peal. For full five minutes we waited, not daring to move. But the din, though it sounded so terrifying to us, had attracted no notice. No shouts of alarm rang out, nor did we hear the rush of hurrying men.

"Now, Muiris," I cried, "strip him. Hurry, man! Hurry!"

In a few minutes we were ready to venture again. We could walk more boldly now, since in the long cloak and steel morion Muiris was quite transformed into one of the Sieur's brigands.

"Mademoiselle Aimée," I whispered, as we stepped out, "you must give me your arm. Think you lovers would walk so far apart. And am I not your lover?"

She said nothing, but placed her arm within mine. I noticed that she was trembling like a leaf.

"Fear not," I whispered, bending down. "Everything goes well. So far there is no alarm."

"It is not that I fear," she replied, but I noticed that she blushed up to the roots of her hair. Ah, how blind we men are!

We went along swiftly, past the door behind which our enemies gambled and caroused. Through long passages which seemed endless we sped, crouching into dark corners when a step warned us that an enemy was near. Several times it appeared as if we were on the point of capture, but always the danger passed us by. We were fortunate in that none of the Sieur's men met us, because I fear I did not make a very presentable Sieur, even though I was now wrapped in his cloak, which we had found in a room which lay in our path. But our stars were in the ascendant. We passed unseen. But through it all my hand rested on my sword-hilt, and not once but many times, I was within an ace of shouting a cry of warning to Muiris who followed behind.

At length we found ourselves out in the open air, and now the most dangerous part of our task lay before us. We must run the gauntlet of the guards posted at the gate. True, the darkness of the night was in our favour, and so there was less danger of being recognised than within the château. But the lateness of the hour was against us. It was hardly probable that the Sieur made it a habit to take midnight rambles amongst the hills. But we must not fail now. A bold bearing might carry us through. And if we were outside the gates, what then? On foot we could make but poor progress. Oh, if we had a couple of good horses how we would make the ground fly! I stooped to whisper my thought to Aimée.

"No, no," she cried, "it would delay us too long. We dare not try to procure them."

I did not urge, for I saw that there was much in her objection. At the gate I cried out in as hoarse a voice as I could assume to the man who came hurrying forward, to open. He seemed to be surprised at the request, and hesitated, mumbling something about the lateness of the hour.

"What, dog!" I cried angrily. "You question me. Open, I say," and I half drew my sword.

He flew to do my bidding. The big gate swung back, and we passed out with leisurely stride beneath the vaulted archway. I felt sorely tempted to run, but that would be neither safe nor dignified. And so we walked as if nothing more important than our midnight ramble troubled us. Better lose a few precious minutes than spoil all by our precipitancy. When we felt we were well away from prying eyes we hurried on and on.

At last as if with one accord we halted. For a while we stood gazing round us. Above us the stars twinkled brightly in a clear sky. Across the mountains the cold, biting breeze came sweeping stingingly into our faces. Around us was the loneliness of the great wastes, which seemed to speak to our souls in that midnight hour for all its mysterious silence. We gloried in the wild beauty, though we were filled with sadness. We drank in the pure air of freedom which we had thought we would never breathe again. We stamped on our memories every feature of that mighty picture spread out before us, a picture rendered all the more precious by contrast with the horrible dungeon we had left.

Behind us shooting its tall turrets into the air the château stood perched on its rock. Down below us lay spread out, bathed in the silver moonlight, rocky gleann and deep pine forest. Afar off I caught a glimpse of some mountain lakelet, its waters silvered by the moon's rays. Ha! was that the glimmering of a fire gleaming out so redly in the distance. My wandering thoughts flew back to our camp at Ivrea. Mayhap that was one of our watch-fires. Perhaps some of Dillon's brave fellows beguiled their watch beside it. If I failed, down there I would meet my death. But no. How could it be? Ivrea lay far, far beyond my range of vision.

The voice of Aimée Neffer recalled me to a sense of our danger.

"We must not tarry here," she said. "Our enemies may discover their master. We must be far on our way before they do."

"Oh, that we had horses," I cried. "How we would make this ground fly!"

"You do not blame me," said the girl, a wistful note in her voice. "I acted for the best."

"Blame you," I cried, and caught her to my breast in a passionate embrace. I kissed her, not once, but many times. For a few seconds she lay quiet in my arms, then broke away with flaming cheeks and heaving bosom. And I, ashamed, bitterly repenting my mad action, stood before her with bowed head.

"Mademoiselle," I cried, "can you forgive me? I was foolish, mad, carried away by my feelings. Bitterly I repent this thing. Oh, believe me when I say that not even in my thoughts would I harm you. But do not let the madness of a moment condemn me to an unworthy place in your thoughts."

She came over to me, and placed both her little hands within mine.

"I forgive you, M. de Grás," she said softly. "I understand how that foolish action has pained you. Spite of it I would be willing to commit my honour to the keeping of one of the most chivalrous gentlemen I have ever known."

"Ah, mademoiselle, how you shame me!" I cried, raising her hand to my lips.

"Let us forget it," she said.... "Hasten! Hasten! Let us away from this place."

We hastened forward again, fearing every moment to hear the alarm behind which would tell of our escape. But no clamorous bell clanged out. Silence only reigned. On, ever onward we pressed, wading through quagmires which trembled and shook under our feet, splashing through brawling streams, forcing our way through gorse and heather. Now we walked ankle-deep in water which bore with it in its bosom the iciness of its glacier birthplace. Again we toiled bent-backed up stony paths which hurt and tortured the feet. To Muiris and myself with our stout, heavy boots it was a painful journey, but to our fair companion it was simply misery. Her shoes were little protection against the sharp stones and shingle of the way we were pursuing. But she never murmured, never complained, only pressed on by the most unfrequented paths known to her. At last I stopped.

"Mademoiselle," I cried, "this cannot be. You must not walk farther. You must permit us to carry you. Muiris and I will relieve one another."

"No, no," she cried, "I could not be such a burthen to you. It is several hours' journey yet to the chaumière of Gaspard, whither we are going. How could you carry me for such a distance?"

"But you cannot walk farther," I urged. "Believe me, we will make quicker progress. And we are not pursued."

She looked down at her poor, bruised feet, and laughed.

"Ah, what a burthen I am," she cried. "Only a poor, weak girl. I, who pretend to be your rescuer. My friends, it would be better that you should go on alone. I will point you out the way."

But we cried out in horror at the suggestion. Leave her, who had brought us out of the place of bondage, to face unknown perils alone! Muiris swore roundly that if it were necessary to carry her every inch of the way he would do so rather than leave her there. Or if she refused to be carried, we would remain by her. Finally she consented, and beckoned me to her side.

"I claim your assistance, brave knight," she cried playfully.

"After my foolishness," I asked, "you will trust me."

"Even so," she replied, and more softly . . . "I will trust my knight in all things."

Raising her in my arms we went forward again. She was a light burthen, and we made fair progress. We went on for about an hour in this fashion, O Briain relieving me from time to time. Then we found the way becoming steeper, and more difficult even, than it had been before. Thinking that it was better to rest before attempting the toilsome climb, and feeling that I might safely do so, I called a halt. Seating ourselves on a bank of ferns we rested our weary limbs.

CHAPTER XX

PURSUIT—DEFEAT IN VICTORY

A LONG time we remained there enjoying the grateful rest. We told ourselves that we were safe, that no enemies were on our track. We told ourselves that the unfortunate Sieur had not been rescued from his unpleasant abode, or if he had been, and our pursuit taken up, that our enemies had missed us. And so the minutes fled on.

Suddenly a shot rang out. It was difficult to tell how near or far away it might be, owing to the myriad echoes which it roused up. We listened to them dying away. Then we looked at each other furtively. No one spoke. It seemed to be as if each feared to give confirmation to the other's thought. We had been so certain that our enemies had missed us, that that shot sounded in our ears as the very crack of doom, blasting our hopes, bringing the airy castles we had built tumbling down about our ears. But might it not be the shot of some solitary hunter who had chosen the night to steal on his prey? And because we cling to hope sometimes with such blind faith, I almost persuaded myself it was so. But we would not take any chances; and so I turned to the others and told them we must go on. Muiris pulled me aside and whispered:

"You heard that shot?"

"Yes," I replied, "and I fear that we are pursued. But not a word. We must not alarm mademoiselle needlessly. After all it may be only a hunter. If not she will know too soon."

Forward again on our march. We now carried our fair guide in a kind of sling which we had fashioned during our halt from a pair of stout saplings we had hewn down in the pine-woods, and our cloaks. It was only a poor makeshift, but we were rather proud of it. It divided the labour of carrying Aimée, whose feet were now so badly swollen that she could only limp painfully along. Seated in her rough sedan-chair, elevated on our shoulders, she could keep a sharp watch for any threatened danger. We were getting along rapidly, and I was beginning to think that the echoing shot had meant nothing after all, when suddenly a startled cry came from Aimée:

"Great God, we are pursued!"

Almost involuntarily we halted, and looked back. Behind us away on the side of the mountain which overlooked the valley we were traversing, we beheld quite a dozen men outlined in the bright moonlight. Their cries came faintly to us. We saw a couple of them raise their pieces to their shoulders. Their shots woke up the slumbering echoes. But we could laugh at their bullets. They were only throwing them away. But we could not hope to outdistance them for long. Soon they would be close up on our rear.

"M'anam do Dhia!" cried out Muiris, "we are taken in front."

He spoke truly. Some distance in front, but on our left hand, came a second party. At the moment they were crossing an open tract of mountain. For a few moments they were visible to us, then disappeared into a thick grove of pines. We counted six men. They had seen us also, for we heard shots being fired as if in signal to the others. We judged both parties to be at least half a mile away yet, and it goes without saying that they could make quicker progress than we could, hampered as we were. Unfortunately the ground offered little advantage for defence. Oh, how my heart ached to have to fly before those rascals! But there was nothing else to do.

"If we could only reach shelter," I cried, "we might keep them at bay. But in this plain——"

"We must surrender, or sell our lives as dearly as possible," finished O Briain grimly.

But Aimée Neffer broke in: "About half a mile ahead there is a place where the mountain is rent in twain by a frightful chasm called La Gorge. It is crossed by a little wooden bridge. If we could reach it——"

I had heard enough.

"On, on," I cried. "We must try to cheat our pursuers."

Forward we dashed, the sling swaying from side to side threatening to unseat its occupant. I shouted to her to hold tightly, and she answered bravely. Ah, there was brave blood in that Vaudois maid! No puling, timorous girl she! As we came level with the flanking party they were little more than a gunshot away. They were now in full view, and shouted loudly to us to stop. But we paid no heed. We heard a couple of shots ring out, but the aim was uncertain. Ahead of us rose up the precipices which bounded the gorge, scarcely two hundred yards away. If we could only reach it. The ground had become rougher and more broken. Huge granite boulders were strewn round as if they had been thrown from the cliffs above by some giant hand. In front a few yards away lay safety; behind us, ever nearer and nearer, rang out the yells of our enemies. For the moment we were hidden by one of the granite masses.

"Muiris," I panted out, "these devils must be kept back. I will make a stand here. Do you press on with mademoiselle. When you cross the bridge see if it could be broken down. Do what you can, and when you are ready a shrill whistle will warn me. Give me your pistols. You will not need them."

"No, no," cried Muiris, "I will stay."

"Muiris," I cried sternly, "who holds the Duke's orders? Besides, you must go on with mademoiselle."

We threw aside the sling. Its use was past. Aimée stood beside me. As she heard my instructions to Muiris she uttered a cry of anguish, and laid her hand on my arm.

"Oh, Piaras, Piaras!" she whispered, "must you do this thing?"

"Mademoiselle," I said, smiling into her eyes, "I will rejoin you in a few minutes. Have no fear."

But I pressed her hand to my lips with fervour. Perhaps it might be my farewell. She turned away lingeringly, and I whispered to Muiris:

"If I should not come within fifteen minutes destroy the bridge, and go on with mademoiselle."

He caught my hand in a firm grip, and turned away. Gallant old Muiris! I believe there were tears in his eyes. I watched them go, Muiris half leading, half carrying his companion. Though she had borne herself so bravely, the hardships of the journey had told heavily on her. She was indeed paying her debt.

Ensconced behind a large rock which commanded the path our foes must come, I waited. If I could keep them back till Muiris had crossed the bridge, all would be well. If not—if, seeing through my ruse, they should overwhelm me at one fierce rush? I shrugged my shoulders—'twas as good to die thus as otherwise. My friends would have got a good start; they would escape.

But the enemy were close up. They had no suspicion of my ambuscade. They rushed on unthinkingly. I waited till they were well within pistol-shot. Then my pistol spoke out, and was answered by a loud cry. In confusion my foes drew back. I could hear the Sieur cursing loudly, shouting to his men to take cover and advance cautiously. Keeping well out of sight I crept away to another rock and waited. I had not long to wait. Soon I perceived a couple of dark forms flitting from rock to rock. Again I fired and carried out my former manœuvre. A Mhuire! would that whistle never come? If the Sieur once perceived that there was only a solitary individual in front, which he must inevitably do, he would quickly crush me by his swift advance. And then I threw up my pistol and fired at a figure darkly outlined before me. I heard the man's sharp cry of pain, and then the voice of the Sieur rang out:

"Forward, men; this is but a trick. Are you afraid of one man?"

Ah, this was the end! For what could I hope to do against the swarming enemy? I had barely one shot left, and then my sword. Well, I might die in a worse way. But suddenly shrilling through the air came a long drawn-out whistle. The signal! Springing to my feet I raced ahead. Behind me a couple of shots rang out, but the bullets flattened themselves against the rocks or sang through the air over my head. I could hear the footsteps pounding behind, but the bridge was well in sight. Beyond it I saw Muiris O Briain and the girl. A Ri an Domhain! Could I pass it in time? A backward glance showed me that my pursuers had scattered out. Close at my heels came a tall fellow who had raced ahead a good distance in front of the others. I heard the cry of Aimée calling to me to take care. Suddenly I halted, and springing aside, crashed my sword, which I had drawn with a sudden wrench, down on his head, as he raced past unable to stop himself. With a choking cry he fell, and leaping across his prostrate body, I raced across the bridge, which trembled and shook beneath my weight.

"Down, down with it!" yelled Muiris, as I reached the other side. "I have cut the lashings."

We bent ourselves to the work. The bridge was merely a rough structure of pines lashed together, with smoothened timbers to make a footway. Along the sides ran a hand-rail breast high. It was lashed with stout ropes to several large pines which grew close to the edge of the gorge at either side. These lashings Muiris had cut away with his sword. If we could cast the bridge down into the depths below we would be safe from pursuit, for the chasm was too wide to cross by leaping. But our enemies were perilously near. As we strained and tugged at the structure we could hear the Sieur urging them on. He had seen our purpose, and was screaming shrilly:

"The bridge! The bridge! They are breaking it down."

It was yielding. Another push or two would send it hurtling down into the dark depths below, where a furious torrent swept and foamed along. And then with a grinding crash it toppled over. We were safe, but two minutes more would have lost all.

Our enemies had reached the edge of the cliff beyond, and stood cursing and fuming. We could see the Sieur, his ugly face distorted with rage, shaking his fist across at us. Suddenly he turned and gave some order to his men which we could not hear. But its significance was borne in on us as we saw them throw their pieces to their shoulders.

"Down! down!" I shouted, dragging the girl to the ground.

The volley crashed out, and I heard a sharp exclamation from O Briain, but thought little of it. Drawing the still loaded pistol from my belt, I fired, but missed. Rising to my feet, I shouted:

"M. le Sieur, we will meet again. We may be more evenly matched then."

He answered with a string of curses, and shouted back:

"Speed the day. You will know what it is to have made an enemy of Gustave de la Genèvre."

Turning I gave my arm to Aimée Neffer. She limped along painfully, and I was about to propose a rest when we had gone a short distance, but

O Briain, who had been walking along silently, staggered. If I had not caught him with my disengaged hand he would have fallen.

"A Mhuire!" I cried. "What has happened?"

"Piaras, a mhic," he said, and he spoke with much difficulty, "my time has come. A bullet has entered here;" and then I perceived that he held his hand tightly pressed against his side. When he took it away the blood gushed out. That cry! Now, now I remembered.

"Muiris," I cried, "we will bind up your wound."

Even as I spoke I knew how useless it was to try to stanch that gaping wound.

"It is impossible," he said. "My days are spent. I am tired, and cannot go farther."

Gently we laid him down, his back propped against a tree. Aimée Neffer was weeping silently, and I—my eyes were hardly dry. To think that poor Muiris had come to these mountains to die. I thought sadly what an ill-omened fellow I was. Never again would I hear his hearty laugh; never feel his strong hand-clasp.

But he was speaking. It almost seemed as if he divined my thoughts. And mayhap he did. Such flashes of illumination come to the dying.

"Piaras, a mhic," he said, and I had to bend to catch his words he spoke so lowly, "do not blame yourself. You remember the day we spoke in the hospital. I had a feeling then that my time was near. The end has come, as I hoped it would, from the soldier's bullet. And I have done my duty. This little girl," and he raised his poor hand and laid it caressingly on Aimée Neffer's dark head, "knows how well. Is it not so, a chailín dubh dílis?"

But she could not answer because of her tears.

"What! you weep!" he cried. "Ah, child, is it not better so? Is it not better that death should come thus with friends by my side? Why weep then? My duty is done, my life is spent. I go to meet those friends I have known. A poor soldier alone in the world, it is better that I should go. You will tell my brave comrades of Dillon's, Piaras, how I died. Ah, they loved me. How many a brave day we saw together. Ah, Piaras, was I not right when I said yon day that I would never see our country again."

"Alas! alas!" cried Aimée, fondling his poor hand, and I ground my teeth together to force back the bitter cry which rose to my lips.

Then his mind began to wander. He was back again in the valleys of his native Clare. Again he roamed, a child, through the long, golden summer evenings, spoke of friends long dead and laid to rest. Now his voice rang out with the wild peal of battle, as in fancy he led his men forward in the whirling charge against the enemies of his race. Suddenly he shouted: "Trasker, look to yourself. . . . I seek only vengeance." And now he seemed to be gazing down on the upturned face of his enemy, as he muttered: "Maire! wife! You are avenged."

Ah me, how sad it all was, standing there with the night wind murmuring mournfully round, the vast mountain solitude broken now and again by the whisperings and mutterings of the dying man. And I had thought that we were the victors. With my brave old friend lying there, his life ebbing away, how cold, how empty seemed our victory.

Suddenly he sat erect.

"Piaras," he cried, and his voice rang out strongly, "all's well. The enemy are driven back. I can die happy now. Do not fear. . . . Give me your hands, for it grows dark."

We placed our hands silently in his, and I heard him whisper:

"Iosa, Muire, déan trócaire ar m'anam."

'Twas the end. With scarcely a tremor the gallant soldier passed away. He had gone on his last march.

For a long time I stood gazing down at his face. At last Muiris O Briain was at rest. Death had passed him by on the battlefield; it had come to him here on the mountains, far from the land of his youth. No more for him would bray out the trumpet calling to the maddening battle-charge. His sword might rust in its scabbard. Muiris O Briain would not need it more.

Gently I disengaged my hand from the stiffening fingers, and touching the girl on the shoulder, assisted her to rise.

"Ah, how luckless I am," she cried, with a heart-broken moan. "To my friends I bring only misfortune."

I comforted her, and after a time she grew calm. Then with the dead branches strewn round I covered over the body of our poor friend, and piled stones above him. With heavy hearts we turned away, leaving brave Muiris to the repose he had so well earned.

CHAPTER XXI

REFUGE—A DEBT WELL PAID

The grey dawn was breaking as we stood before the little cottage of Gaspard. He sprung from his bed at our knock, and flung his door wide to us. He welcomed us heartily. 'Twas but little he could offer us, but that little he would give gladly. I thought how differently he had acted on the former occasion I had met him. Then he had watched only for the chance of sending a bullet through me. Now as he stood in the open doorway, he even regarded me with a smiling face.

Aimée related to him all that had happened, and asked that he give us food. He set before us cheese and black bread, with goat's milk and wine. We ate heartily, for though our hearts were sad we felt that we must keep up our strength. We knew not what the future held, nor what further demands might be made on our strength. When we had eaten, I bade Aimée retire to the inner room that she might rest. After telling Gaspard to keep guard outside in case of alarm she retired, remarking to me:

"This place is far from the château. But it is well to be on one's guard. The Sieur de la Genèvre is a revengeful man. He might even find means to follow us here."

For a time I sat gazing into the blazing log-fire which Gaspard had kindled. Around me silence reigned. From the inner room I could hear the gentle breathing of the fair sleeper. I thought sadly of the events of the past few days. What would be the outcome of all this miserable tangle? A few miles up the mountain slept poor Muiris, my best friend, victim to the mad scheme of the Duke. Ah, how well the Chevalier de Frobin had spoken when he said the Duke would avenge him! How now could I hope to succeed against the powerful mountain traitor? Suspected, alone, how could I venture back to his stronghold? Was it not better to return and hand up my sword and life into the hands of the Duke? But tired, overtaxed Nature demanded its due, and sitting there I fell asleep.

. . . .

I awoke with a start. It was well on into the day, for the sun was shining brightly in through the tiny window. I had started up with the sound of a shot ringing in my ears. For several seconds my dazed senses refused to act. Then the sound of a struggle came, and the thud of a heavy blow, followed by silence. I leapt to my feet. With a bound I was at the door, but it was hurled in, and a man sprang across the threshold. A glance showed me who it was. The Sieur de la Genèvre, his eyes bloodshot, his clothes torn and covered with mud. With a heavy blow he sent me to the ground, and springing over me dashed in the door of the room where Aimée Neffer lay. As he caught sight of her a terrible oath burst from his lips.

"You jade," he shouted, "this for your treachery!"

The crack of his pistol was followed by a sharp cry of pain.

"Devil!" I shouted, springing on him. "Defend yourself."

He cast away the empty pistol and turned to meet my attack. To the winds were now cast skill and science. Only the terrible, primitive passions of savage man were uppermost as we grappled and tore at each other's throats. Like animals we fought, tugging, straining, rending. All my wild passions were let loose—the veneer of civilisation gone. Revenge now I would have for the death of Muiris. Aye, bitter, bitter revenge. And for that poor girl who lay within that room. Recklessly, blindly I fought, putting forth all my strength to break down the resistance of this frothing fiend. His squat body held bull-like strength; but I would wear it down, worry him, crush the life out of him. Oh, what a merciless, ravening savage a man can become!

Suddenly I felt him yield a little. I gave utterance to a wild, cruel laugh. I was wearing him down. The fight was in my hands. Gradually I felt him weaken, heard his breath grow more laboured. Then with an effort which caused my muscles to crack as if the strain were too much for them, caused my breath to come in a sobbing gasp from my labouring chest, caused the veins to stand out on my forehead like whipcord, I raised him in my arms and cast him against the wall. With a sickening crash he fell to the floor and lay still; and I, spent, exhausted by this final effort, reeled backward against the table.

A feeble moan recalled me to myself. It came from Aimée Neffer. I rushed to the bedside, starting back in horror as my eyes fell on the blood which saturated it. My soul cried out in anguish. Muiris first, now this gentle, innocent girl. I threw myself on my knees by the bedside, and soldier as I was, inured to scenes of blood and sadness, my frame shook with wild, terrible sobs. What had I done that I should cause all this? God of Heaven, was I accursed?

I felt a hand caressing my bowed head, and heard a soft voice whisper, oh! so lowly in my ear:

"Mon ami, why do you weep? 'Tis not meet that a soldier should. Tears are only for women. Look up, Piaras. I may call you Piaras now."

I raised my anguished countenance and looked into her eyes.

"'Tis I who have brought you to this," I cried with

fierce self-accusation. "Had you not aided me you would not be here."

"Ah, how glad I am!" she said, a happy smile lighting up her beautiful face. "How happy that my debt is paid. How I prayed that I might yet aid the man who had aided me in my distress, who had rescued me from the hand of an enemy. If my life has been the forfeit, what matters it? The God of Mercy granted my prayer. The rest is nothing."

What a noble, generous woman she was, this dark-haired Vaudois maid! All the doubts and suspicions I had felt rose up before my mind accusing me. How unworthy, how ignoble they all appeared now! I rose to my feet.

"Aimée," I cried hoarsely, "I have been blind, ungenerous. I have stabbed you with my vile suspicions. Yonder at Le Coq Doré I believed you capable of betrayal. I did not know. Can you forgive me my wretched doubtings?"

She looked at me with shining eyes.

"I have already forgiven you," she said. "Ah, Piaras, what will not we women forgive to those we love? For I have loved you, Piaras. May I not confess it now, in these last few moments of my life? Were it otherwise I would bury my love in my heart, and let you go your way unknowing. Have you any love in your heart for poor me?"

Love! I had not thought of it. My mind, filled with other affairs, had not had room for more gentle thoughts. Ah yes! On the mountains above I had kissed her, taken her in my arms, but it was not the feeling which animates a lover which had caused my action. Rather was it the action of a man carried away by a wave of gratitude for one who had risked much for his sake. But now looking at her lying there, listening to her gentle pleading, I felt that I could have loved her, felt that I could have repaid her by my devotion.

She was looking at me as if her eyes would pierce my very soul.

"Ah, I know, Piaras," she whispered. "Perhaps I have asked much. Love comes not at our bidding."

I stooped my head and pressed my lips to hers. Deception, you say. Perhaps! Perhaps! And even if it were, can you not forgive the gentle crime? Would you do less? Would you shrink from making the last few minutes of one who had lost all for you less lonely by the medium of a kiss? If you would, Piaras Grás can say no more. I can only take on my shoulders the guilt of the gentle crime, feeling that its punishment will be outweighed by the sweetness and consolation which it brought to his poor friend, dying there so far away from home or kindred.

A step behind me caused me to look round. The shepherd Gaspard had staggered into the room, his face white and haggard. He stood transfixed with horror as he beheld his young mistress. Then in a voice in which grief and rage struggled for the mastery he demanded who had done this thing. But she motioned him to her side. Tears coursed down his rugged cheeks as she took his hand within her own.

"Poor Gaspard," she whispered. "I am going from you. You will go to my father when I am gone. You will tell him all, and bring him here that he may bring me back to the old home. You will do that, Gaspard?"

The poor fellow could not speak, but he raised up her hands and covered them with kisses. She motioned towards me.

"Promise me, Gaspard, that you will do everything he asks."

He bowed his head in silent assent, and staggering away covered his face with his hands and groaned aloud.

"Piaras, Piaras," she whispered suddenly, "raise me up. The time is here. There is but a few minutes more."

I raised her in my arms. I heard her give a little sigh of contentment as she laid her head against my shoulder.

"Ah, Piaras," she whispered, "how happy you have made me. . . . At last the debt is paid."

Her voice sank lower and lower. I heard her murmured prayer: "Lord, have mercy on my soul." For a few seconds she was silent. Then again I heard her whisper:

"Piaras, a kiss—the last."

My lips met hers in one long, last kiss. Her dark head sank on my shoulder. A sigh, and the soul of gentle Aimée Neffer had gone across the border. Gently I laid her back on the bed. Her poor lips seemed yet to smile. Yes, I thought sadly, she had died happy.

I turned away from the bedside. Gaspard was still there, his head bent down. His back was towards me. I touched him on the shoulder. He started round at my touch, and seizing my arm in a grip of iron, demanded hoarsely:

"Who has done this thing? Oh, tell me, tell me, that I may drive my knife through his black heart."

"He lies without," I said. "The Sieur de la Genèvre."

"Oh, let me to him," he shouted violently, and rushed from the room ere I had time to prevent him. I dashed after him. He had flung himself on the Sieur, who still lay insensible where he had fallen. In his hand, upraised to strike, gleamed his long knife.

I seized his arm.

"Gaspard," I cried, "this man is my prisoner. Remember the command of your dead mistress."

"Diable!" he cried, struggling furiously. "This dog must not live."

"His life is mine," I said. "Your mistress shall be avenged."

"Oh, my poor mistress! How bitter shall be the news!" he cried, bursting into a passion of tears.

When it had passed, he told me how the Sieur, accompanied by two followers, had crept on him. How he had shot one, and crushed in the skull of the other by a blow of his musket-butt, only to fall before the Sieur.

We bound the limbs of the still unconscious wretch tightly together, and then I bade Gaspard go to seek the father of Aimée, telling him that I would watch till his coming. 'Twas a long and lonely vigil there in that silent cottage by the body of the maiden who had loved me—the saddest I have known. Her murderer had long recovered his senses, and addressed bitter taunts to me, flung vile insults at the pure, unsullied fame of his victim. No expression of regret passed his lips, only the foul mouthings of a fiend. But I pushed a cruel gag into his mouth and thus stopped the slanders of that evil tongue.

The moon had long risen over the peaks of the mountains, and still Gaspard had not come. Out in the pale moonlight I waited. A slight noise caused me to turn. Before me I saw the figure of the Sieur. In some manner he had managed to free himself and was fleeing towards safety. With a shout of rage I dashed after the flying wretch. Was this devil going to escape me now? His taunting laugh came back to me as I raced along. He ran with the speed of a deer, and I feared that he was escaping me. On the brink almost of a tall cliff he stopped and looked back, laughing derisively.

"I have cheated you, monsieur l'éspion," he shouted. "Who wins now?"

I gnashed my teeth in my rage, but a sharp report cut through the stillness of the night. I saw the Sieur throw up his arms and stagger forward. And then a small body of armed men advanced into view. Gaspard rushed towards me.

"Ah, monsieur," he cried, his voice ringing with fierce joy, "old Gaspard's bullet has avenged his mistress after all."

The Sieur was dead; my mission ended. But at what a cost? How much happier I had been had I never heard of him. Alas, how powerless we poor mortals are before the stern decrees of Fate!

To the stern, black-bearded man, the brave mountain chief who had so nobly struggled amongst his mountain fastnesses in defence of his cause, I told the whole story. He listened in silence, gazing down sadly into the white, beautiful face of his daughter. He shed no tears, but I knew that his father's heart was wrung with anguish. When I had done,

"Monsieur," he cried, "my sword has been often drawn against the French power. In the passes where I rule the name of Frenchman is hated. But I offer you my hand. Take it. It is a tribute to my daughter's friendship and love. Across her dead body we can forget the enmities which divide us." His voice shook. "Pray God that we may never meet in anger for my daughter's sake."

I gave him my hand. For a long time we stood there, the Franco-Irish officer and the Vaudois chief. By all the ethics of politics we were enemies, but we stood clasped hand in hand, drawn together by the friendship, the love, the sacrifice of a girl. I heard the strong, stern man groan:

"Oh, Aimée, Aimée, ma petite, you have gone from me, and I am alone."

Stooping he kissed the cold, pale lips. Then he became the iron soldier. In stern tones which told naught of the agony which gnawed at his heart, he ordered his men to prepare a bier to bear away their mistress.

In a few minutes all was ready. I walked behind the rough bier beside the lonely man for a few miles. Then I whispered to him that I should go. Henri Neffer turned to me.

"Monsieur," he said, "let us clasp hands once more. Death has made us friends. She who lies there was not mistaken. In you she had found her ideal. I thank you, noble Irishman, for your conduct. We may not meet again, but I shall never forget. Adieu."

I wrung his hand in silence. Ah, how little I had done! We never met again. After that night of sorrow, Henri Neffer passed out of my life. Bareheaded I watched the sad company till the peaks had closed round them and hid them from my view. Then, sad and heavy-hearted, I turned my face towards Ivrea.

CHAPTER XXII

AGAIN AT IVREA

The morning reveille was sounding shrilly through the camp as I, weary and footsore, made my way towards the quarters of the Duc de Vendôme. I had conquered, won back my former place, but I felt little of the elation which conquerors feel. As I thought of those two poor friends who had lost their lives, I felt that my victory had been won at too great a cost. A Dhia! could I call a victory that which had reft me of two such friends!

I had not long to wait. In a few minutes I heard the measured step of the man who had sent me forth, and then he stood before me. Saluting I waited for him to speak.

"Ah, M. de Grás," he cried, "you have come back! I had thought that you had failed."

"Would to God I had," I cried out bitterly. "Ah, why, Milord Maréchal, did you select me for the task?"

He looked at me coldly, searchingly. Perhaps something in my face conveyed some idea to him of what I had gone through.

"It was not I who selected you for the task," he said at last. "It was you yourself, monsieur, who undertook it."

"Aye, you are right," I cried. "'Twas I who undertook it. But, milord, had I foreseen the consequences, had I known of the two dear lives which would have gone out that I might live, how gladly I would have faced your platoon. Alas, milord, how well you have revenged yourself."

He frowned.

"Diable!" he cried, "I am not wont to be spoken to thus. But you are a brave man. I can forgive much to bravery. I will forget what you have said."

"Milord," I cried, "would to God that I could forget those two true friends whose lives have paid for mine. How hollow it is to speak of success! For I have succeeded. The Sieur de la Genèvre will trouble you no more. Above in the mountains he lies. But, milord, my heart is sad. It weeps over the graves of my friends."

"Of whom do you speak?" he inquired.

"Of Muiris O Briain who accompanied me, and of one other, a gentle mountain girl. Do you blame me then when I say that it would have been better had I faced your platoon, that you have well avenged the death of your friend, accident though it was?"

For some time the Duke was silent. He seemed to commune with the past, for his eyes held a far-away look. At last he said:

"I understand now. But think you I had no love for that friend to whom your sword gave death? Monsieur de Grás, I have also had my friendships. Few they were, for I have few true friends. If you mourn your friends whom you loved, do I not mourn also. But enough. This O Briain of whom you speak. Where does he lie?"

"Far up the mountain by La Gorge," I replied.

"You can guide a party to the place?" he queried.

I nodded silently.

"It is not right that a French officer should sleep so far from camp. I will send for him. Now go. We will speak of this matter further. But remember, M. le Lieutenant, if you have your memories, I have them also."

He spoke kindly. Saluting, I turned away. I too had come to understand. I had seen only in my commander the roué, gamester, shallow-hearted courtier. He had revealed himself to me as a man who could feel deep friendships, who could understand the bitterness of another, a man who could honour the bravery of a poor soldier. I could not bring myself to hate him. His kindly action regarding O Briain went far to rehabilitate him in my eyes. A man who could act thus could not be all bad. And I had thought him bad to the core. How we misjudge each other!

'Twas several hours later when I, at the head of a strong party of Dillon's, set out on the sad errand up the mountains. We found him peacefully sleeping where I had piled his carn. As we looked on the cold features I saw the tears course down the cheeks of many a war-hardened veteran who had charged behind him in the red blaze of battle. And then the march down the silent mountain passes, the rays of the moon lighting up our way.

We hollowed out for him a narrow grave, and laid him to his final rest as the dawn broke. The Duke stood beside that lowly grave where the humble soldier slept. I did not wonder now how he had gained the love of his soldiers. As I listened to the crashing volley which knelled my comrade's last requiem, I thought how full of sorrow and bitterness had been his life. Far from the land of his birth he slept his soldier-sleep. Sleep on! Sleep on, gallant Muiris! May your rest be unbroken in that Italian land, old friend!

For some days I heard nothing more from the Duke. With a peculiar delicacy he left me to myself till the edge of my grief should have blunted itself a little. Then one day an aide summoned me to his quarters again. He received me with marked kindness, and informed me that I was reinstated in my former rank. He had received information of the discovery of the Sieur's body, whose successor had sent in his submission to him. I smiled bitterly as I listened, but made no remark. And then he asked:

"You spoke of a girl the other day, M. le Lieutenant. May I inquire who she was?"

"Mademoiselle Aimée Neffer," I replied. "The girl whom I rescued from the Chevalier's house, and about whom we fought. She to whom I owe my miserable life. The purest, bravest girl I have ever met, whose memory is to me as mine own honour. But, Milord Maréchal, we will not speak further of her."

He bowed.

"I will respect your wish, M. le Lieutenant," he said. And I gripped the hand stretched out to me.

"Have you any request to make?" he asked.

"No, Milord Maréchal, save that we may forget."

And then I left him.

CHAPTER XXIII

DESPONDENCY—SHELDON'S AGAIN—THE CALL TO
IRELAND

IVREA at length yielded to our arms. The town and citadel once more resounded to the tramp of the victorious French. Duc Vendôme had added fresh lustre to his name, to which he still further added by the capture of Verrua in the following year. I was still with his staff. My heart still cried out for my old squadron which was now attached to the Army of Flanders, but I was too proud to ask any favour from the man who had wounded me so deeply. Besides, I had grown quite indifferent as to success in my profession. I had lost enthusiasm. The shadow of the unfortunate events with which I had been connected still hung over me. I went on in a dull, routine way, performing such duties as fell in my way well, but with little of that fiery zeal which counts for so much in the soldier's trade. I almost felt tired of life. The urgings of ambition troubled me not at all. I had become dour, silent, with no wish to push on. It is a dangerous state to fall into, but how many of us experience the like after the death of a loved friend, the failure of some great project. Even so we live on because our nature urges us to do so. We conquer and thrust aside our black thoughts. So it was with me.

Gradually the remembrance of these events faded. The memory of these two loyal friends who had stood beside me in danger's hour became—no, not effaced, they could never be that—but softened. They would be always to me precious memories, but not to darken, not to force me to despair, only to urge me on to nobler, better things. From their graves they seemed to beckon to me, to whisper in my ear: Piaras, look upwards. Live not in the past. The future lies before you. We have been your friends in danger. You owe it to us that you strive onwards, upwards.

Thus spake the gentle Vaudois maid and the poor soldier from out the past, and I listened, gave ear to their urgings. My black, sullen moods left me. I became once more a man, with all a man's glorious ambitions. Do you blame me, my friends? Have you never felt such blessed urgings? Has no loved voice rang in your ear during the silent watches of the night telling you to lift yourself from the abyss of some great sorrow. If not you will turn from my pleading in disgust, you will condemn me as heartless, ungrateful. But should it be that you have heard such voices, such urgings, then, my friends, you will understand and sympathise. Be assured, however, that man must not live always sunk in the slough of despond.

'Twas some time after the surrender of Verrua that the Duke said to me one day:

"M. de Grás, you have now been serving with my staff for many months past. I have decided to transfer you back to your former regiment."

I could hardly believe my ears. To have the chance of rejoining my old comrades. I could have thrown up my cap with joy, but that would have been a very unsoldierly proceeding before the Maréchal Duc de Vendôme. I contented myself with silence. He looked at me keenly.

"Eh bien, M. le Lieutenant, you are silent," he said. "Is it that you wish to remain here?"

"Milord Maréchal," I cried, "Sheldon's is my regiment. My career commenced in it. In its ranks I wish to continue."

He smiled at my eagerness.

"Eh, I thought so," he remarked. "I have watched you for some time past. I do not think you would be successful here. I would be glad to retain you, but since it is your desire to go I will dismiss you. I have naught to say against a soldier's desire to rejoin his old squadron. Moreover, it is the desire of Monsieur de Nugent that his squadrons be up to full strength. I have written to him informing him, mentioning your service here, and suggesting that you be promoted to a captaincy. 'Tis the least I can do, for I feel that I have done you much injury. And I owe it to you to say that I have convinced myself that in that old affair with the Chevalier de Frobin, you were blameless."

I could hardly speak from astonishment. I would have been more than pleased to receive my transfer, but to be recommended for promotion, and by the Duke. I do not know how I stumbled through my thanks. And then to hear him apologising to me, the poor lieutenant, he, the proud Louis Joseph, Maréchal Duc de Vendôme. Time: ah, what an avenger it is! But it could not rouse up those sleeping ones from their quiet graves.

Before I quitted Italy I rode away to that lonely spot beside Ivrea where rested the ashes of poor Muiris O Briain.

"Muiris," I cried, as I knelt beside the little mound, "I am going far away from this Italian land, but I shall not forget you wherever my wandering steps may stray. Farewell. Farewell, old comrade."

Turning I mounted my horse and spurred away, and as I rode I thought of that other grave somewhere amidst the hills. She had loved me with all her pure heart. And I—— Well, perhaps it was better so.

A few weeks found me back with my old comrades. They welcomed me as one from the grave. Alas! many gallant cavaliers I had known were absent from the muster. They had paid the last great penalty, for our brigadiers recked little of death. With our dashing squadrons I charged on that disastrous Whit Sunday across the plains by Ramillies village, when owing to the imbecility and stubbornness of the Maréchal Duc de Villeroi, our army was forced to ignominious flight before the allied forces of the Duke of Marlborough. Beside us on that unfortunate day fought our countrymen of Clare's Infantry Regiment. In the house of the Irish Benedictine nuns at Ypres hang the two colours which they snatched from their hereditary enemies. With them we shared the glories which brave men may gain even when incompetence nullifies their efforts. Like them we suffered fearful losses. So great were they that for months after that day our squadrons were unfit to take the field.

I had little thought that our losses would effect my future. But who can read that hidden time? One day our colonel sent for me to the house in which I was billeted in Brussels. I found him with several other Brigade officers. Bluntly he came to the point, for Christopher Nugent was a man of few words.

"Captain Grás," he said, "you know how heavily our regiments have suffered. We have been discussing the best means of filling up our ranks. We consider that it is necessary to recruit from Ireland. It is a service of much danger, one requiring caution and secrecy. Failure will mean death for the man engaged in it. I have thought of you for the duty. Consider well before you answer, and if you shrink from the task, we will not consider you less brave."

It did not take me long to decide. Too well I knew the difficulties and dangers which would surround my work. Even so I would give much to see again the brave old land which called to me across the waters. Raising my head, I replied briefly:

"I have decided, mon colonel."

"And what is your decision?" asked Nugent. I could see that the others had craned forward in their eagerness.

"I will go," I replied.

"Maith an fear!" came the cries from the others, but Nugent simply said: "I knew you for a brave man, Grás."

"When do I start?" I asked.

"In a couple of weeks you sail from Dunkerque," said the Colonel. "Your work must be done as circumstances will dictate. But be careful and watchful. Remember what your success means to the Brigade."

"I will remember," I replied, and, saluting, hurried away, followed by the encouraging cries of my chiefs. I held my head high as I trod the old streets. Above me the sky was blue and cloudless. Around me the breezes seemed to chant a pæan of joy. At last! At last! dear homeland, I am to see you again, even though it be as an outlaw, a stranger amongst my people!

CHAPTER XXIV

IN DUBLIN—A GENTLEMAN OF LEISURE

"Help! Help! kind sir."

The words, uttered in a woman's voice, from which terror could not banish its sweetness, fell on my ear. I had been strolling along the High Street on my way to Tom's Coffee House, which stood hard by the Castle.

Quickly I swung round on my heel. For several seconds I could perceive nothing in the darkness, and then in the murky light cast by a smoky oil-lamp I caught a glimpse of several struggling figures beside a sedan-chair. With a shout of warning I dashed forward, drawing my sword as I ran. But there was no cause to use it. On hearing my cry, three or four figures disengaged themselves from the struggling mass and disappeared down the dark opening of a laneway.

Sword in hand, I hastened forward and stood bowing to the occupant of the chair, whose progress had been so rudely interrupted.

"Madame," I said, inquiringly, "I pray me that you have not been hurt."

"Ah, sir, what might not have befallen but for your kind assistance." The voice was sweet and tremulous, but in the semi-darkness I could not make out the face of the speaker. "The streets are so unsafe at night. We risk much by venturing forth. Had you not been near!" And she stopped as if in terror at the thought.

"Madame," I hastened to reply, "the darkness and unsafeness of the streets have done me an unwitting service in bringing me to your aid. And, may I say, you would add much to my pleasure should you deign to accept my escort to your home."

"Sir, you would add to my sense of gratitude and obligation." She paused. Mayhap she was confused by her own boldness.

But with my hat sweeping the ground in an elaborate bow, I turned to the bearers and bade them proceed on their journey. The pair of stout fellows, who though roughly enough handled by the footpads, had received little more than a few scratches, set off down the High Street.

I fell in beside the chair. I had no desire to press my attentions on its occupant, and so strode along in silence. But we had not proceeded far ere she called me to her side, and engaged me in conversation. I learned that she had been to a concert in the Tailors' Hall, and on emerging into High Street had been set on by four ruffians, whom my opportune arrival had put to flight. One of them had even tried to drag her from her seat.

What with footpads, beggars and bands of roystering young bucks, the streets of the good city of Dublin were unpleasant enough in the sixth year of the reign of that august lady, Queen Anne of England.

Beneath swinging signs and smoky oil-lamps, through the Winetavern Street, with its wide-open wine-shops and coffee-houses, we wended our way, lighted by the flaring flambeau borne in the hands of a runner, who went ahead, past the Marshalsea on Merchant's Quay, our ears filled with the supplications of its unfortunate inmates, and on to Usher's Quay, where we halted. And here I assisted the fair unknown from her chair, and as I stood aside bowing low, she placed her hand on my arm, and with graceful words thanked me for my gallant conduct, expressing the hope that we might meet again. Then, giving me her hand to kiss, she tripped lightly up the steps of the tall mansion before which we had stopped, and with a farewell smile disappeared within its portals.

How beautiful she was! How daintily she carried herself, with an artless grace which impressed itself on my mind. I who was so unused to the society of her gracious sex; whose life had been spent in the rudeness of camp life and amid the panoply of war; what would I not give for another glimpse of this fair girl who had so unexpectedly crossed my path? With a sigh, I turned away and resumed my way to the Coffee House, whither I was going when her cry for help fell on my ears.

But as I thought of what I was, a bitter laugh broke from me. What right had I, Piaras Grás, the emissary of a foreign Power, to indulge in thoughts of such as she, in all probability the daughter of some adherent of the Ascendancy? I, an outlaw, in my own land, engaged in a hazardous enterprise, which brought my neck within reach of the halter every day. Whose days were spent in perpetual warfare against the existing powers; whose nights were passed in the company of men who would gladly have placed me for tender keeping between the paws of the "Black Dog," from whence my progress to the execution place would be speedy and certain. Fool! fool! to allow myself to be carried away by the pretty face and winsome air of one who would, doubtless, willingly assist her father, or brothers, or acquaintances, in laying by the heels the pestilent wretch who dared to defy the Powers by law established, and glory in the deed. What though she were fair to look upon? Was it likely that she was any better than those other intriguers and butterflies of fashion who fluttered their way through the city's ballrooms? With a shrug of my shoulders, I dismissed the subject from my mind.

As I strode along, the bustle and activity of the civic life around me absorbed my attention. Anon,

I jostled in the darkness up against some pedestrian hurrying on his way. Again my ears were saluted by the shrill "Make way! make way!" of the sedan-carriers bearing some fair citizenness to home or meeting-place. Redly flaming flambeaux passed hither and thither, while rumbling vehicles jolted along the stony streets. At last, I turned into the Castle Street, and was soon engaged in a dicing game with one of the military officers who frequented Tom's noted Coffee House.

Sitting there in the midst of these men, coolly rattling my dice-box, who would imagine that my days were passed in such devious ways? With what a shout of joy these officers and burly citizens would have thrown themselves on me had some voice suddenly called out: "Behold! a spy of the French King is amongst you." How eagerly they would have laid hands on me!

But who would have suspected that the respectable Ebenezer Swetenhall, gentleman of leisure, who had served in Her Majesty's Armies, had ever been guilty of such nefarious practices—had ever been other than a loyal subject of the reigning dynasty? He, an upholder of the glorious Revolution—who would have dared to whisper a word of suspicion? Who dared to doubt him?

As I played my ears were constantly open to the stories related by the habitués of the place. Now it was some delectable piece of social gossip, again some item dealing with the movement of the Pretender's adherents, culled from the pages of "Pue's Occurrences." But be the item what it might, my sang-froid never deserted me. My laugh mingled with theirs. My glass was drained to the perpetuation of the new dynasty and the confusion of the Jacobites, all the while that I rattled my dice or raked in the stakes of my opponent for the nonce, the gallant Captain Wildair of the Queen's Dragoons.

But the echo of a soft voice rang in my ears above the varied sounds of the coffee-room; the vision of a fair face came between me and my red-faced opponent. Unable to content myself, I finally threw down my box, and bidding the captain good night, walked home to my lodgings in the Corn Market. Soon after I was slumbering soundly and seeing again in my dreams the face of the fair unknown.

CHAPTER XXV

A WHISPER FROM THE PAST

I HAD been in Dublin for several weeks past, commissioned by my chiefs to raise recruits to fill up the gaps left in the ranks of our bold Brigade by constant campaigning. With money in plenty, I had taken up my abode in the Corn Market—a bold, roystering gentleman, who had seen much service on the Continent, who was prepared to pass a bottle or turn a jest with the gayest, or lose his money at the gaming table without turning a hair. It served my purpose to comport myself like the bucks who plumed themselves and strutted round the inns and taverns of the city. Captain Swetenhall, late of Her Majesty's Army, was hail, fellow! well met, with all of them, and would not be suspected of designs subversive of the Government of the realm. And so I was a well-known figure at the different taverns, and at the malls, where fashionable society disported itself. With such recommendations, I had soon secured the entrée into the houses of the best society of the metropolis.

All the while I went amongst the people, doing the work which had brought me hither. Many a piece of good silver passed from my hand into the palm of some youngster, who burned to shoulder a musket in the ranks of the Brigade. Oh, it was a merry game, to which the danger added zest.

So from day to day the work went on. Picking up recruits when and how I could; consorting with men whose very existence was, in the eyes of the law, a crime; rubbing shoulders with the wealth and fashion of the city. Secretly an opposer of the law; openly its most blatant defender.

But never after that adventure in the High Street did I catch a glimpse of her whose face haunted me. I had fought stubbornly against these constantly recurring thoughts, had endeavoured to efface her image from my mind, but the struggle was vain. Again and again I had told myself that it was madness that I, who carried my life in my hands, should dream such dreams. But the fires smouldered on, ready to burst into flame when the first breeze should fan them. Many a time I strayed almost unconsciously past the stately house on Usher's Quay, but never a sight rewarded me.

And then, when I had almost flattered myself into the belief that I had conquered my foolishness, I again met her. It was one evening, as I strolled on the Mall, arm in arm with two other officers of the garrison, who had taken me under their tutelage, that a sedan-chair stopped, and a lady, young and beautiful, descended from it. We were just passing by at the time, and, whether by accident or design, she dropped her fan. Stepping quickly forward, I picked it up, and returned it to her. As my eyes rested for an instant on her face the knowledge came to me that I had found my fair unknown.

She thanked me gracefully, excusing herself for her gaucherie, and was turning away, when suddenly she stopped and looking straight at me inquired if we had not met before.

"Yes, mademoiselle," I replied, "in the High Street, where I had the honour of doing you a service."

"Ah, yes," she returned, "I remember now. You are the gallant gentleman who came to my assistance on that dreadful night." . . . And then she added smilingly: "And I do not even know the name of my preserver."

"Captain Ebenezer Swetenhall, very much at your service," I replied, bowing.

"Ah, Captain, I have heard of you. May I hope to see you at my Lady Brudenel's ball on Thursday evening next? Mary Sickles would like to repay some of her obligation."

Sickles! The name brought the blood rushing to my face. The remembrance of the unfortunate incident of five years before flashed across my mind. Could it be that she had any connection with my old enemy? Ah, surely not! Surely so rare a blossom could not spring from so rough a stem! The thought was a disquieting one, but I thrust it aside, because I wished to do so. It was five years since that night in Cathair Domhnaill. Let the past lie buried in its ashes. Let me live only in the present. With a glance I assured myself she had not noticed my abstraction.

"Possibly, fair mademoiselle," I replied, "should the Fates be kind."

Then, raising to my lips the hand which she extended to me, we parted—I to resume my interrupted promenade, and be quizzed mercilessly by my companions, to whose questions I returned evasive replies; she to mingle with the merry crowd of Mall players.

When I returned to my lodgings late that night, I found a little perfumed note awaiting me, containing an invitation to the ball to be held in the house of the Lady Brudenel.

. . . . . .

The stately mansion at Usher's Quay was ablaze with light as I mounted the broad staircase and was greeted by the hostess. Strolling through the rooms costumed quietly in dark blue velvet, braided with silver, I was greeted on all sides. The élite of the city were there assembled. The entrée to Lady Brudenel's entertainments was much sought after, evidently. Here, a noted churchman chatted animatedly with a well-known lawyer; there an alderman, rotund and well-nourished, was holding forth to an orator, whose well-rounded periods held the senators in awesome admiration what time his voice sounded through the vaulted chambers of the House. From the inner rooms, set apart for the votaries of Dame Fortune, could be heard, by the attentive listener, the sharp rattle of the dice. Scattered here and there were many of the young bucks and dandies of the city, amongst whom I noticed my friend, Captain Wildair, looking very different now from the red-faced, ungainly cavalryman with whom I was wont to play. Resplendent now in coat of claret-coloured silk, his dark-green waistcoat braided in gold, he flaunted it with the best. Ladies in stiff brocades and rustling silks hung on the arms of be-laced and be-wigged beaux, as they moved on towards the apartment set apart for dancing.

I had come alone. I had been much surprised by the receipt of the invitation, for though such a well-known figure about town, I had no previous knowledge of the lady of the house. Instinctively I connected it with my conversation with the fair Mistress Sickles. Her words were the principal cause of my presence. Ah! what fools we men are when a pair of sparkling eyes are in question!

My glance roved over the gay and brilliant throng, but nowhere could I mark her graceful form. I was turning away impatiently when her well-known voice sent a thrill through me:

"Will the Captain Swetenhall honour me with his arm while I go and seek my aunt?"

With a low bow and a murmured "At your service, mademoiselle," I offered my arm to my fair questioner, while we made our way through the crowded rooms. Having found her aunt, none other than the hostess of the evening, I conducted her back again to the ballroom, where we were soon treading it through the graceful measures of the minuet.

How my heart thrilled with delight as I gazed on my companion! She was dressed in some light clinging material of a creamy colour, which floated about her in graceful folds, and stood out in bold contrast to the huge panniers and hoops of the other fair dancers. Her glorious auburn hair was dressed rather high over her smooth, white brow, while her soft brown eyes held a dreamy look. As she moved gracefully to the strains of the stately music, I feasted my eyes on her beauty. Surely for such a maid one could willingly surrender all, and think himself well repaid.

At last the dance was over, and we moved away to a quiet alcove. During the next half-hour I drank in the tones of her sweet voice as she chatted of the men and women of her circle. How I watched her every movement; her every gesture! How I watched the sparkle of her eyes and revelled in her sunny smile, as she related some merry anecdote. Sitting there in her presence, all thoughts of my mission were swept aside. I gave myself up to the full enjoyment of the passing hour. I was but as a shadow thrown across her path. A few weeks more and my work in the capital would be ended, and then away to push my task farther afield, and I would have passed out of her life as if I had never been. At the thought I sighed involuntarily. But my mood changed, and I was once again the gay gallant.

The minutes flew by quickly; ah! so quickly; and then she left me to go and assist her aunt in her duties. And I, poor fool, sat going over again in thought the happy minutes which I had spent, alternately hugging to myself this beautiful dream of my imagination; and then upbraiding myself for allowing thoughts of love to come between me and my duty.

Several times again that night I met her, and each time my admiration and worship grew deeper. And as I made my adieux at the head of the stairs, where a crowd of gallants fluttered round her, and bent over the little hand which lay in mine, I swore to myself that I would always treasure up the memory of her fair face in my innermost thoughts.

But as I made my way down the crowded stair, I was recalled from my dreamings to the ever-present sense of work as the voice of an exquisite young dandy whispered in my ear: "To-morrow evening at seven. By the seashore at Bullock. Everything is ready."

CHAPTER XXVI

BY BULLOCK STRAND—A LOYALIST VOLUNTEER

Riding beneath the pale light of the twinkling stars, my face hidden beneath a velvet mask, I pricked towards the seashore. All had been arranged. In twos and threes the gallant lads who had taken the French silver would have taken their way to the rendezvous where the smuggler awaited them. Sweeping along, the mournful cry of a curlew came to my ears like some voice warning me of danger and disaster. But little I recked of warnings. My plans were well laid. No suspicion lurked in the minds of the dullards who watched over the interests of the State.

A few seconds and I stood on the pebbly strand, looking out over the heaving waters towards the black shadow which marked the spot where the smuggler lay with all sails set ready to spring forward on her journey to the distant Gallic coast. Beside me was the bluff old captain, watching the embarkation of his living cargo. As the brave fellows took their places in the boat, I wrung their hands in a tight grip. Then with a subdued farewell the muffled oars fell into the rowlocks, and they had taken the final step on the road which so many of their compatriots had travelled before them. Quickly the embarkation was carried through, and then, with a final hand-clasp and a "Slán Dé agat," the skipper took his place.

Alone I stood on the shore watching the boat moving out across the dancing flood. The moon had risen and now sailed in all her pale glory across a cloudless sky, tipping with silver the wide waste of waters; burying her shafts in the tiny wavelets which came trooping in at my feet.

Hardly had the boat quitted the shingly beach, when a loud shout rang out: "Stand, in the Queen's name!" A couple of shots pealed out on the night air, and I heard the trampling of many feet rushing towards me. Their approach had been so silent that they were within fifty yards of me before I could move. But in an instant my pistols were out, and firing at the dark mass of men, I sprang towards my horse, which was quietly standing near by. With a bound I was into the saddle and spurring hard towards safety. As I fled, a scattered volley rang out, but by good fortune I escaped unhurt.

Making a detour to throw them off the scent I rode rapidly citywards and reached my lodgings as the bells were clanging out the hour of nine.

"A narrow shave, that," I mused, and changing my dress, I hurried down to Tom's, where I had arranged to meet my dragoon friend, Wildair, with whom I had made a wager at cards.

Punctually to the time appointed I was in my seat, dealing my cards lazily. Who amongst all that gay company, looking at my smiling face, listening to my light stories and jests, would have imagined that a short hour before I had been engaged in the damnable work of speeding a company of "wild geese" on their way, that I had been galloping along the road pursued by the hissing bullets of the soldiers of their royal and sovereign lady, or that with foul and evil intent I had turned my arms against the forces of that gracious ruler.

So it was that when about two hours afterwards an officer, all mud-bespattered, strode into the coffee-room, I was the first to turn towards him.

"What's the matter, lieutenant?" I drawled lazily, while I flicked the dust from my lace cravat. I recognised the new-comer as an infantry officer, one

Lieutenant Jones, a tall, lanky, red-haired Englishman. "You seem to have had rough service."

"Matter enough," he growled angrily. "A damned traitor sending off recruits to France."

And then he launched off into a description of the affair. Not a muscle of my face twitched as he told how they had marched to Bullock, where they had information a number of traitors would rendezvous that night. With breathless interest, I listened to him as he drew a lurid picture of the scene by the beach, with the boat rowing away to the sloop lying in the offing. How they had fired at the solitary figure standing on the beach; how he had returned their fire, leaving two of their men badly wounded; and then how this most disloyal wretch had galloped off. My masters, it was glorious standing there in the midst of these men listening to the recital of my own misdeeds.

When the lieutenant had ceased, as much for want of breath as of further facts, I was among the first to recover from the astonishment created by his recital.

"I' faith, my friends, he was a daring ruffian," I ejaculated. Then, turning to the lieutenant, I inquired: "Lieutenant, I doubt not you would know that damned ruffian again."

"Zounds, Captain, you are wrong there," he growled testily. "Though the moon was shining brightly and we could see him clearly enough, his face was covered with a black mask, which hid it completely. He was tall and well built, tall as yourself, Captain," with a laugh, "but that gives us little to work on. There are many such men in Dublin. But," and he swore a mighty oath, "I will yet lay him by the heels, and then a short shrift and an airy dance awaits him," and he laughed loudly at his own pleasantry.

"Bravo! bravo! lieutenant," I cried. "May we soon see this Jacobite cock between your claws." A sentiment which was greeted with loud shouts and cries of approval.

In view of the exciting intelligence, few of us felt any desire for further play. In groups we stood discussing the occurrence. The centre of a group, I examined it in all its aspects, suggesting ways and means which might be adopted for the capture of this wretch who had so daringly entered into the very citadel of authority. I suggested the formation of all those present into a volunteer troop, who would assist the military authorities in patrolling the roads, and keeping a special eye on Bullock.

"After all, gentlemen," I said, "this is a matter which concerns us all. We ought to be prepared to give our assistance in the matter."

My suggestion was warmly taken up, and there and then this crowd of loyal gentlemen offered their services for the furtherance of the project.

"Now, my friends," I exclaimed, "it is necessary that we name someone as captain. One who is active and resourceful——"

"Who could we find more active or resourceful than yourself," a voice interrupted. "Swetenhall, Swetenhall for captain."

My name was acclaimed from all sides. With appropriate words I thanked them for this mark of the esteem in which they held me. After some further conversation and with mutual good wishes for the success of our undertaking, we left the Coffee House, and wended our different ways homewards through the dark streets.

Hardly had I shaken myself free from the crowd of poor dupes than my leisurely walk was changed into a quick stride, which soon brought me to my lodgings. Hurrying to my room, I wrapped a long, black cloak round myself, and slipping a pair of loaded pistols into my pockets, sallied forth once more into the streets.

A few minutes' walk brought me to Fishamble Street. Plunging into the thick darkness of a narrow archway, I groped my way forward. Knocking cautiously at a door, darkly outlined in the gloom,

I waited. After a few minutes it was opened. A whispered word secured me entrance, and then I made my way down a long, narrow passage, into a room lighted by a single candle. At a blazing fire were seated two men smoking. The taller of the pair was none other than the young dandy who had spoken to me on the staircase at the Lady Brudenel's ball. Looking at his easy, good-natured face, with its sleepy blue eyes, and allowing your eyes to travel over his foppish attire, from his Ramilie hat and wig to the fine lace which almost covered his delicate, effeminate hands, you would hardly imagine that Charles Jans was other than a brainless fop. But beneath that easy-going exterior was hidden a reckless, dare-devil nature, which often stood me in good stead. The other, more soberly dressed, was a prominent merchant, Roche by name.

Throwing myself into a chair, I related the events of the evening. My adventure by Bullock drew forth exclamations of surprise and dismay. But when I related the proceedings which had taken place in Tom's they laughed heartily.

Both of them were rather inclined to doubt the wisdom of my allowing myself to be named chief of the volunteers. They feared it would expose me to dangers which I would find it hard to combat. But I soon set their fears at rest.

"Egad, my friends," I cried, "nothing better could have happened for us. Ebenezer Swetenhall, the captain of a troop of volunteers, burning with desire for the capture of recruits for foreign service, can move where he lists, can go into all places, will be told everything. His zeal will be his passport. Should he be seen conversing with any of the disaffected, he seeks information. Should he speak to anyone suspected of smuggling, he is probing for knowledge as to intended flights of 'wild geese.' And so he will be above suspicion. But you, Jans, must take my place at the embarkations. I, the zealous Swetenhall, will be too busily engaged with my gallant troop in hunting you down to take interest in other matters. But we must find some other place for our rendezvous."

"Gad, you are right, Captain," said Jans, "that last squeak was too close to be pleasant. What do you say to Howth?"

With our heads close together for fear of lurking spies, we discussed the whole matter, and finally decided on Howth. Jans was to take my place at the embarkation, while I, by hints, would draw off attention towards Bullock. When we had settled everything to our satisfaction, after a final toast to our success, drank in good French wine, which Roche drew forth from a cupboard in the corner, I left them; they to make their way out on to the quays, I to return by the way I had come. As we parted the bells of old Christchurch boomed out the midnight hour.

As I turned once again into Fishamble Street, I almost ran into the arms of Lieutenant Jones. As I noted his suspicious glance fixed on me, I felt a quiver of apprehension pass over me. What if he should suspect?

"Ha! ha! Captain," he laughed boisterously. "I thought you were safe in bed long ago. Do you often go to Fishamble Street?"

"No, lieutenant, not often," I replied. "Sometimes I visit a friend of mine."

"Gad, what an hour for visiting!" he exclaimed, with a cunning leer.

A Dhia, how I hated the fellow! Had it been otherwise, how gladly I would have struck him in the face. But caution must be my guide at present. So I inquired with my most elegant manner:

"Lieutenant, is it necessary that I publish the hours at which I choose to visit my friends?"

"The Captain Swetenhall visits when and where he chooses," and he bowed mockingly. "But the gallant Captain will injure his reputation should he keep such late hours in such dark places."

I started and looked keenly at him. Was there a hidden meaning conveyed in his words? But his face was impassive, and with a shrug I dismissed the matter. I would let it pass for the present, but later——

"A truce to this, lieutenant," I said. "The night gets colder and I will be going home. Good night." And, with a bow, I passed on my way.

But could I have seen the malevolent look with which the lieutenant followed me, or heard his muttered: "The gay Captain visits late and in curious places. We will see; we will see," I would have been rather startled.

CHAPTER XXVII

LOVE IS NOT FOR ME—CHECKMATE TO AN ENEMY

My mission was drawing to its conclusion. Another day would see its finish, and then the metropolis would know the dashing figure of Captain Ebenezer Swetenhall no more. My recruiting had been completely successful, and the final draft of men would sail from Beann Eadair the next evening. Then, ho! for the soft breezes and the purple heather of my native south.

I felt a wonderful feeling of relief that the end was so near at hand. A feeling of uneasiness had begun to take possession of me. Since that untoward meeting with Jones in Fishamble Street, I felt that I was being watched secretly; that my every movement was dogged, my every action weighed. Shadowy and intangible as it all was, I knew that suspicion was being directed against me. But no whisper of it had reached my ear. To all outward appearance my position was as secure as ever, my character as unblemished. Whenever I met Jones, I felt his beady eyes fixed on me with a suspicious gaze. I was convinced that much of the intrigue was being fostered by him, but I could not afford to bring him to book.

But though I knew all this, it did not cause me to recede a single step from the plan I had mapped out, nor to reduce my recruits by a single man. I would carry through my project in its entirety though every spy in Dublin was at my heels. My recruits were faithful, and no whisper had reached the ears of my enemies.

A SWORDSMAN

So it was in a happy frame of mind I dressed for the ball to be given in the house of the Grattans. Would I have the good fortune to meet the fair Mistress Sickles? I asked myself. Since the night at Lady Brudenel's I had not seen her, and was looking forward eagerly in the hope that that fickle dame might cast her favours in my way.

A dandy of the dandies, I made my way through the fashionable throng who were assembled, and soon was the centre of a group of young bucks, who laughed uproariously at my sallies. While the fun waxed apace, I managed to convey a slip of paper into the hand of my fellow-conspirator, Jans, who laughed and jested—the merriest of the crowd. The words it contained were few, but pregnant: "Everything goes well. My gentlemen volunteers will proceed to Bullock to-morrow evening. Howth will be clear for you." Then I tore myself away from the merry fools. As I turned I met the gaze of the red-haired Jones fixed on me. His eyes held an inscrutable look. A voice seemed to whisper: "Take care, Piaras. The lieutenant watches you like a hawk. Guard yourself well."

But the thoughts of Jones and his surly looks were soon forgotten in the presence of the gracious girl who occupied such a large place in my thoughts. Wandering aimlessly through the rooms, I saw her surrounded by a circle of cavaliers. She rose at my approach and came towards me, a smile of pleasure lighting up her face. Side by side we wandered away from the sportive throng. Seated beside her I felt myself almost carried away by the passionate love which surged through my veins. I was sorely tempted to pour out the burning words which would put my fate to the test. But honour held me back. Even though I was convinced that her answer would be the fulfilment of all my hopes, what right had I, an adventurer, a soldier engaged in such a dangerous game, to speak of love to her? Living a double life, would it be worthy of me to offer her my love? What right had I to entangle her free, joyous existence with my wayward fate? No! love was not for me, and I put the temptation from me. But I could not refrain from saying:

"Mistress Sickles, to-morrow I depart from your fair city. Duty demands my presence elsewhere. May I say that the remembrance of your kindness to me, an unknown stranger, will be with me always."

"It grieves me much to hear you are going from amongst us," she replied earnestly. "I had hoped that our acquaintance would be of longer duration. I will treasure up in my heart the memory of the inestimable service you did me—will never cease to respect the name of a brave and gallant gentleman."

She bent her dear head and I could almost have sworn I heard a sob. Unconsciously my hand stole out towards hers, but I drew it back. And then she was herself again, chatting and laughing merrily.

At last I conducted her back to the ballroom. As we went, I whispered recklessly into her ear: "Let us enjoy this last dance together," adding to myself: "and to-morrow, forget."

With laughing eyes, she whispered back:

"Be merry while we may. A soldier's philosophy, Captain Swetenhall," and then we swept away into the dance.

But I had other work to do that night. When I had resigned her to the partner who came to claim her hand for the next dance, I made my way to the card-room, where the final act would be done which would ensure the complete success of my project. As I approached, I heard a loud voice raised in angry tones:

"Gentlemen, I tell you, the Captain is not all he seems. Can any of you tell me who he is? He came amongst us from the devil knows where—says he served on the Continent. Perhaps he did, but was it with our forces? Lately, I have watched him closely, and know that he keeps very strange company and visits in strange places. I notice that he rides often in the direction of Bullock, which has not a very loyal reputation. What if he should be a Jacobite spy?"

I walked into their midst before they had recovered from the consternation into which they were thrown by his words. Everyone had gathered round the speaker. For the moment cards and dice were forgotten.

A deep voice broke the silence: "The Captain Swetenhall is a brave and loyal gentleman." All eyes turned in the direction of the person who had spoken, none other than Jans. I stepped forward into the group, who mechanically made way for me.

"The lieutenant was discussing me," I suggested, with a comprehensive glance round.

No one replied. None of them seemed willing to take up the matter.

"Gentlemen, gentlemen," I went on, "I await your pleasure."

At last Jones stepped forward. "I did not think the Captain was within hearing," he said. "If he has heard words hurtful to his self-esteem, I cannot help it."

"The room is public," I replied. "The lieutenant should not talk so loud."

Turning to the others, I said: "May I inquire in what particular way my actions interest you, gentlemen?" My voice was cold as I glanced around.

"Egad, Captain, we thought you kept strange company—that you ride in the direction of Bullock over much," Jones replied.

"Zounds, gentlemen," I asked, ignoring him, "if it be my pleasure to ride in the direction of Bullock, is there anyone here to say me nay? The sea air is pleasant, the scenery pretty, and there is information to be gained."

A murmur came from behind. I knew I had gained a point and hastened to drive my advantage home.

"My friends," I resumed, "as I came in the

words 'Jacobite spy' seemed to grate on my ear. Perhaps I was mistaken, but the words have an ugly sound. I would be very careful in using them. I have given proofs of my zeal and loyalty sufficient to stand against unsupported assertions and covert suggestions." I looked full at the lieutenant. "My loyalty to the Government of our Most Gracious Sovereign has been unquestioned. Should any gentleman feel hurt by my preference for particular places or particular company, I am pained. If Lieutenant Jones must see a Jacobite spy in every honest gentleman who comes amongst you, truly I am sorry. But a truce to this foolishness! If I have ridden often in the direction of Bullock, you, my friends, will ride there to-morrow evening."

Instantly, these poor fools who had been wavering in their allegiance to me, clustered round, won over by my bold words. As for the lieutenant, nonplussed by the turn of events, he held his peace. The trick had turned to me, but who would call the game?

In a few words, I explained how a rumour had reached me of a contemplated sailing from Bullock. The rumour was of the vaguest, but I had thought it best that we should take precautions, and proposed we should ride in that direction. Perhaps we would have the good fortune to lay our hands on some of the rebels. With wild huzzas they greeted my proposition, some of them in their enthusiasm drawing their swords and waving them over their heads. Then, turning to Wildair, who was present, I said:

"Perhaps, Captain, the military patrol will ride with us?"

But he replied: "I am a soldier, and at the command of my chiefs."

An uncompromising reply. Yet, I knew the spark had taken—that Beann Eadair would be as safe from the unwelcome attentions of military as from volunteers.

CHAPTER XXVIII

A WILD-GOOSE CHASE—A LITTLE SWORDPLAY

'Twas a right merry party which sallied forth from the city on the following evening. The authorities had taken alarm, and a score of troopers, under the command of Wildair, accompanied us. Thus it was that I rode along beside him, engaged in merry converse. Along the dark and silent road we swept. Woe to any unfortunate recusant knave who should cross our path. But silence and loneliness prevailed, save only when the shrill, raucous cry of some sea-bird came through the void.

Within a short distance of the seashore the order was given to dismount, and we crept forward. When we reached the beach no living thing met our gaze. The full moon shone down on a lonely strand and glinted on a placid sea. The wavelets whispered and cooed to each other the endless tale which they have told and re-told since the world began. Our swords would rest idly in their scabbards that night. My ruse was completely successful.

Turning to my companions, who stood round, disappointment written on all their faces, I remarked:

"Egad, gentlemen, our ride has been for nothing. The rats have kept to their holes to-night. I pray you may be more successful on a future occasion."

Dead silence greeted me. I doubt not their suspicions were intensified. But a commotion made itself heard in the rear of the troop of dandies and soldiers. With two or three furious strides, Jones launched himself forward, his whole bearing betraying the rage he felt. Silently, I waited for his words.

"Begad," he cried, his voice quivering with passion, "we have been brought on a wild-goose chase. The gallant Captain who rides so often to Bullock has heard some old hag's tale and we must needs follow him here. Or perhaps the tale formed itself in his own imagination. Methinks he knows over much and hears tales which never reach the ears of others. A loyal gentleman, forsooth, one who has given proofs of his loyalty. But I have had eno' of such loyalty."

I had made no attempt to interrupt him. Turning to the others, I remarked:

"Comrades, I crave your pardon for the upturn of this affair. I' faith, we might have had better luck. But the lieutenant seems to be angry."

"Egad, yes," he shouted, thoroughly aroused by my tone. "Yes, angry about you and your fine stories. What is known about you? But, your pardon, you are a loyal gentleman."

Shrugging my shoulders, I remarked courteously:

"I regret most sincerely that the gallant lieutenant should be so angry. I regret also he does not know me. But, gentlemen "—and my voice sounded as smooth and unruffled as if I were in the presence of a lady—" no one credits asses with the possession of much brains!"

The lieutenant fairly shrieked. Almost choking with fury, he cried: "I demand an apology."

"Ah," I said, reflectively, "an apology. But, then, asses do not understand apologies."

With a yell, Jones sprang towards me, his sword flashing in his hand. Several of the others held him back, while I remarked coldly: "Lieutenant Jones is in a most devilish temper. Let him calm himself."

Then turning to Wildair: "May I ask you, Wildair, to act for me?"

In a few seconds all was arranged, and our swords crossed. Along the shining blades, which twined and interlaced like living things, the moon's rays played lovingly. With their clashing was intermingled the fret-fret of the restless waters as they kissed the shore and retreated to return again in endless procession. Round about in groups stood the spectators, soldiers and dandies, watching with straining, dilated eyes, the tierce and parry of the sinuous weapons.

It was all over in a few minutes. My red-haired opponent tried to beat down my blade. Slowly I retreated before his wild onslaught, contenting myself with a parrying of his attack. Then slowly, slowly I began to press him backwards. He was completely at my mercy. In his blind fury he recklessly exposed himself. Should I kill him? the question went surging through my brain. But, then, what did his suspicions or innuendoes matter to me now? My task was finished. On the morrow I would turn my back on Dublin, and so I spared him.

He made a fierce lunge at me, which I swiftly parried, and then my blade leaped out, and passed through his left shoulder. With a groan, he staggered back into the arms of his second, calling out in a voice shaking with pain:

"Swetenhall, beware! I'll meet you again."

Perhaps I regretted at that moment the thrust had not been lower.

Glancing round the circle who surrounded me, I inquired:

"Can I place my sword at the service of any other gentleman?"

But no answer came and I resumed my garments. I had won through.

CHAPTER XXIX

AN OLD FRIEND

THE darkness of a June night had long thrown its dark shadow across the land as weary and travel-stained I urged my lagging steed along the rough road leading towards the little hamlet of Cathair Domhnaill. Several days previously I had ridden forth from the good city of Dublin, and away with flowing rein towards the country of my early days, amongst whose heather-clad hills and wild gleanns I had wandered in those dear, dead days when life was new, and spread out its beautiful vista before me.

At early dawn I had been in the saddle speeding forward towards the district round which my further work would lie. Amongst the mountains of wild Ui Rathach and Corca Laighdhe I would find many a one eager to help me. Brave boys in plenty would grip my hand, and welcome the chance which I would offer them to take their place beside their former friends and companions in the ranks of the Brigade. I felt that every mile which I left behind carried me nearer to the haunts of friends. Even so, caution was necessary. The country was full of spies watching with longing eyes for the golden reward which the capture of such as I would throw in their way. I had, therefore, avoided the larger towns which lay on my route as much as possible, preferring to keep to the villages and hamlets, and now I was almost at my journey's end.

As I rode up a steep incline an odd shimmering light marking the position of the little hamlet broke on my vision. Reining in my horse, I sat gazing down on the place which I had left five years before, a fugitive from the one-handed justice of the Williamites. Again in fancy I could see the scene before the little inn where I had struck down the undertaker, Sir Michael Sickles. Had he succumbed to his wound, I wondered. Would I meet brave old Micheal Mor, whose hand had saved me from the consequences of my deed. Would he know me? I smiled at the thought. Verily it would take a keen observer to recognise in the tall, broad-shouldered Captain Hall, with his black beard, trimmed Vandyke fashion, and his waxed moustachios, the stripling who had fled that night.

For the better carrying out of my plans I had taken care that the gallant Swetenhall should lose his identity on the road, and one would be scarcely likely to connect me with the Dublin roysterer. Striking spurs into my horse, I dashed ahead. No need for me to hesitate. I knew every turn and twist of that road as if I had travelled it but yesterday. My steed gathered together his flagging strength, and bore me swiftly towards the village where he knew instinctively he would halt for the night.

In a few minutes I pulled up before the door of the inn, and, dismounting, threw the reins to the giolla who came hurrying to meet me. Then I stepped across the threshold. I had little difficulty in recognising my old friend, the landlord, who came to meet me. A little older, a little greyer, Micheal had borne the years well. It was easy to see that he had no suspicion as to the identity of his guest.

In a loud voice, as befitted one of my class and character, I asked if I could have supper and lodgings for the night. With the alacrity of a good host Micheal answered that his house was at my disposal, and he inquired what I would wish to have placed before me for supper.

"Whatever you please, good landlord," I replied, "an' you serve it quickly, for I have ridden far to-day."

Quickly a meal was set before me, and, having satisfied the cravings of my hunger, I sent for the landlord to inquire if my room were ready. He came instantly and conducted me to it. As we were mounting the stairs I stepped to his side, and asked if I could have private speech of him. Hesitatingly he replied that he was always ready to oblige his customers; that he was ready to hear me. But I answered the security of my room was necessary. At that he regarded me long and earnestly. But I was well disguised, and no inkling of the truth crossed his mind.

When we had entered into the neat little room he had assigned me, I closed the door carefully, and, turning to Micheal, who was eyeing my every movement, I asked in a low tone if we were safe from eavesdroppers.

"Why do you ask?" he demanded sharply.

"Because, good landlord," I replied, still in the same low tone, "these are dangerous times. And I doubt not you know the proverb, 'the ditches have ears.'"

"Speak on, good sir," he said; "you need have no fear," and he placed the candle which he was carrying on a small table.

"Do you remember," I began, "a night five years ago when a young fellow who had broken the foreigner's law fled from the soldiers?"

Micheal was wary. He might be placing himself in danger by avowing his knowledge to an unknown stranger, and so he replied:

"Such an incident may have happened, but what would I know of it?"

"This young fellow, indeed he was only a stripling, escaped," I went on, ignoring his question, "and it is whispered that it was by the aid of a certain innkeeper."

"He must have been a bold man," he remarked, carelessly. "But it is seldom I hear of such things. The cares of my inn keep me busy, good sir."

"The duties of a good host are numerous," I proceeded. "And the 'White Rose' has a good one. But methinks landlords have ears, and they like to use them. But we were speaking of this young man. Micheal, he escaped to An Currán and from there to France, thanks to this innkeeper and some other good friends."

At the familiar address he started and paled.

"Oh! Micheal, Micheal," I went on, enjoying his trepidation, "you should not show your hand so plainly. Were some spy to see you now?" And then dropping my bantering tone, "But fear not, no harm will come to you through me."

He stared at me, his eyes wide with astonishment.

"Dia linn!" he muttered, "who can this man be who knows me so well?"

With a deft movement I removed my beard and hat, saying at the same time:

"Do not speak or cry out. Piaras Grás stands before you."

With tears in his eyes he embraced me, whispering:

"Thank God that I have lived to see this day; that my old eyes have once more beheld your face. A mhic mo chroidhe, I had never hoped to see you again. But, Master Piaras, why have you come here and in such a fashion?"

I told him of my work in Dublin, and of all which had happened there, dwelling in particular on the final embarkation from Howth, of the complete success of which I had been told by Jans on the day I had left the city. That merry young gallant had laughed loudly over the discomfiture of the authorities to which he had contributed so much.

"Now," I concluded, "I have come here to my native place to carry out a similar work."

"Master Piaras," said my brave old friend, "it is

dangerous work. The whole country is full of spies, but you can depend on me to the last. No spy shall ever learn your secret from me."

I grasped his hand. "I know you for a true friend, Micheal," I said.

With a final " Dia dod' bheannachadh," he turned to go. But I stayed him.

" Remember, Micheal, a chara, Piaras Grás has disappeared. In our public relations your guest is the Captain Hall, an English gentleman travelling for his pleasure."

Then with a loud " Good night, Captain," he left me, and in a few minutes I was sleeping soundly, as befits the man who has ridden fast and far.

CHAPTER XXX

LOVE WHISPERS AGAIN—AN INVITATION

For some days I rested very quietly at the "White Rose." Then, with all the fervour and energy of which my nature was capable, I threw myself again into my work. Day and night I was afoot. To-day in Béarra; to-morrow in Beanntraighe. While the moonlight danced on the waters of Currán Lake I received the fealty of many a bold glensman. Beneath the shadow of old Carrán Tuathail many a swift mountaineer fresh from his mountain fastnesses bound himself to follow the soldier's career. To wake and funeral I wended my way, and there in the midst of the lowly graves where their fathers slept I heard the vows of fidelity of the mourners, and sealed the bargain in silver pieces. And then at night-time, with only the bright stars or the pale moon looking down, a little vessel would creep out of some lonely inlet, just as five years agone I had crept away, and out across the seas with its flight of "wild geese."

It was during this time that I saw my dream-maiden. I had been abroad all day among the peasantry whose dwellings lay round my old home. Chance rather than inclination had led me there. I had got word that a large number of people would assemble to accompany the remains of one of their number to the old churchyard. This report had brought me hither. The seed had been sown amongst them, and I knew I would reap a rich harvest.

My task completed, I turned homewards. The quiet of the evening had come, and the sun sinking to its rest away in the west had begun to lengthen the shadows across the grass. The mellow whistle of the blackbird perched in its leafy shelter came to my ears. The murmur of the babbling brook filled the air with its music, while the lowing of a distant cow floated adown the soft breeze. Everything was quiet and reposeful.

Strange how in such a scene the thoughts of other days come to you—sights and scenes from the long-gone past: faces which have passed your way; the echo of a kind word; the memory of a soft glance. Strange how the note of some church bell, as mellowed by the distance, it comes stealing through the air, brings with it the bitter-sweet remembrances of those other years.

It was so with me. Again I felt stirring in my heart the unconquerable longing to see the place where I had spent my earliest days, the halls which had echoed to my childish prattle, but now, alas! gave back the echo of a stranger's voice. Almost unconsciously I turned in the direction of my old home. A ride of a few miles brought me within view of it. There beyond it stood calm and majestic, its grey, ivy-covered walls lit up by the last rays of the dying sun. How well I recalled those days when as a boy I had wandered through its spacious rooms! How well I remembered that day when old Micheal Mor had hoisted me on his broad shoulders, and carried me up the winding stairs of its tall tower! How I remembered the great hall with its antlered deer-heads; its burnished arms and weapons of war and chase!

With a bitter sigh I turned away from the contemplation of it all, and, proud man that I am, inured to war's red work and rude alarms, I confess I felt the hot tears start to my eyes. But with an effort I dashed them away, and spurred my horse to the gallop. To what purpose my vain regrets? All had passed, and I was but a wanderer having no fortune but my sword, no home but the rude barrack in some foreign town.

My road led me to the little cottage where my father had dwelt when the Williamite adventurer had driven him forth from his ancestral halls. The unbidden tears rose again as I looked. Nothing remained of this other home of mine save roofless walls crumbling to dust beneath the rude blast of the unpitying storm. For a long time I stood amidst its ruins, then mounted and continued my way, my heart bursting with grief. The Gráses had indeed been uprooted. Nothing remained to tell what they once had been but a few grass-grown mounds in the quiet churchyard beyond, and the memories which lived in the hearts of the people who had known and loved them.

I was recalled to myself by the trampling of horses. Raising my head I caught sight of several riders coming towards me. But as they trotted past I looked more closely. With a sudden, fierce throb I recognised one of the riders. There could be no mistaking that noble head with its aureole of rich auburn hair, that graceful form which sat its horse so perfectly. The mad, wild blood went coursing through my veins like fire. I had again found my love.

But the thought came with its cold logic: Duty lies before you; love must be a thing apart. Was it not better that I should school myself to forget. The dream had been a beautiful one; but one impossible of fulfilment. She had, no doubt, merely wished to show her gratitude for the slight service I had rendered her. Probably long ere this I was forgotten. A Dhia na bhfeart! what right had I to count on remembrance? A soldier thrown across her way by some mischance of wayward fortune.

No! I would forget my madness. I would live for my profession, and for it alone. Fool! fool! to think that I was stronger than Fate; could laugh at love.

. . . .

The days followed one another, and I was still at the "White Rose." No suspicions had been aroused by my proceedings. The administrators of the law seemed to be blissfully unconscious of my presence, and the people were true. I came and went without let or hindrance as if never a Government existed.

But one day I was startled out of the quiet tenor of my ways. I was seated in the common room of the inn at dinner. Suddenly I heard a heavy step, and, looking up, I saw a burly, red-faced man enter slashing his boot-tops with his riding whip. In stupefied amazement I sat gazing at him. Was I mad or dreaming? Surely it could not be he, the man whom I had last seen with the blood streaming from the wound my bullet had made that fatal evening five years before. Surely my wits must be playing me false, or could it be that my shot had not been fatal? This certainly was Sir Michael Sickles, my old enemy, substantial and full-blooded as of old.

With an effort I resumed my meal. Out of the corner of my eye I watched his movements. I could see that he was watching me, and, with a sudden resolution forming itself in my mind, I looked up and gave him "good even." But no gleam of recognition leaped into his eyes. In the black-bearded man he did not recognise the former Piaras Grás. Surlily he replied, and, seating himself opposite me at the table, called loudly for wine. Micheal Mor himself brought it, and gave me a warning look as he inquired:

"Can I do anything else for you, Captain?"

But I only shook my head in reply to this unnecessary question.

Sir Michael sat in silence for some time. Neither did I speak. I had no desire for conversation with this enemy, who had again come into my life. At last he broke the silence.

"You seem to be a stranger in this country, sir."

"Yes," I returned. "I am a stranger. A wanderer tired of the gaieties of cities, I seek a little relaxation far from them."

"Have you been in Dublin?" he inquired.

"Yes," I replied; "I was there for some time."

He bent forward confidentially. "You are a military man, Captain. I heard the landlord address you as such. You must visit me at my place, Snaidhm Castle, where we could enjoy a quiet game of piquet or écarté. I know all you officers play. Egad, Captain, it is not fitting that you should spend your time moping at an inn. You will, I warrant you, find my place more congenial to your tastes."

Here was a dilemma. I almost laughed at the strangeness of it—invited to my early home by the man who had usurped it, the man against whom I had turned my pistol. All my ideas as to the fitness of things cried out against the acceptance of such an invitation—my position as an emissary of the Brigade; the memories of the olden time. Could I accept? And, on the other hand, dare I refuse? My refusal would perhaps rouse the enmity of the baronet, and expose me to many petty annoyances which would seriously interfere with my plans. It might set this inquisitive baronet to making inquiries into the things which interested a gentleman travelling for pleasure, still unwilling to visit his kind. Better to avoid his unpleasant inquiries. The acceptance of the invitation held some danger, but at least my acquaintance with him would do away with lurking doubts, would brand me with a kind of official sanction. And so with an airy politeness which I was far from feeling I accepted. With a vigorous hand-shake he left me, telling me he would expect me on the following evening.

When he had gone, I sat in my chair cursing the unhappy chance which had driven him in my direction. Once or twice I thought of not presenting myself at the castle, but that would only make matters worse. There was no escape. I should see the thing through. When I told old Micheal of the affair he shook his head, and muttered: "I like it not, I like it not. God grant nothing evil comes of it."

CHAPTER XXXI

THE DAUGHTER OF MY ENEMY

It was with a curious feeling that I presented myself the following evening at the residence of Sir Michael. As I followed the servant through the spacious old hall my thoughts were very bitter. But none should know what a tempest was raging in my heart. Bitterly I regretted having come, as I gazed on each spot hallowed by memories.

And then I was in the presence of my host, uttering words the purport of which I could hardly tell. But he was too stolid to notice my perturbation. Gradually I recovered my self-possession, and was soon chatting of the life of the gay metropolis. I found it a very safe subject, for it was seldom he visited it. At last dinner was announced, and I accompanied my host to the dining-table. My self-possession almost deserted me again as a girl advanced towards us, and was introduced by the baronet as his daughter. But I recovered myself quickly, and bowing low, raised her fingers to my lips.

With my brain in a whirl, I seated myself. It was as I had half suspected. This fair girl whose image I had enshrined in my heart, whose every grace and charm had entwined themselves with the tenderest recollections of my life, she whose memory I had vainly endeavoured to cast out of my thoughts, was the daughter of my enemy, one of the hated race who had torn our lands and livings from us, and sent us forth wanderers.

How much better that I had never known? Then I might have treasured the memory of her dear face in my secret thoughts—treasured it where neither time nor care would have effaced it. But now my dream was ended; my idol shattered. The jewel which I had treasured was torn from me by the ruthless hand of Destiny. So be it. I would bow my head to it, and laugh and smile as if I had never known.

Somehow the meal ended. Sir Michael, who had enjoyed himself thoroughly, grew drowsy and snored loudly in his arm-chair. Thus the burden of the conversation fell to myself and my fair companion. As we chatted, I noticed that her eyes often regarded me thoughtfully. Perhaps some note of my voice called up a half-forgotten memory. But coolly indifferent, I sat as if I had never guided her twinkling feet through the mazes of the dance, or listened to her sweet voice before that night.

During one of the lulls in the conversation she asked, suddenly:

"Captain Hall, you have been in Dublin. Have you ever met with a gentleman named Swetenhall?"

"Swetenhall! Swetenhall!" I murmured, reminiscently. "I may have, but cannot recall. What was he like?"

I felt almost criminal as I asked the question.

"Tall, handsome, dark-complexioned, wearing a small black moustachio. Altogether foreign-looking. I knew him well. He did me a service once which I can never forget."

"I regret I cannot give you any information regarding him, Mistress Sickles," I replied, slowly, while my eyes sought the table. "I meet so many men in my wanderings, I cannot remember."

She appeared disappointed, but made no further reference to the matter. Soon after I took my departure, and the last remembrance of that fateful visit is the face of the daughter of my enemy as she stood in the open doorway beneath the flickering light of the candles bidding me adieu, while the soft night breeze ruffled the stray curls of her hair.

And that night in my dreams I seemed to see her with her hands stretched out to me appealingly, while a far-away murmur came to me: "She remembers. She remembers."

. . . . . .

I avoided Snaidhm Castle after that visit. Never again would I look on the face of my love, now lost to me. As well might the wolf and the lamb lie down together, as the son of the Grásach to look on the daughter of the Williamite undertaker. Faugh! the thing was impossible. Thus I fortified myself.

I had taken precautions that my enemy should not find me at the inn. Several times he called, but I was absent on each occasion. For several weeks this game of hide-and-seek continued, and then one evening as I was strolling along beneath the shadow of the woods I heard the swift tramp of a horse behind me, and stepped aside off the narrow path to give it passage. But the horse halted beside me, and a voice uttered my name. Looking up, I perceived that the rider was none other than my enemy's daughter. For an instant I was confused, then my hat swept the ground in salute. Silently I stood before her. But she asked me to assist her to dismount, remarking, naively: "It is so much easier to talk when walking."

I assisted her from the saddle, blaming myself for a fool. But she could not help being the daughter of my enemy, and she was very fair and winning. So we walked on together in silence, beneath the widespreading trees, our feet making no sound on the soft earth.

She seemed to be thinking deeply, or mayhap she was waiting for me to begin. But I had no desire to commence the conversation. At last she broke the awkward silence:

"Captain, you have not visited us lately. Did you not enjoy your first visit, or is there any other reason why you do not come again to our poor house?"

"Believe me, Mistress Sickles," I said, earnestly, "there are reasons why I cannot visit your house. I regret that these reasons exist, for your sake as well as my own; but they raise themselves barrier-like."

"Why not?" she urged. "Time must lie heavily on your hands. You have been used to the gay society of Dublin, and though we cannot offer you the enjoyments of a gay city, let us contribute in some measure to the brightening of your stay amongst us. Surely, Captain, you will allow us?"

Steadfastly I answered: "It grieves me much to think that I cannot, mademoiselle, but I ask you not to urge it. The refusal pains me."

But she would not be satisfied, and continued urging, and at last I said:

"If you knew the man whom you are urging, fair Mistress, you would hardly press me. If I were to tell you that I am playing a double game, what would you think? If I were to tell——"

But I shrank from the avowal of my former relations with her father. No; let her live in ignorance of my secret.

"Ah, Captain, you are trying to frighten me," she said, with a ringing laugh. "Trying to make me think you a very wicked personage. But you make me all the more eager to gain your consent. You will come, Captain Hall; promise me."

Could one fight against such urgings, against such trust and confidence? I could have fought the blandishments and cajoleries of Sir Michael himself, but against the urgings of this fair enemy I was not proof.

With something very like a groan, I consented, and assisting her to mount again, we parted.

CHAPTER XXXII

FOR THE HEAD OF A TRAITOR—LOVE COMES TO ME

When I reached the castle the following evening, I found the baronet reading an official-looking document. He greeted me boisterously, and then continued his reading, leaving me to my own devices. But I was not long left in loneliness, for the door opened, and Mary, looking bewitching in a gown of white silk, came in. She had hardly greeted me when her father turned round.

"Gad, Hall," he burst out, "here's a fine business. Some d— rebel of a Jacobite down here recruiting for the Frenchies. There, read that," and he pushed the paper he had been reading towards me.

Rapidly I ran through it. It offered a sum of five hundred pounds for the capture of a French officer who was known to be recruiting in Kerry. With a laugh I pushed it back to him.

"What do you think of it, Hall?" Sir Michael asked. "A Jacobite spy amongst us, eh. But," with a fierce oath, "I'll lay him by the heels. No one of their breed shall run loose round here for long."

"I am sure of that, Sir Michael," I replied, dryly. "No one could doubt your zeal and activity."

Was it fancy, or did I catch a look of intelligence flash from the eyes of Mary as she stood watching me?

Dinner was announced, and for the time spies and Jacobites were forgotten. But several times Sir Michael growled out his intention of "laying the spying scoundrel by the heels." Looking at the coarse, bloated features of the baronet, I felt a great wave of pity surging through my heart for the gracious girl condemned to a lonely life with that fierce old roysterer whose only enjoyment seemed to centre round the dinner-table and the wine-bottle.

Dinner over, Mary excused herself, while I sat on, an indifferent listener to the conversation of the baronet. But quickly his company palled on me, and leaving him dozing, and enjoying his wine between the dozes, I strolled out into the night air. The night was warm, and heavy with the scent of woodbine and hawthorn.

I had gone farther from the house than I knew, when the rustle of a gown startled me, and a soft voice said:

"Captain, I expected to find you still with my father, but he told me you had gone out. A penny for your thoughts."

"Yes, you shall have them, Mistress Sickles," I replied, turning quickly; "you shall have them if you care to listen. But I warn you they are unpleasant enough."

We were quite alone. I had fought a battle with myself that day, and had come to a decision. I would tell her all. Mayhap my confidence would be ill-placed, but the stories I had heard from Micheal of her goodness to the poor, down-trodden people had decided me. I was convinced I could depend on her truthfulness and honour.

"Yes," I went on, gravely, "I will tell you my thoughts. They are those of a man who is playing a double part. Mistress Sickles, I have been playing a double game. Myself and the Captain Swetenhall whom you used to know in Dublin are one and the same person."

Quickly I removed the black beard, and stood revealed in the moonlight. I marked the pallor of her face as she gazed at me with wide-open eyes. But she said nothing.

"When your father," I resumed, "gave me that

document to read to-night he little guessed to whom he was showing it. He little guessed he was showing it to the very man whom it concerns—the man whom he has sworn to capture. Yes, Mistress Sickles, I am the French officer who has come amongst you recruiting for the Brigade. But I am no spy. I have taken every means I could to further my cause. I carry my life in my hands, but I have not stained them with dishonour. I came here this evening fully prepared to reveal all to you, because I do not wish to enter your father's house again. I feel it would be dishonourable. To-night I bid farewell to this house; then let the agents of the law seek me out. No one knows my secret save yourself. I know I can depend on your honour not to betray it. You are the daughter of a loyal supporter of the Ascendancy, but even so, I trust you."

I ceased, waiting for her answer. Raising her head, and looking me in the face, she replied:

"Captain Hall, though you are a French officer, though ten times five hundred pounds were on your head, though I am the daughter of Sir Michael Sickles, your secret is safe with me."

She laid her hands in mine, and I was sorely tempted to take her in my arms and kiss her upturned face. But I restrained myself.

"And Mistress Sickles," I resumed, "before I leave you, perhaps never to see you again, let me tell you another secret, more painful than the other, but one which needs must be told."

"Why tell it if it pains you?" she hastened to ask.

"Because I wish to act as an honourable man. Years ago," I hurried on, "this castle and all its lands was in the possession of the Gráses. From father to son they followed on in unbroken succession for countless generations. Then came war, with all its disastrous consequences. The Grásach espoused the losing side, and was driven forth."

"And my father was given his possessions," she

whispered, with a catch in her voice. How lovely she looked! And I was going to lose her.

"Yes," I went on, gently, "your father became the possessor of the lands of the Grásach, while he, a ruined and broken man, lived out his life in a little wayside hovel. Years rolled away, and then one evening as the son of that broken man was mounting his mare in the village of Cathair Domhnaill yonder, Sir Michael Sickles strode up and demanded his mare from him, offering the price which the law allows, five pounds. But the offer was repelled, and rather than allow his beloved mare to become the property of Sir Michael, the son of the Grásach shot her, and as the knight threw himself on him with drawn sword, discharged his other pistol at him. That night that stripling, for he was little more, whose life was forfeit, escaped to France."

"You—you are the son of the Grásach?" she whispered.

"Yes, I am Piaras, the son of the Grásach. Can you wonder now that I must away from your house—that I cannot enter under its roof again? I was a mad fool ever to have come, but my madness is over."

"But why—why have you told me all this painful story of the bygone years?" she asked me.

"I tell it to you because I love you, have loved you from the first. Because I could not live a lie in your pure presence. Because before I go I want to carry away the knowledge that you have forgiven my deception which, God knows, was not of my making. Mistress Sickles, will you tell me that I am forgiven, that I may carry into my exile the memory of your sweet pardon? Mary, a mhuirnin, I love you, but love is not for me."

"Why is it not for you?" she breathed softly, bending towards me. . . . A Dhia! how fair she looked in her shimmering robes of white. . . . "Is it because I am the daughter of Sir Michael Sickles? What have I to forgive? Say rather what have you not forgiven. Have you not declared your love for me, the daughter of your enemy? Since those happy nights we spent in each other's company in Dublin I have loved you. What care I that you are a French officer! I love you, Piaras."

"But, Mary—I, an outlaw with a price on my head. I, an opponent of the law which your father administers; an enemy to everything which you have been taught to hold dear."

"What matters it to me if you be an outlaw? What if there be a price on your head? I care nothing. I love you."

And there beneath the stars, with the night wind sighing round, I took her in my arms. My mission, the reward for my capture, Sir Michael, all, all were forgotten in the joy of these few minutes. Ah! what can equal the trustfulness of a good woman; what equal the purity of her faith in her idol!

And later as I stooped from my saddle to imprint a good-night kiss on her upturned face, she whispered into my ear: "Have faith in me. Your secret is safe. I love you."

CHAPTER XXXIII

THE PROTECTION OF THE LAW-ABIDING

AFTER that evening I kept far from the house where love had come to me. With feverish impatience, I pushed on my task. Recklessly I faced the danger which was around me, but it passed me by. Often I was within an ace of capture. Many times I quaffed my wine with the officers of the military patrols which had been scouring the country for me, and toasted with them the speedy capture of the miscreant. Many a time I sent them on a long chase after some will-o'-the-wisp which had existence only in my own imagination. Everywhere I went the little white proclamations which set the price on my head flaunted themselves in my face. But the price was still unclaimed. The black-bearded Captain Hall was still at large.

But though I kept away from the castle, my dear one hovered near. Evening's close often brought her to my side, and then we would wander away into the grand old woods, to whisper again, 'neath the spreading pine or gnarled oak, our vows of love.

One evening, when I had been about six weeks in the Ui Rathach country, she came to me, her eyes full of anxiety, and told me that one Lieutenant Jones, a red-haired soldier she had known in Dublin, had arrived at the castle. She had heard her father talking with him, and discovered that he had been sent on special duty to hunt down the recruiting-agent. I smiled grimly as I listened. The lieutenant had made a quick recovery.

"Piaras," she whispered, nestling closer, "you will be careful for my sake. I have an uneasy feeling about this Jones. I shiver with apprehension as I think of your dear life exposed to the traps and wiles of spies and informers."

"Fear not for me, a ghradh gil," I said, kissing her fondly. "Lieutenant Jones will find his work cut out for him. I am not tired of life yet."

And she was content with my assurance.

At last an error almost led to my undoing. Perhaps I was careless; that my constant immunity had rendered me less wary than I might have been. Thus it came about that I enlisted a fellow whom I met by the wayside. As I tendered him the piece of silver something seemed to whisper that I was a fool to trust him, but his glib tongue deceived me, and I refused to listen to the voice within. But whatever subtle instinct moved me, I shrank from giving him the name of our rendezvous.

A few days later as I was riding leisurely on my homeward way I stopped at a roadside inn, and throwing my rein across the tethering-ring outside, entered. I called for wine, which was served to me at a little side table. Hardly had I seated myself, when the jingle of accoutrements struck on my ear, and almost immediately the room was filled with troopers, foremost amongst whom I recognised my whilom recruit, now clad in dragoon's uniform. Instantly I saw my danger. It behoved me to act quickly. Pulling my hat over my eyes, I finished my wine without any undue appearance of haste. Lounging carelessly towards the door, I had almost reached it when a voice rang out:

"Hold! Stop him! It is the Jacobite spy!"

With a blow of my fist I levelled the trooper who sprang to seize me, and was through the door like a flash. In an instant I was astride my horse and speeding down the road, with the troopers yelling like demons behind. The chase was furious. Nevertheless, I held my own in the first mad burst. But my horse was jaded, and began to lose ground. Unless I secured shelter, and that quickly, I would be captured. In my extremity I took a desperate resolution. We were not far from Snaidhm Castle. I would take refuge in the house of the law-abiding Sir Michael, and trust to good fortune to carry me through.

Urging my horse to his greatest speed, I dashed up to the castle, well in front of my pursuers. A servant came hurrying forward, who led away my horse. I was ushered into the presence of the baronet, who was not alone. I was not surprised to recognise in his companion my quondam opponent, Jones. I bowed to the baronet, who welcomed me, and offered me a seat beside him, introducing me at the same time to his companion. They had been playing cards.

"Gentlemen, gentlemen," I cried, "do not allow me to interrupt your game. Mine is a mere passing visit."

Sir Michael offered me a hand, but I declined, and sat watching the play, all the while listening intently. I was not mistaken. The soldiers had tracked me to my refuge. I heard their clatter as they dashed up to the door. Their voices sounded in the hall. I knew the moment had come. Removing the beard from my face, I sat revealed.

"Swetenhall, by Heaven," burst forth the astonished Jones.

"My friends," I said quietly, "I have been pursued here by soldiers. You can hear them outside in the hall. Sit quietly and continue your game. I give you warning that if by word or sign you betray me to them, your lives will pay the forfeit. My pistols are loaded," showing them. "Now play on!"

It was a tight corner, but I imagined I knew my men. In the shadow I sat, my pistols pressing against their stomachs. We had not long to wait. The door was thrown open, and the officer of the patrol appeared. He addressed Sir Michael.

"Sir Michael, we are in pursuit of a French recruiting officer for whose capture a large reward is offered. For the moment he has escaped us. Has he entered your house?"

The long barrel of my pistol pressed into the stomach of the unfortunate baronet, who growled out:

"I know nothing of him. Why do you come here disturbing a loyal gentleman and his friends at their cards?"

"Your pardon, Sir Michael," said the officer, "but the Queen's duty must be attended to. The rebel may have taken refuge here."

"Sirrah, what do you mean?" roared Sir Michael, urged thereto by a prod of my pistol. "In my house—the house of a justice."

"I ask your pardon, Sir Michael," said the abashed officer. "I could almost have sworn he entered here, but we must have missed the scoundrel. With your permission we will withdraw. Perhaps we will pick him up again. Good night, Sir Michael."

"Good night," growled the baronet.

Just as the officer was turning away, I caught a movement on the part of Jones. Instantly my pistol pressing against his stomach reminded him of his peril, and he sank back again in his chair.

For several minutes we sat in silence. I heard the troopers departing. With a laugh I turned to my fuming companions.

"A close shave, my masters," I burst out jovially, as I put up my pistols, "but all's well that ends well. I am deeply grateful for the kind assistance you have given me. Had you acted in any other manner I would have been very pained at the result. But, Sir Michael, will you not ask me to have a bumper?"

With a furious oath, he filled out a bumper of wine, and pushed it towards me.

Leisurely sipping it, I turned towards Jones, and inquired, suavely:

"And you, Lieutenant Jones, how are you, and my other Dublin friends? I am glad to see you recovered from your slight indisposition."

"Oh, you damned villain!" he grated through his set teeth. "Had I only known!"

"I can assure you, lieutenant, it would have sadly inconvenienced me had you known," I replied, laughing. "I was quite aware of your good intentions."

"Oh! you dog of a spy," he snarled.

"Easy! easy! lieutenant," I admonished him. "Do not allow your temper to get the better of you."

Then I bade them see me off. I judged the patrol to be well on its way by now, and beyond reach of recall. Even so, I did not wish to give them the chance of possible treachery. At the door I gave them a cordial good night, and mounted my horse, which a servant brought round. Sir Michael said nothing; he seemed to be stupefied by the rush of events. But Jones could not restrain himself.

"Swetenhall, or whoever the devil you are, look to yourself," he shouted. "I'll see you dancing at the rope's end yet."

Whereat I laughed, and giving rein to my horse, was away into the night.

I had not gone far when I caught the flutter of white draperies, and heard my name uttered. In an instant I was by the side of my loved one.

"Ah, Piaras, Piaras," she upbraided, "why will you run such terrible risks? I saw you enter the house, and when the soldiers rode up knew whom they were seeking. I feared for you, but knew my presence could not help, but on the contrary might do you harm. Ah! the agony and despair of these few minutes. In terror I watched from my window, fearing every moment to see you led forth a prisoner. When I saw them leave I almost fainted with joy. And then when I saw you ride off, I stole away and came through the woods. Piaras, it wrings my heart to see you in such peril."

"A mhuirnin dilis," I breathed into her ear, "what kind fate has sent you into my life? A poor soldier of fortune, having only his sword. But, come, love, the night grows late. The daughter of a loyal gentleman should not give speech to seditious persons, and at such hours. Come, I will see you home."

She urged me to go, saying the danger was too great. But I silenced her remonstrances with a kiss. With my horse's rein thrown across my shoulder, I led her back by the way she had come, and told her of the stratagem by which I had cheated my enemies. As she lay in my arms before we parted at the edge of the old wood she asked:

"Piaras, when will this terrible danger be at an end?"

"A few days more," I answered, "and then away to merry France. A mhuirnin, it is little I have to offer you for your boundless love and devotion. Fortune or rank I have none. Turn back even now. I shall not blame you, nor bear you one bitter thought. Fortune and rank can be yours for the asking. I can give you nothing but my loyalty."

But she answered steadily: "Piaras, I love you. Riches, honours, I desire them not, so that you are near. I will follow you to the ends of the earth."

A kiss sealed the compact. I watched her floating draperies as she disappeared amongst the shrubberies. Then I turned and resumed my way.

CHAPTER XXXIV

THE FROWN OF FORTUNE

Though the fox cheats the hounds for many a day he is caught at last. I felt that the coils were tightening round me, but my work went merrily on. Under the very noses of the authorities I enlisted my recruits. In a dozen different disguises I wandered up and down Ui Rathach, to-day a parson of the Established Church; to-morrow a friar. In Cathair Saidhbhin a gay dragoon, in the town of the Little Skiffs a burly, loud-voiced corn merchant.

I had quitted the "White Rose," fearing to compromise old Micheal, who wept bitterly at my going, and now dwelt wherever chance offered. But one day my luck took a sudden turn. Fickle Dame Fortune had showered her favours on me; she was now determined to show me the reverse. It was but a few miles from Snaidhm that the blow fell. With a recklessness born of the constant presence of danger I tried a cast with the capricious dame, and eschewing all disguise, trusting to chance and the fleetness of my horse, went forth. For several hours I pursued my way unmolested, and had just parted from a tall peasant who had brought me word of a mountain hosting where my presence was eagerly awaited. Promising to be with him on the morrow, I turned to continue my way to the house of a neighbouring sympathiser, when suddenly I heard the tramp of a mounted patrol coming towards me. They were hidden by a bend in the road, and were close up before I was aware of their presence. As they swept into view, I turned my horse's head to flee, but frightened by a pistol shot which rang out behind he reared, and threw me heavily. In an instant, lying half stunned, I was surrounded. As I rose to my feet I perceived my friends, Sir Michael Sickles and Lieutenant Jones, the latter of whom shouted out loudly : " Surrender yourself, in the Queen's name."

An instant I thought of resistance, but as I glanced round at the drawn swords of my captors I saw how useless it would be. Could I use my pistols I carried a couple of lives in my hand, but what then—to fall hacked to pieces beneath the strokes of half-a-score sabres. No! Piaras Grás would have another day.

With a shrug of my shoulders I turned towards Sir Michael, who was pompously reading an official-looking document, and glancing at me from time to time. No need to tell me what it contained. Had I not read through its dreary waste of words a full score times? Did it not flaunt itself in my face from every tree-trunk in the countryside? Could I not repeat it almost word for word?

"Hall, otherwise Swetenhall, describing himself as a Captain late of Her Majesty's Army; age twenty-eight or thereabouts; height five feet ten; good teeth; brown eyes; black hair, worn rather long and curling; black moustachios waxed to a point; erect military carriage. Probably will appear under various disguises. To anyone capturing and delivering into the hands of the authorities the person of the said Captain Hall, otherwise Swetenhall, who is engaged in recruiting for French service, the before-mentioned sum (£500) will be paid."

Courteously bowing, I inquired: "Monsieur le Baronnet, may I spare you the trouble of so much reading? I am the man you seek, 'Hall, otherwise Swetenhall,'"

"So, sirrah," he sneered, folding up the document, "we have laid you by the heels at last."

"Monsieur le Baronnet," I replied, "you hold the winning hand," and I glanced round the circle of hostile faces.

My sword and pistols were taken from me, and mounted on my horse, which one of the soldiers had caught, I was led back to my old home. Through a long corridor I was led and into a small room with barred windows. There, bound tightly in a chair, they left me. As I heard the key grate in the lock I felt I was indeed a prisoner.

My position was unpleasant enough sitting there unable to move hand or foot. The cords cut into my flesh, and I suffered tortures from the manner in which my blood stagnated owing to their tightness. I knew they had posted a sentry beneath my windows, for I could hear his footsteps crunching through the gravel, while the door was also guarded. Dar m'fhocal, I thought, they have taken good care of me. Well I knew that my stay here would be a short one. Probably I would be sent the next morning to some of the neighbouring towns to await transportation to Dublin, and then, in fancy, I could see myself standing bare-headed, gazing down on the upturned faces of an angry mob filling the whole expanse of Stephen's Green, with the grim outline of the gallows looming up behind me. Little as I wished to make a spectacle for a Dublin rabble, I could see no chance of escape without outside help. Powerless in the midst of my enemies, I could only await the turn of events. Several times I thought of Mary, who would have doubtless learned of my capture, but with such a strict watch on my prison what could she do?

I must have fallen into a doze. Suddenly I awoke with a feeling that I was not alone. Through the windows the moon was sending a fitful ray. The sounds of the house had died away. Even the monotonous step of the sentinel outside my door had ceased. With a start I realised that someone was in the room. The soft swish of a woman's dress came through the profound stillness. A soft hand was laid across my mouth, and a dear voice whispered in my ear :

"Hush! Do not make a sound. I have come to save you."

With eager, trembling hands she unloosed my bonds. For several minutes I could not stand erect owing to the cramped position in which I had been for so long. When at length, after vigorous chafing, my blood had begun to flow freely again she gave me her hand and led me out through the door, which she locked carefully behind her. There stretched on the ground outside the door lay the sentry breathing heavily, his carbine beside him.

"Drugged beer," she whispered.

Noiselessly we moved down the corridor, our way lit up by the moonlight, which struggled feebly in through a tall lancet window. In whispers she told me how she had managed to slip into the beer intended for the sentries a powerful narcotic which her father sometimes made use of, and then, when the household had retired, secured the key of my prison. The task had not been very difficult because of the junketing which celebrated my capture. Under the door of the dining-room we could see the light of the candles which had not yet been extinguished, and hear the stertorous sounds proceeding from the baronet and his companion, Jones, who were sleeping off the effects of their carouse. Like a pair of shadows we stole past. Through long corridors and down broad staircases we sped. Only once did we halt, when she left me to put the key again in Sir Michael's private room, from which she had taken it earlier in the night.

At last we were in the open air, and then pressing her to me in a tender embrace, I sped away through the darkness towards a mountain cottage where one of my trustiest friends dwelt, which I reached ere the dawn had come.

CHAPTER XXXV

CONSUMMATION—FAREWELL

Five days had passed since my escape. During that time I had not been idle. Everything was ready for the final stroke which would bring my work to its fitting conclusion—which would crown it with the guerdon of love. The word had gone round to my gallant fellows, and beyond in the little creek where my "wild geese" would rendezvous the swift smuggler lay waiting to spread her white sails to the breeze which would bear us away to the kindly French shore.

I had learned that mo chailin aluinn would be present that evening at a ball to be held in the neighbourhood of her own home. Accordingly my arrangements had been made. That night would see the fulfilment of all my fondest dreams.

It was within an hour of midnight as I drew up my horse in a lonely thicket beside the road along which Sir Michael and my love should travel homewards. I was well screened from the view of anyone who should pass the way. But the road was a lonely one, and my vigil proved long and solitary. At last my patience was rewarded, and in the distance I heard the rumble of a coach. The moment for action was at hand.

As the coach came into view I rode out from the shadow, and my loud "halt" rang through the night air. An upraised pistol gave force to my command. With the swiftness which terror lends, the coachman threw his horses back on their haunches. My pistol still covering them, I ordered himself and his companion footman to throw away such arms as they might have. With alacrity they obeyed, and several blunderbusses went hurtling into the thick heather which bordered the road.

The head of Sir Michael was thrust from the coach window, and with a full-mouthed oath he demanded the reason of the stoppage. I advanced towards him.

"Sir Michael," I replied, "I have taken the liberty of stopping your coach. I have come in the fulfilment of a duty. Your daughter has done me the honour of giving me her love. I have, therefore, come to demand her at your hands, well knowing there was little use of asking your consent beyond in your castle, where you were surrounded by the instruments of your power. But here now, where we are more equal, I ask her from you. She loves me, and I have sworn to make her happy. But should she, even now, at this eleventh hour, wish to draw back, I will not say her nay. Never shall it be said that I forced an unwilling bride to my arms."

"An unwilling bride! Sirrah, what do you mean?" Sir Michael roared. "Who are you who dares to stop a justice on the highway?"

"I am one whom you know well," I replied calmly. "One who was recently a prisoner in your house. An outlaw; a traitor, an' you will, Sir Baronet, but still an honourable man. But what says your daughter?"

"My daughter, sir, can have nothing to say to such as you. An outlaw—a scurvy knave with a price on your head. Out of my way, sirrah."

"Let her answer for herself," I answered unruffled.

So saying I dismounted, and swinging open the door of the ponderous vehicle assisted her to alight.

But I had not noticed a dark figure stealing up behind. It was the cry of my dear one which warned me. Turning I saw the red-haired Jones rushing on me with drawn sword. Raising my pistol I fired.

With a cry of pain he dropped his sword and staggered back, his sword-arm hanging useless.

"That will be a warning, lieutenant," I remarked.

"Mistress Sickles," I went on, "you have heard the proposition I have made to your father. I could wish that the time and place were more appropriate, but the Fates are against it. We await your answer. Be it what it may, I, at least, will abide by it."

As I looked at her standing there in all her beauty, the jewels in her hair glittering in the bright moonlight, their sparkle half hidden by the gauzy veil which covered her head, looking so stately in the folds of her creamy silks, I felt I could face dangers unknown for her sweet sake. And I confess that a tremor of apprehension ran through me. Had I lost her by my quixotic proceeding? But the next moment I despised myself for the unworthy thought.

Sir Michael turned to her, and, in a voice trembling with rage, exclaimed:

"Mary, I forbid you to reply to the insulting proposal of this footpad who comes to demand you at the muzzle of his pistol. Whatever relations you may have had with this gentleman, this outlaw, I know nothing of. Whatever they may have been I forgive them. But do not disgrace yourself by giving ear to the words of this man who is dead alike to all feelings of justice or honour. Come; let us go, and have done with this farce."

She made no movement to obey, but placed her hand in mine.

"Father," she said simply, "I love him."

"Shameless girl," he cried furiously. "I forbid you to have anything to say to this wretch. He a spy, a low-bred scoundrel, whom nobody knows."

"I am the son of the Grásach whose lands you hold," I answered proudly.

With a yell of rage he pointed a pistol at my breast:

"You—you, one of the accursed brood," he snarled.

But with a cry my beautiful Mary threw herself before me, shielding me with her body. Sir Michael's hand dropped to his side. She stretched out her hands appealingly to him.

"Father," she cried, "I have been a dutiful daughter to you. I have obeyed you in everything, but I cannot obey you in this. My heart is given to him."

For a long time he stood with his head bowed down. Then he said hoarsely:

"Go! go! away out of my sight. You are no longer daughter of mine. Go with your wretched outlaw! Go! ere I am tempted to empty my pistol into his vile body."

She threw her white arms round his neck with a cry of anguish.

"Father, father," she whispered piteously, "you will not send me from you like this. Only one goodnight kiss to carry in my memory."

And then I saw this Williamite undertaker, this hard-drinking Sasanach, this boicin whom I had despised, strain her convulsively to his breast, while he rained kisses on her upturned face. And as I looked a feeling of respect for him grew up within me. At last, as if ashamed of his weakness, he freed himself from her clinging arms and turned to me.

"Sirrah, you have conquered," he said, "you have stolen my daughter from me. I had other aims for her than to be the bride of an outlaw. Go! I cannot say more to my daughter's lover."

I bowed. I had grown to honour this usurper of my father's patrimony within the last few minutes. He had risen to a height of self-denial of which I did not think him capable.

"Sir Michael," I said, "your daughter is safe in my keeping."

Then I sought my horse.

A groan caught my ear. It came from the unfortunate Jones, who was leaning against the coach forgotten in the tension of the last few moments. He was trying to stanch the blood which rippled slowly from his wounded arm. To him, even, I could afford to be generous. In spite of his hoarse protests I roughly bound up the wound, and thus left him.

With the queenly head of my cailin donn pillowed on my breast, my arm encircling her, we galloped away. Once I looked back, and my heart went out to that silent man standing there alone, gazing after us. After all, rough adventurer, rude riever that he was, he had loved her. Silently I registered a vow that never through me should come sorrow to this tender nestling of his who had come to me in all her glorious trust and confidence.

Very fair and winsome she looked as an hour later we stood before the white-haired old priest in the fisherman's little cottage, and heard the words which made us one. Very proud and happy standing there by my side in the creamy silk and soft laces which she had worn to the ball, little knowing that ere the morning dawned it would be her bridal robe.

The first flush of the dawn was breaking through the eastern clouds as our little vessel, her full flight of "wild geese" aboard, leaped forward on her course, her white sails spread to the freshening breeze.

Long and silently we gazed at the fast receding shores of the homeland. All around us was the loneliness of the mighty deep. Yonder the "ring of day" was widening and ever widening, driving away the shadows of the sullen night.

Stooping, I murmured in her ear:

"A mhuirnin, mhuirnin, have you any regret?"

She nestled closer to me, and looked up into my face.

"Not while you are near, Piaras," she whispered softly.

And then I bent and kissed her.